Ski Mask Money

Renta

**Lock Down Publications and Ca$h
Presents
Ski Mask Money
A Novel by *Renta***

Renta

Lock Down Publications
Po Box 944
Stockbridge, Ga 30281

Visit our website @
www.lockdownpublications.com

Copyright 2022 by Renta
Ski Mask Money

Lock Down Publications
Like our page on Facebook: Lock Down Publications
@
www.facebook.com/lockdownpublications.ldp
Book interior design by: **Shawn Walker**
Edited by: **Cassandra Barrett-Sims**

Stay Connected with Us!

Text **LOCKDOWN** to 22828 to stay up-to-date with new releases, sneak peaks, contests and more…
Thank you.

Submission Guideline.

Submit the first three chapters of your completed manuscript to ldpsubmissions@gmail.com, subject line: Your book's title. The manuscript must be in a .doc file and sent as an attachment. Document should be in Times New Roman, double spaced and in size 12 font. Also, provide your synopsis and full contact information. If sending multiple submissions, they must each be in a separate email.

Have a story but no way to send it electronically? You can still submit to LDP/Ca$h Presents. Send in the first three chapters, written or typed, of your completed manuscript to:

LDP: Submissions Dept
Po Box 944
Stockbridge, Ga 30281

DO NOT send original manuscript. Must be a duplicate.

Provide your synopsis and a cover letter containing your full contact information.

Thanks for considering LDP and Ca$h Presents.

Dedication

This book is dedicated to my world, my best friend. My Queen. My wife. My mother. My Diamond. Alexandria Ridge, this one for being my sound board all those long days and nights. The nights when I couldn't sleep, so you stayed up playing spades with me on your phone. This one for you, Love, 12:30 shit.

Acknowledgements

Honestly, I want to merely say, *"Say, mane, I love y'all!"* Yet, I pen these acknowledgements to not only give you me, but to introduce the world to my *family*. If you took the time to read this book, especially if you purchased it, you're part of my family.

Let me ask you something, "If you could close your eyes and become who you'd be five years from now, what would you become?" Some people would become lawyers, others doctors, and some, merely successful entrepreneurs. Yet, and still, I know a lot of you would manifest yourselves into a successful drug lord. I was once he. My aspirations were only to be Scarface. Meech. Until I glanced passed the shine and discovered a failure's dream. You are what you manifest.

What's the business world? It's the author who never intended to be an author. *Trust No Man*, by the OG Cash changed my life. No Cap! How I met the man behind the name *Ca$h,* changed me even further. Showed me how a boss can get to it, even while at the bottom. So, hail to the Boss Man for opening my vision to another dimension. LDP, wud up!

Special love and shout-out to the Queen, Shawn Walker— if you can see it, so it be so, mama!

Though my love has no order, my praise to God should've been first, yet, no matter the God you praise, if he can't understand you, who he/she created? Shid, you're serving the wrong one! God understands 'cause he overstands! So, I give thanks to mine for it all! For if he hadn't manifested me the God, I would still be trying to find me! No Cap!

My Queens: Mama *Black*, the woman who birthed me, I love you, Baby, and I know you're lookin' down on ya boy, smiling hard as a mu'fucka. I'm tryin', Queen!

Mama Helen? Mannn! You're the epitome of love and loyalty, and if this world were mine... I'd give you more than the flowers, the birds, and the bees!

Mama Leah? I see you fighting, woman! I'm proud of you and want you to know if every woman was bred how you are, the world would be a greater place.

Mrs. Me ... What's up! Baby, I don't have the words sufficient, so I'll just leave it at, *Till death!* Cleo, Shay, Carla, B., Snow Storm, Kanika, Mrs. Niel, Mama Sharon, Nisha, *My first protector!* Sayyyyy ... I salute you ladies and I'm gone hold it down!

Say ... Say, RNO-BITS, *my favorite shoota!* What the bidness? You up, Playboy! RNO-Bam Bam- *Jaylon Barriere,* Fam, you're the only nigga I know who tries to pronounce your name with a roll of the tongue like you French or somthin! Turn yo' shit down, bro! Lol!

OJ, Lil C , Green Eyes the Bandit, White Boy T, Fleek – *My lil nigga I'm lookin' for!* Wydell, RNO-Klutch-A-Mill—*The hardest nigga I've ever heard on the M-I-C! No Cap!*

Papa, Katta, Thugga, E-Man, T Gizzle, BOS, Scoopy the Ape, DayDay, OG Jones, Dino, Pumpkin, East TX, TuTu, Yard Style- *Love you big Bro, Shout out to wild Thang!* Quick the Slick, Solo- my twin, Bingo the Krock, LeLe, BC, Too Black!

Say ... and all my brothas I ain't name ... Shid , I don't even gotta say your names, y'all *know* how my heart beats for my guys! Head up, chest out, Fam! If they don't see the beauty in our struggle, we'll put it in their face!

RNO!? Y'all know I rep this RNO shit! Y'all know if it ain't real, it ain't me! Speak no names, receive no indictments! We're here, RNO shit!

I saved the best for last though! My readers ... My ppl ... I no longer say *fans*! I'm all the way in with y'all, family! I love y'all!

It's you who's kept it one hundun and rocked with me no matter what, and I owe you a debt that will be paid! My word's law! 2:21!

RNO
Renta

A REAL NIGGA'S PRAYER

Lord, I'm calling on you from the pavement, the same streets that demands blood as a payment, for initiation.

A living vampire that's sucked the spirit from the village it takes to raise a child.

Now, young niggas run wild, claiming a purpose that's purposeless. Searching for worth within worthlessness, and not giving a damn if it's death that they're flirting with.

Have mercy, God ... For I've sinned against all ten commandments.

Sitting front row within the school of hard knocks; Mama wants me to get my education.

The science of the trap, an extra clip for the strap, and, trust no one. Shid ... I'm ready for an early graduation.

Protect my squad, OG, for we were forced into this life of fleeing from the police ... the same people that's supposed to protect us, is leaving us dead in these cold streets.

Chalk outlines and bloodstains speaks ... to our families with muted speech.

Hood politics intermingled with "Reganomics," it was a plot from the beginning, an illusion of profit ...

Contain us to blocks and corners before injecting the vein with narcotics.

Now, our offspring fear trust, the Willie Lynch theory that has youngin' clutching a dirty heater...

Mama danced with the devil so long that she stood at the alter and exchanged vows with a dirty needle.

God!

I seen a man cry, way before I saw a man die. Man had the weight of the world on his shoulders— I cried.

When I realized that man was he, and soon, that man became me ... A crooked cycle on repeat.

A multitude of Jesus' that breaks unleavened bread with Judas at the feast. For thirty pieces of silver, a smile ... betrayal ... then, a kiss on the cheek.

11

This, during Passover ... on my block where the rock gets passed over, to the youth that has dreams of no longer being passed over.

The alphabets swarm the block, shawty can't pass the rock. . . Past over.

Now the future looking bleak, and he now realizes he can't see ... life through a crystal ball.

Lord ... have mercy, I need you to hear me, 'cause I'm drowning where broken dreams drowns me.

I don't wanna die in the same streets they crowned me, beheaded by the same ones that found me.

My culture ... a phase of metamorphosis. The caterpillar became the butterfly, but youngin' went from LA gears to Air Jordans ...

He became the plug before being unplugged by another that had the dreams of mad fortune! Spinning the wheel of fortune, life in jeopardy, shot shots in the air that were the opposite of Air Jordans.

I'm just praying, God, that as I do this time, my Queen holds it down. Give her the gift of a sound mind, and the loyalty of a real bitch, a diamond with the right shine.

Let not my seed suffer, for the sins of the father ... on my knees at the bottom, in the blood of every real nigga I pray, Amen.

- Gambino-

"'A foolish pleasure, whatever / I had to find the buried treasure / so grams I had to measure'"

- Biggie Smalls-

A NIGHT IN PARIS

Everyone deserves access to a clean water supply! These words were scrawled in cursive across a forty foot long, silk banner that hung suspended from the vaulted ceiling, and those seven words were the reason the large crowd of rich, and some famous, had flown all over the globe to socialize at the function in the city of lights. The charity was being held in the name of the diminishing water supply in foreign lands, and the room was bustling with energy as the clinking of champagne glasses intermingled with the laughter of the rich.

In various places, sporadically stationed throughout the massive room, bulky cases were covered with silk cloths, awaiting to be unveiled. The night was perfect for the invite-only gala that was being hosted by one of France's most affluent men, and even with the fifty-*thousand*-dollars *per plate* dinners being served, the mood was festive. Rafique Amedeo was the perfect host, and since he was the founder of the prosperous foundation that benefited the lavish life-style of the capital and largest city of France, that night, he planned to embark upon one of his most lucrative ventures.

The room was decorated in the city's usual grandiose trappings, the vaulted ceiling hosting multiple dripping, crystal chandeliers, and the floor was made of imported marble. The gold and burgundy furnishings were majestic, but the most breathtaking pleasure, outside of the rich and expensive wines, were the startling views of the Eiffel Tower. The French interior designer had left the floor-to-ceiling windows bare, so one could capture it's beauty by way of moonlight. The massive iron tower was erected nine hundred and eighty four feet into the heavens, and though it was never meant to remain standing after Paris's exhibition of 1889, let alone be a landmark for the city, that night, in contrast with the thousands of twinkling stars in the sky, one could understand why the French had kept its structure. The waters of the Seine River glowed, rippling beneath the illumination of the moon and the view had stolen Gambino's attention, holding it prisoner. The man stood six foot two inches with creamy skin the hue of buttermilk pie. His head was framed with a mop of silky curls due to the mixture of his Creole bloodline, and he knew *how* to use his handsomeness as a weapon. Standing silently at one of the many windows, he allowed his vision to feast upon the night, and well aware of being admired, Gambino allowed a soft smile to curve his lips. He lusted on the memory of the night before, when he'd fucked Tamia, Rafique Amedeo's wife, into a beautiful submission. Bringing the snifter of Brandy he'd been nursing to his lips, he slightly tilted the pear shaped glass, allowing the liquor to wet his tongue.

"What's good, Playboy, how's life of the upper echelons treating you? How much longer till showtime?" A deep, Texas accented voice spoke through the micro ear piece in his ear. It was invisible to the naked eye, but the speck of a device was high frequency technology, and the nude latex design blended perfectly with the hue of his flesh. Gambino's eyes roved the room with a slow observation to ensure he wasn't the object of anyone else's fascination before they settled on his admirer. Tamia was enchanting the crowd with a dazzling smile as she undoubtfully made her way in his direction. His eyes swallowed her. She was a darker version of Salma Hayek, but with a dangerous curve to her ass.

"Everythangs everythang, my guy, just ready to rock this baby to sleep so we can get the hell back to the states. These cheese eatin', champagne drinkin' mu'fuckas got my drip out of whack," Gambino mumbled his response, before running a manicured hand down the lapels of the cocaine-white tux coat he wore. The black satin trim of the jacket matched the black tailored tux pants that sat perfectly against the suede white Versace loafers that encased his feet. "Did the other piece finally show up?" he whispered. Silence followed the question and just as Tamia was sashaying toward him, his stomach filled with a sickening feeling. *Somethings off, I can feel it! Maybe I should call it off?* He wondered, but even as the thought crossed his mental, the answer he feared most echoed in his ear.

"Naw, we're still missing that piece of our puzzle and that's unusual, family, what you think?" the voice spoke in the ear piece.

14

Gambino glanced up just as Tamia entered his space, and with no time to consider the decision, he cast fate to the gamble.

"It's a beautiful night for art." He gave the code to move forward with the plan. There was no response, but he knew his squad would go in headfirst with the business, there was no turning back.

"Excuse me? I didn't quite hear you, Monsieur." Tamia smiled with the question. Gambino's vision took an erotic odyssey as his eyes rode the wave of her model-like stature. Lady wore a deep red Valentino Haute couture dress that covered her entire left side, but left her right shoulder, breast, and all the way down to her hip, bare. The red pastie that covered her nipple was in the shape of a pair of red glossed lips, and the vision caused Gambino to fantasize of how he'd sucked the long flesh of her surgically enhanced titties.

"Art. Your presence, just you as a woman, it's art." He paused to lick his lips. "It's a beautiful night for art." He played to her vanity. A woman's craving to be physically appreciated was the foreplay that he'd use to seduce her into naivety, and as Queen's full lips parted into a flash of perfectly straight veneers, the laughter in his ear was evidence that his deceptive charm hadn't gone unnoticed with his team. He smiled as he raised his glass in a toast. "For the many children this cause will benefit."

Tamia obliged with a raise of her own champagne flute of the bubbly stuff before they both took tasteful sips. She gazed at him with mischief in her eyes, but as he studied her, Gambino couldn't help but wonder if the woman knew her husband was a cutthroat venture capitalist who stole from the poor from beneath the guise of Good Will and Shell companies. Tamia's eyes twinkled beneath the soft reflections of the many chandeliers, and just as her husband took his position at the podium they'd erected for his moment of glory, lady's innuendo told Gambino that by the end of the night, he'd have her in his bed.

"I see you *enjoy* my dress." The seduction was thick like the accent of her French as Gambino's vision fell to her exposed breast, before licking his lips and returning her gaze. The bun her hair was pulled up into made her eyes seem chinky.

"No, I don't"— He paused to gauge her reaction, and just as he'd expected, disappointment formed her pretty lips into a cute pout. "I think, for you to wear *anything* that hides from the world … such a masterpiece of a body?" he stated questionably. Smirking, Gambino downed the rest of his drink. C'est pire qu'un crime, c'est" ,une faute" he whispered in French. *It's worse than a crime, it's a blunder.* He remembered the phrase. Ms. Lady smiled so big, Gambino wondered if it hurt the fillers in her lips.

"You don't think it's a bit"— she paused to glance down at her exposed breast— *"Revealing?"* The seduction was back as she inconspicuously ran her fingers down her soft flesh.

"Honi soit qui mal y pense." Gambino insured her that anyone that thought evil of it should be ashamed.

"Then, maybe – maybe you can peel it off of me? Soon?" Tamia shed all pretense.

"Good evening, ladies and gentlemen, it's a pleasure to have you here, with me, in the grandest city on earth!" The sound of her husband's voice castrated their *sexversation.* A generous round of applause could be heard, followed by gleeful cheers. Both Gambino and Tamia turned to face the stage as Rafique Amedeo proposed he and his partner's intent.

"Tonight is a very special night for us all. Me and my friends of the *Unseen Blessings* Foundation are proud to have you here for a cause that will better so many. As we speak, there are millions of men, women, and children in the countries of Kuwait, Egypt, Israel, and even Saudi Arabia who have such a low internal water source, that if the withdrawal increases, the surface water will shrink to nothing. There are villages in Africa that still don't have direct access to a steady source of clean water." He spoke passionately with a sad shake of his head.

"So, me and the Unseen Blessings staff plan to donate fifty million for the effort of easing the economic depression worldwide!" He slammed an open palm against the podium. A blast of cheers erupted with a round of applause. As he spoke of having pipelines laid from a clean water source, Gambino's eyes swept the crowd. *This what money does, huh?* He smirked at the thought. He already knew the waterlines the man spoke of being laid in those far away countries would do exactly the *opposite* of what ole Rafique was promising. Those water lines would be laid *to steal* the *oil* from places rich in resource. "Now, for this evenings show cases!" Rafique Amedeo's voice boomed over the cheers of doctors, politicians, and multi-million dollar corporation owners. Gambino watched as the silk cloths were peeled from the bulky cases to reveal stunning displays, each case encasing precious stones from different corners of the world, and as the cloths were pulled from the paintings on the walls, soft intakes of breath could be heard over the murmurs of the delighted crowd. Anything from Sandro Botticelli's renaissance work, to the works of the Dutch painter, Rembrandt Van Rijn, and even a Picasso original were on display, but the captive of Gambino's vision was a chest high glass case.

Without a word, he slipped away from Tamia and made his way over to it, lust filling his gaze at the sight of *the Millennium Star*, a flawless two hundred and three carat gem worth two hundred eighty- five million dollars. It was a stone of De Beers, a preeminent diamond company. Many thieves had attempted to capture its beauty, but just as it's always been, beauty was an elusive conquest, and in the case of this beautiful stone, many had found themselves a captive of many a prison systems.

"Beautiful, isn't she?" Tamia's thick accent tickled his ear. Gambino merely nodded while wondering when she'd snuck up behind him.

"Twenty minutes and we'll be on our way—in forty five minutes, you need to be anywhere except where you're at, Bruh," the voice spoke through his earpiece.

Without the slightest indication that he'd heard what had been said, Gambino spoke cryptically, knowing his squad would over-stand. "Yes, it's gorgeous, but I wonder why they placed it *here*, by the corner window?" He indirectly gave the location. "What if a thief was lurking?" His word play came off as a question for Tamia, but he had to stifle the humorous laughter that threatened to spill from the suggestion.

Tamia's soft hand touched his arm, but when he fixed her with his gaze, he frowned in confusion at the expression of discomfort on her face. "I'll meet you at the château in thirty minutes," she mumbled, before nodding toward an approaching man. Gambino glanced up just in time for—

"Darling!" Rafique Amedeo declared with a broad smile on his face. His eyes briefly darted to Gambino before reclaiming his wife. He took her face in both hands before pulling her close and kissing both her cheeks. When he stepped back to admire her, he noted the sickening expression on her face. "You look under the weather, Madame, are you okay?" He asked concerned. Tamia shook her head sadly before speaking in rapid French to let him know she had taken ill and would be leaving early.

Gambino suppressed his laughter. *Bitches! From the United States to France, pussy does it to us every time!* He thought before excusing himself.

***

Fifty Minutes Later...

Four men, three divers, and the driver sat silently in an ink black speed boat. The water craft gently bobbed upon the frigid waters of the Seine River as its occupants pulled their oxygen masks down over their faces. The pitch-black wet suits they wore glistened beneath the glare of the moon, and as the lead diver strapped a waterproof pack to his back, he couldn't shake the unease he felt.

They were usually a five man crew, but for the first time in their time of chasing the bag, one of their crew was absent. That was unusual, and even more, the code they were all taught to text in case of emergencies hadn't been seen.

The man sat on the edge of the boat, gazing out into the distance as ripples played over the surface of the black water. Out in the darkness of what *could* be a perfect night, the Eiffel Tower loomed high into the twinkling sky.

"You men ready? I don't think Malcom gonna make it." One of his team proposed. There were nods of confirmation, but he, the leader and the man communicating with Gambino, had his gaze fixated on the towering design of iron. It was said that during the war between France and Germany, the French had a radio surveillance post at the top of the tower, and he wondered if it was still up there. Finally, he turned his eyes to his team, he trusted each man with his life and knew they'd hold it down for the house if it came down to that. He slid his gloves on and with a confirming nod, he leaned backward and fell into the water with little to no sound.

***

The red dress slipped from her slender frame and pooled around her pedicured feet. The summer house sat next to the Loire River in the city of Orleans, the city that New Orleans in Louisiana got it's name from, and it was one of the many homes her husband owned around the country. They stood out on the balcony of the two story manor house, the stars were bright in the heavens as adultery was committed beneath a full moon. Gambino was ass naked and the only barrier between his saluting dick and Tamia's moist lower lips were the lace panties she wore.

Lady wasted no time peeling them away and tossing them over the railing. "You gonna fuck me or what?" Her accent was thick in her English.

"Peine forte et dure!" Gambino spoke with a crooked grin. *Strong and hard punishment!* The phrase sent chills down lady's spine. Tamia dropped down onto her hunches, her ass cheeks almost touching her calves, before gazing up at him to find him gazing down at her. Her legs were spread apart as her fingers played with her clit, and with the other hand she gripped his nature in a python's grip. *Who would've thought a nigga from Fifth Ward of Screwston would find himself in Paris gettin' swallowed up by a millionaire's wife!* He thought as his eyes fell to the see through heels she wore. "Damn!" He growled as her wet lips wrapped around the head of his muscle. Her fingers were slick with her nectar as she removed them from her essence and used both hands to massage that dick while tongue kissing the head with a sloppy technique.

Gambino reached down and undid the tight bun of her hair, watching it tumble down about her face—he lusted. She devoured him. Without a break of the sluttish kiss she was giving him, Tamia reached behind him, gripping his ass cheeks, and pulled him closer so his dick could slide deeper into her wet captivity. It was war!

"You want me to nut in your mouth?" Gambino growled as his dick pulsated in her mouth. Tamia gazed up at him with an evil glare when he twisted her hair around his fist and begun to slow grind in and out of her mouth. "You wanna feel me splash at the back of your throat, Tamia?" He talked his talk as that animal within overpowered the gentleman's façade he'd earlier portrayed. In seconds, he was fucking her mouth so deeply that he could feel the back of her throat, but lady was determined to prove she was a big girl! She *glared* while applying a slight squeeze to his nuts. "Shiiiiit!" He growled.

Tamia slipped her other hand from behind him before it returned to her clit, creating a hurricane that caused her to moan against his nature. The quicker her fingers danced, the quicker Gambino fucked her mouth. His jaw muscles were prominent as he gritted his teeth against the pleasure and growled at the vision beneath him. Below the glow of the moon, he could see Tamia's juices leaking from her cut, and saturating her fingers, as her suction became so powerful, her jaws caved. Her lips locked tightly around him, she could feel that distant hum and knew his climax was racing through his body like a bullet train. The thought of that nut splashing against the back of her throat unleashed the whore in her as her fingers became a blur against her clit.

"Mmmmuah! Mmmuah!" Her moans were passionate. Gambino's knees almost buckled as his soul surged through him, but at the last minute, he pulled his nature from her wet imprisonment—*Smop!* Her lips popped from the suction. "Aaaahhh," she moaned, mouth opened wide to catch his escape. With both hands she milked him, his juice squirting all over her lips—her chin,—and even her chest.

20

"You nasty little bitch, I think I love you!" Gambino growled as he watched her run her tongue over her lips in a freak-nasty sexiness.

Tamia ran her pointer finger over her chin until his thick stickiness became a small mountain against her manicured nail, and staring him deep in the eyes, she placed it in her mouth and sucked it off with an enjoyable moan—"Mmmmuah!" She climbed to her feet and turned to face the moon before leaning forward. Placing both hands on the rail, and with a deep arch in her back, she tooted her juicy little ass up into the air. Glancing back at him, lady ran her tongue slowly across her top lip. "She's yours, monsieur, if only for the night—à la belle étoile," she whispered in French. Under the beautiful star or in the open air at night? Gambino allowed her French to translate in his mental.

Tamia rested her chin on the surface of the cool metal before reaching back with both hands and spreading her cheeks apart. "Make me cum," she whispered.

***

The fire emitting from the torch glowed brightly, turning the water a turquoise green around them as sparks cascaded from the fire cutting through the metal grate that denied them entrance to the sewage tunnel. The water was frigid as one of the divers focused a water proof LED light on the mildewed metal, watching as the fire cut through the last bar that held the grate in place. The heavy metal slipped away, and floated toward the bottom of the river. The lead man pointed toward the opening of the underwater passage and nodded.

***

"FOK ME-FOK ME-AHHUM," Tamia cried, before biting her bottom lip. Gambino stood behind her, pounding his nine inches inside her. He'd placed her left knee onto the rail, his left hand gripped her thigh, and his fingers were tight around her flesh while his right hand pushed down on the small of her back. He dug deep, pumping viciously in and out of her pussy as his inward stroke became so powerful, a smacking sound emitted from his pelvic as it connected with her ass. Tamia had never experienced *raw* fucking before, and the sensations did something foreign to her libido. Her eyes rolled to the back of her head as Gambino pipped her.

"Give me this pussy! Your husband's weak ass ain't fuckin' you right, he don't know what to do with this pussy, does he? Tell me, tell me he ain't fuckin this pussy right! Tell me, you little slut!" He growled as he raised his hand high and brought it down on her ass cheeks.

"Oh, Godddd, yess-nooo, he-Ahhh-he can't, he doesn't fok me like- like-ohhh, youuu-dooo!" she sang, as his strokes became manic, deep, faster. Her cum was thick as it coated him, but he was possessed inside her. Gambino switched his stroke to a crooked angle, the head of his nature knocking at her walls as he rolled his hips with his thrust. The friction drove lady over the ledge of the steep mountain of climax and her body shook in pleasure as she reached down and squeezed his nuts. "I can't-can't stop-cuming," she moaned deeply. Gambino reached up, claiming a handful of her hair, yanking her head back. "Yess-yassss!" She cried as she released onto him. Gambino's plans were crooked, he wanted to repay her for putting him and his people onto the lick of their lifetime, and making her cum over, and over, and over was merely a portion of the payment. The rest would be a surprise.

***

CLICK CLACK! The sound of the bullet being jacked into the chamber echoed throughout the tunnel. The divers had made it out of the waterway and were standing in ankle-deep, putrid, sewage water. Each man had worn waterproof packs on their backs that protected their supplies from the frigid water.

"In and out, fam, let's take these rich mu'fuckas down and get our asses back to the states before we find ourselves locked in some French Republic Jail. I heard they're still into hangings down here and I ain't trying to see the gallows in my future," the leader spoke, after he'd peeled his breathing mask off. His catlike green eyes captured his people, everyone who saw how strange the contrast his mocha skin was to the brightness of his eyes found him to be a paradox. The man smirked. They'd traveled all over the globe to get to that bag and each man had their own agenda, and it was a known fact that the man they referred to as *Cat Eyes* was out for one thing—*The Millennium Star* Diamond. His eyes seemed to glow with just the thought of it, and as he tightened his grip on the mac .90, he knew he'd kill for it. His mind vaguely noted the spare pistol he'd stuffed down inside his wet suit as he slipped a Friday the thirteenth mask over his face. Nodding at his shooters, Cat Eyes was ready to get it poppin'.

"Let's get to this money, family, don't let *nobody* get in the way of that," he demanded, before turning and making his way toward a side tunnel that would either lead them to failure or their happily ever after.

***

They'd wound up in a spare room of the Villa, one that was draped in gold and black satin. Gambino lay spread eagle on the huge mattress as Tamia rode him reverse cowgirl. Her pale skin seemed to glow within the darkness of the room as she rode his dick backwards. He watched as she leaned forward and placed both hands on the mattress, and without warning, he felt the strangest sensation. Tamia's lips wrapped around his big toe, and she suckled it as she began bouncing her lower self-up and down on his shaft. Her cream oozed down his manhood as he watched his length play disappearing acts with her pussy, and with each rise on his nature, her cheeks spread wider, and he could see the tightness of her pink *exit* hole. The tight embrace her kitty gave him wreaked havoc on his self-control and as she sucked his toe, Gambino had a head on collision with euphoria.

"Arrrggh!" He growled as he bucked beneath her.

***

"This is rare, flawless two hundred and three carat stone that has a rich history. It's dubbed the Millennium Star and the price tag on this beauty could make a generously rich person blush." Rafique Amedeo spoke passionately as he and a group of admirers stood around the glass case. The stone inside, sparkled brilliantly under the glow of the low lighting of the room.

"Excuse me, Raf, would it be too much to ask to have a private word with you? It'll only take a moment," a tall, handsome, European man spoke from behind him. Rafique glanced back at him. The man was a partner of the Unseen Blessings Foundation and though Rafique despised him, the man's money made him an asset in terms of global matters. The oil tycoon's wealth was abundant and Rafique loved nothing more than money.

"Pardon me." Rafique excused himself with a smile and a nod. The two men retreated to the far side of the room and as a waiter passed by with a tray of cocktails, they helped themselves to their pleasures. Nursing shot glasses of liquor, they stood before an ancient painting inspired by Claude Monet. The portrait was a beautiful work of impressionism and both men could appreciate its beauty. "Beautiful, isn't it?" Rafique whispered, as he raised the snifter of Cognac to his nose, inhaling deeply.

"Yes, Monet was a genius in capturing spontaneous reactions on a canvas." Tom agreed.

"Touché, I agree"—Rafique paused and tossed the smooth liquor back. He winced as it burned a slow-welcoming trail down his chest—"But, I wasn't speaking of Monet's talents, I was speaking of the new venture we'll be embarking on in a few weeks. With the expertise of your oil company, we'll be able to *filter* oil from certain parts of Bahrain, Cambodia, and as far as Africa. By the time they realize we've laid a mainline *and* a reverse pipe, we'll be somewhere on the Mediterranean, on our yacht's, enjoying Scotches by the coast of Asia." He chuckled.

Their plan was to lay a waterline and create a direct inlet from the ocean to create a stronger water supply. Globally, water is abundant, but unevenly distributed amongst countries, and the Unseen Blessings Foundation planned to join the hundreds of other *thief* companies that took advantage of poverty stricken countries' naiveté. They planned to lay the waterline and *underlay* a second line that would swallow oil from those distant lands and deliver it to an offshore rig.

Rafique's associate smiled a tight smile as his nervous eyes scanned the painting. The associate's name was Tom Norris, and he was a spineless man who would forever live in Rafique's shadow. Tom loved the painting, especially the artist's play on colors, but his appreciation dissipated when he heard a soft cough of impact. He felt Rafique's body jerk beside him, followed by a splash of color that sprayed against the painting. The wet stain upon the canvas was so dark, he had to lean in a little closer to realize something was terribly wrong.

"Hhhhhuu," Rafique exhaled a long whoosh of air. Tom's vision quickly found him. The surprised, vacant stare of his eyes was testament that his soul had just stepped away from his physical. At that moment, the peace of the night was stolen by the arrival of evil.

"Down! Everybody get the fuck down! Nobody try to save the day, and this will go smooth, get down—now!" a masked bandit demanded, before snatching a blond haired woman by her hair and yanking her to him. He yanked her head back with brute force. "Come here bitch!" He growled. His eyes seemed to glow from behind the Friday the thirteenth mask as he glared out at the crowd.

"Oh my God, please, *please* don't do this," the woman cried as the Champagne flute she held fell from her hand and shattered against the marble floor. The red wine splashed against the white marble, and the glass shattered into jagged pieces. The gunman placed the barrel under the woman's chin. The shocked crowd gawked in surprise.

"In the name of Mother Mary!" a man from the crowd shouted.

As if the process wasn't moving fast enough for his taste, the gunman added his own form of encouragement. *Boom!* The gun released a short flame that entered under the woman's chin, and like the eruption of an angry volcano, her top blew into the air in a shower of dark blood, and pieces of her scalp, and brains. A red slash of blood squirt across his white Jason's mask, resembling a bright scar. The murder had it's intended purpose, and the room of people hurried to their stomachs, facedown.

Tom felt trapped, alone in that dark corner of the room, staring horrified as Rafique fell to his knees, eyes wide, *lifeless!* The red stain that had spread across his white, starched shirt was the evidence of an expired life.

Cat Eyes stood a few feet away, looking like a nightmare gone wrong. He'd strapped the Mac over his shoulder and opted for the Cobra pistol. The round suppressor he'd attached to it made the gun appear monstrous. *Pueww!* The escaping bullet was a whisper when he pulled the trigger for the second time. The slug found home in Rafique Amedeo's melon. *Overkill!* The man's skull exploded in a red spray as his body pitched forward, headfirst into the wall.

"You ain't deaf, white boy, he said get the fuck down!" His demand was vicious.

"God," Tom cried, as he dropped to his stomach so fast, the move appeared comical. Cat Eyes smiled a crooked smirk. "Please don't kill me, man, it was all Raf's idea, I told him not to steal from—

"Shut your punk ass up, fool! I should plug you for snitchin' on ya mans. Just keep your mouth shut" —Cat Eyes cut him off before nodding toward Rafique's still form—"at least share a moment of silence for the dead," he whispered as his eyes blinked shut for mere seconds. When he reopened them, they were slits in the eye holes of the hockey mask. "Amen," he spat, as two flashes of hot lead escaped from the barrel of the burna. Blood and pieces of flesh exploded from the dead man's jaw and neck where the slugs pierced him. Cat Eyes wanted to whack Tom Norris, but Gambino had made it clear that he was not to be harmed. He wondered why as he studied the cowering man. He was soaked in his partner's blood, but the man became a second thought as Cat Eyes lost interest. His eyes swept the room, his men had secured their surroundings and the sight of all the treasures on display made his dick hard.

"Sorry to crash the party, ladies and gentlemen, but I'm kinda fucked up you good people didn't invite me and my folks ... we enjoy the finer things as well." He chuckled with the words. Whimpering and soft prayers could be heard throughout the assembly as he stepped over the dead man at his feet. "What do you want from us," a shrill voice cried out. Cat Eyes chuckled as his eyes molested the room in search of the only thing his every dream had been tormented by. When his eyes feasted upon the Millennium Star, his heart turned cold in his chest. The man was willing to whack *everyone* in the room if that's what it took to possess that diamond—*including his own men.* "Everything! We want it all," he responded.

***

"Let's take a shower, Monsieur, the night is young and maybe you'll enjoy a ride through the country side. We have a vintage, convertible Aston Martin that I think you'll enjoy the speed of as we discuss future endeavors," Tamia whispered, as her manicured nails made a slow trail down his exposed chest. The night was still, as the moonlight illuminated the room. Gambino rested on his back, gazing up at the high ceiling as they lay tangled in the black satin sheets. Tamia's exposed leg rested across his lower half as she lifted onto her elbow to gaze down at him. "Maybe the deed is done?" she asked with a raised brow.

Gambino's eyes never left the spot he'd been staring at—even as a soft breeze blew through the open balcony door and caused the sheer drapes to flutter inwardly. *This lady just had her husband whacked for the insurance policy, and now she wants to have pillow talk with the man she hired to get it done! This bitch's heart is as cold as the polar caps!* His vision held her hostage, and he studied her for a second before the voice in his ear sealed the deal.

"It's done, bruh, ... ten minutes and we'll be rich enough to retire." The confirmation brought a smile to Gambino's face. Coincidentally, Tamia took his smile as confirmation to *her* question, and she seductively smirked as promiscuity navigated her small hand beneath the sheets. His nature instantly reacted to her touch,

27

as she ran the tip of her tongue across her teeth, allowing him to witness the freak stirring in the depths of her gaze.

Tamia straddled him. "I loved him, ya know," she admitted, before positioning Gambino's hardened sword. "But, I must love him as Selene did Endymion," she whispered, as she rose and stabbed herself onto him. "Ahhh," she whimpered, as her lips parted in ecstasy from the painful bliss of his dick throbbing inside her. Her dark hair fell over her shoulders and face as she leaned and placed her hands on his chest. The ride was aggressive as she rose until her lower lips were squeezing only the head of his muscle. With a dark smile on her face, she studied him, her clam squeezed, released, and squeezed again, and again, before she dropped down onto his blade, committing a blissful suicide. Gambino reached up and gripped her titties, squeezing them before pushing them together so tightly, pain burglarized the house of pleasure.

"But Tamia—

"You-foking, you-black, nig-uhhh," she cried out. She gritted her teeth as the ride became frantic.

"Whose Selene?" he asked, as he glared up at her. Endymion?"

"She-mmmmah-she's the goddess of the, the moon!" She fought to explain.

Gambino released her breast and swept her hands from his chest. He pulled her down until they were chest-to-chest and her face was in the crook of his neck. He reached up and ran his hands up her sleek back until he held her in a tight embrace. His arms interlocked under her arm pits, and his hands held a firm grip on her shoulders. Gambino deep stroked her pussy. Tamia moaned a beautiful song as she wrapped her arms around his neck, sucking the bottom of his ear into her warm mouth.

"Mmmm," she moaned as he fucked her from the bottom. Their bodies glistened under the pale light as the sweat—the passion—it all became too much as his flesh slipped from her mouth in an erotic moan. "Dammmmn," she cried as he held her and worked his work. Her cum was thick as it coated him—"She loved a man named Endymion. In Greek mythology, they sa-ayyy, they say that Endymion's youth was preserved by external sleep," she whimpered as his nature drove faster. Confusion invaded his mental as Gambino tried to figure out her play on words until ... "I'm, I'm cummminnnng!" She cried at the same time the revelation dawned on him.

Eternal sleep! Death, he thought, as he felt her nectar ooze around him.

***

They'd sacked up most of the valuables and the shooters were ready to make their escape, but Cat Eyes had saved the best for last. *Pissshh!* He crashed the butt of the gun into the glass case that encased the Millennium Star diamond. The stone glistened in multi-dimensions under the glow of the low lightened chandeliers, and for a brief moment, the man's vision was a prisoner of its beauty.

"Damn," the word slipped from his lips in a whisper.

"Come on, Bruh, we need to get the hell out of here," one of his comrades shouted, as he hoisted the waterproof bag onto his shoulders. Nodding, Cat Eyes reached down and took the diamond by its edges. He smiled as he pulled it from its case.

Beep! Beep! Beep! Beep! Beep! Beep! The sound of a hidden device sounded its alert. Confused, the man behind the mask frowned, and just when he was about to turn and make his escape— *Poof!* From somewhere inside the case, the device released a soft spray. It hit him directly in the eyes—

"Awwww, fuck! Fucccck! I can't see, dawg, I can't seeeee!" He shouted as the gas burned the cornea of his eye and damaged his pupils. He dropped the huge gem as one of his partner's in crime rushed over and tossed the screaming man's arm over his shoulder. Slightly, dragging him away and being his crutch at the same time, he led them to their getaway. "Fuck! I can't see, wait, the diamond—Joey, get the diamond," he cried.

"It's too late, we have to go ... it's too late," Joey responded, as he pulled his wounded solider from the room. "It's too late," he whispered.

***

The End Game
Next Morning

"It's a beautiful night to make looove/ beneath a clear black sky/ the fragrance of Jasmine upon the bed, the Gods, you, and meeee //My body sings a song so sweet, a smile curves my lips in my sleep." Tamia sang an old ballad as she showered.

The steam from the hot water filled the massive bathroom and carried the fragrance of lavender body wash in the air. The lady stood beneath the nozzle spray with her head tilted back so the water could splash directly against her neck and breasts. Running her fingers through her wet hair, the burning water carried the sins of her adultery down the drain as she squeezed a nice amount of liquid soap onto the loofah. Tamia sang her giddiness as she created a sudsy lather over her soft skin. Soft bubbles dripped down her breasts, stomach, and down unto her nether regions.

Placing a foot on the ledge of the tub, her femininity tingled, ached from the thug passion Gambino delivered the night before, and as she used the spongelike material to cleanse herself, Tamia gently massaged that distant aching.

The sound of the door opening to the bathroom brought a mischievous smirk to her full lips. "One more time for the road; perhaps? Sex in the shower will be a delicious way to conclude our night, Monsieur, ruff- nasty sex." She giggled while using the loofah to massage her clit. "Ummmmm!" She moaned as her eyes blinked shut. When they cracked back open, she could see Gambino's silhouette through the frosted glass of the closed shower-door. Anticipation snaked through her veins like an angry serpent in pursuit of its prey. "Will you not join me? Don't you want to be back inside of my wet, hot pus—

Boom! The explosion from the gun was demanding when the first bullet knocked her words back down her throat. The slug slammed into the left side of her chest.

"Ahhhh..." Tamia sucked in a deep breath from the intense pain.

The shocked look in her eyes lifted to the jagged hole the bullet had knocked through the frosted glass. It was through that jagged peep hole that she came eye to eye with a breathing nightmare, and with disbelief dancing in her gaze, the soapy loofah fell from her hand. The woman's vision slowly drifted down to her left breast, where a small hole leaked, three inches up from her erect nipple. In shock, Tamia lifted her finger tips to the wound, gently grazing it, causing a thick trail of blood to spill slowly down her chest. She was oblivious to the splash of blood that stained the wall behind her from the bullet's exit. When she lifted her bloodied fingertips, she knew death was certain. Her confused gaze lifted and through that jagged bullet hole in the frosted glass, she found the devil. Gambino glared at her while aiming the pistol with deadly intent.

"Why" was the only question that slipped from Tamia's blood soaked lips.

"I'll answer when we meet again in hell. Right now, I must hold you accountable for the sin of adultery, "and" being a snake bitch. Tell your husband I said, wud up."

Boom! Boom! The cannon vibrated in his gloved hand. The first bullet knocked her head back and her brains splattered against the white porcelain wall. Tamia was dead before the second bullet punctured her stomach. She fell crookedly, her head slammed into the edge of the tub as her blood intermingled with the water, and the drain swallowed it like a vampire...

"Gambino, you hear this shit?" Joey's voice snapped him out his reflections of the night before.

It took a moment to gather his senses. He'd traveled so deeply into the memory that even though eight hours had passed since he'd whacked Tamia, he could still smell the gasoline he'd used to ignite the house. Gambino honed in on his focus before allowing his eyes to digest his surroundings. The morning was thirty degrees, and though the heater was on, the SUV they sat in felt like an ice box. The entire team were present. The man in the driver seat was a long haired white man named Joey. In the passenger's seat was the man

31

who had stood the team up the night before, and in the back was Gambino, Cat Eyes, and a Hispanic man they'd grown up with named Julio.

Julio pushed his door open before turning to the four men he'd crawled from the slums with—"I'll see you boys back in the states, be safe," he spoke to all, but dapped Gambino up, before sliding from the truck. They were in the parking garage of the airport, splitting up for their safety.

"For sure, my dude, you do the same." Gambino returned the love as he positioned himself behind the driver seat.

"Take care of Vato, you think he'll be okay?" Julio asked with a nod at Cat Eyes. Gambino's eyes found him. Cat Eyes sat directly behind the passenger's seat with his head tilted back against the head rest. His eyes were bandaged shut, his sight still hadn't returned, and that fact scared him. Gambino's gaze returned to Julio, they shared a troubled expression since both knew how Cat Eyes treasured his green eyes.

"Bro's a troopa, he good. Move light, babyboy, a race can't be won until you're across the finish line." Gambino saluted him, and only after Julio had departed did he close the door. "So—where you say you were last night, Malcom?" He addressed the man in the passenger's seat. Malcom seemed fidgety as he thought of an excuse, but resolution stole his ability to think. He exhaled a hot whoosh of breath.

" It doesn't matter, Gambino, it's over for us." The words seemed to freeze time. Joey flinched in the driver's seat at the same time Cat Eyes lifted his head from the head rest.

"What he just say? " he asked. " I thought you just told us you had a flat tire and—

Bam! Malcom slapped the dashboard with all his might, slicing the throat of Cat Eyes' rant.

"I lied, brother, I lied." His voice broke as a lone tear fell from his left eye. All eyes were trained on him, so no one noticed Gambino slip the tool from inside his coat. There was a nagging in his gut that told him shit was about to turn sour. His suspicious eyes began to travel around the parking garage, and he wondered if treachery was lurking. "I lied, Joey, they had me by the balls, man, and—

"What the fuck are you talking about, Malcom, spit it out!" The white cat shouted. Malcom dropped his head in shame as he did the unthinkable. He pulled his gun out of his coat and held tightly to it.

"Woah- woooah, what's up with—

"I was pulled over before we left the states, man. Fuck! A fucking busted taillight—can you believe that shit," he spat, as if he could barely believe it himself. His face was wet with salty tears and he shook his head as if he were in denial. They found a gun on me—the same one that was used in three different murders. My fingerprints were all over it and-and … His words trailed off as he used his other hand to pull something out of his pocket. Gambino tried to see what it was but didn't want to lose the aim he had on the passenger's seat.

"Somebody tell me what the fuck is going on, *fuck!* I can't see shit," Cat Eyes shouted as he balled his fist in frustration.

"Chill, family, chill. Bruh has some shit he needs to get off his chest, mane." Gambino calmed the tension. "Sup, nigga, talk," he demanded, his stare never wavering from his longtime friend.

Malcom had pulled a small piece of foil from his pocket and opened it to reveal a clear white substance. He'd been up the past four days, as high as a NASA Space shuttle, off of Methamphetamine the users had dubbed *Ice,* and the sleep deprivation ate his conscious away. Lifting the foil up to his nose, Malcom vacuumed the ice into his nostrils—the sting was instant.

"Arrrrgh!" he growled as spots blurred his vision. It took a few seconds to compose himself, but after he felt the drain slide down his throat, his bloodshot eyes grew large as he stared wide into nothingness. A thin trail of snot, tainted with streaks of blood, dripped over his lips from the drug burning the interior of his nose. Without bothering to wipe it away, the crazed man suddenly erupted into a fit of hysterical laughter as he began to rock back and forth in his seat.

Blood had leaked into his mouth and coated his teeth as he laughed, and somewhere in the midst of the laughter, the man's cries entered the moment of madness. Tears slid down Malcom's face causing him to look like the Joker from the movie Batman.

"They wanted *you*, Gambino, out of our entire squad, they wanted you! Our last job, the one we did in Pearland? The girl you killed was the Mayor's daughter! You fucked up, G, you fucked up bad, bruh." He cried as the laughter died and his face suddenly became expressionless.

Gambino's hand lifted until the barrel was level with the side of Malcom's head, his heart had turned black, rotting the love he had for the man. *This boy ratted one me? On me?* His mental was attempting to wrap around the reality like an anaconda does its prey. At that moment, he understood how Jesus must have felt as he sat at that table, breaking bread with the same men he knew would deny knowing him—the same niggas who would trade his life with a kiss on the cheek. He gritted his teeth so powerfully, his jaw muscles became prominent.

"You say what, nigga?" He growled as his hand tightened around the cold metal. Malcom chuckled when he felt the kiss of the barrel. He expected no less from his brethren, especially since they were all shooters. He nodded in understanding—*that's* why he was revealing his secrets.

"I've been wearing a wire for the past three weeks, bruh. When that plane touches down in Houston, whether I'm on it or not, they'll be waiting for you, Gambino." His voice held a tinge of sadness.

Gambino's heart began to pound against his ribs, he wanted so badly to dome dude, his hand shook from the war his common sense waged against the animal in him.

"You-you sold us out?" Joey spat the question as if it were the foulest taste he'd ever had on the tip of his tongue. His hands gripped the steering wheel so tightly, his knuckles turned white.

"I can't believe this shit, mane, fuck you turn rodent on us, bro? The same cats you starved with. We're going to prison, fam, damn," Cat Eyes spat in disgust. " I'm gonna be the only blind nigga with a 300-hundred-pound gorilla man named Tank for a celly! This shit fucked up, bruh! This ain't how it's 'pose to go, you really a rat, Mal?" He was in disbelief. He'd stood beside Malcom in gunfights, witnessed the man lay entire traps down, he just couldn't believe dude had turned into Master Splinter.

"Don't go back to the states, Gambino, run, fam, just-disappear. I'm sorry, bro, it was either me or—

"You sorry! Nigga, you just told us you turned— Gambino sliced through his explanation, and had the intent to go in, but his words died a quick death when Malcom's strange laughter filled the truck.

Before anyone knew it, he'd cocked the gun with force before staring down at the Beretta nine millimeter. Gambino and Joey watched as their longtime friend lifted the tool. Gambino's finger twitched on the trigger. "Be easy, Malcom, the trigger on this bitch so whorish, all I gotta do is tap it and it's gonna bust for me." He tried reasoning, but when Malcom turned to face him, the look in his eyes was as empty as a woman who'd had a hysterectomy. Their stare-off would become the monster that haunted Gambino's nightmares in the years to come.

"I'm sorry, bruh, I-I'm sorry," he repeated. And before Gambino could wrap his mind around what was about to happen, Malcom's hand became a blur. Life took on a slow motion effect as the man lifted the gun and – *Boom!*

CHAPTER ONE
PENITENTIARY LIFE

Three Years Later – Estelle Unit State Prison

"Last call for chow, last call!" C.O Givens shouted, as she held the door open for the inmates to leave the wing. She'd worked the compound for the past two years and though she hated it, she stayed because tuition was kicking her ass. She was a married woman, and her husband could've easily paid for her entire four years of higher learning, but Givens had gotten married six months *after* she'd gotten the job and had been raised to never depend on a man for what she could do for herself.

"Damn, Mrs. Givens, it's something special 'bout you and I'm trying to discover it. You still letting the color of our uniforms be a boundary? I know you don't keep curbing me for playboy that put that ring on ya' finger. I can tell by the way you walk, homie ain't fuckin you right." Tay, a dark skinned inmate talked his talk. He and a group of men he considered family were the last group to leave for the cafeteria, and as usual, he was shooting his shot.

Officer Givens rolled her eyes. The thuggish young man was attractive to her, but she'd never jeopardize her occupation for a moment of pleasure.

"Boy, Bye! Don't start with me today, *please*. I'm not in the mood," she retorted. Tay smiled a crooked smile with a raised brow, and she could see it in his eyes, he was about to get slick with his tongue.

"*That's* what I'm sayin', mama, you strut round this den of crooks, flashing that big ole diamond on ya' finger, but the frown on ya' face, and these moods you claim to not be in, makes me wonder if you're married to the ring *or* the man who got'chu in this mu'fucka lookin' like marriage is the worst decision you ever made."

"Come on, Tay, dawg, that hoe ain't talkin' 'bout shit," Lil K shouted as he, Thug, LeLe, Papa, and Too Blk made their exits.

"Yo' mama a hoe! You always got something to say, Lil K, you ain't nobody!" Her response was sassy.

Tay chuckled when Lil K gave her the finger and mashed off. Tay headed for the door but paused and glanced back at her. Again, Officer Given's rolled her eyes at him before crossing her arms over her chest. *This dude!* She thought of his persistency.

"Crazy part 'bout it is, just 'cause my clothes are white and yours gray, you overlook what *I* see in you, but accept what he *don't* see," he jazzed. He shook his head as if to say: *Shame on you*, before turning and heading to catch up with his people. Givens gave him the finger as soon as his back was turned before securing the gate to the cell block.

"You okay, girl? Don't let him get to you. He thinks he's the ladies' man of the unit." A female officer spoke from the guards picket. Officer Branford was a chocolate, thick, stallion of a woman who seemed to take her job a bit too serious.

Givens gave her a weak smile with a feminine wave of the hand. "Girl, please, I ain't pressed. I don't let nothing these dudes say bother me. At the end of the day, I'm just doing this to pay for school and after that…" She shrugged. "Anyway, girl, let me go do this security check so I can sit my butt down. I've been on my feet all day long and my feet hurt," she playfully whined, as she gave a pouting face. She waved with her fingers before making her way down the wing's runway and allowed her eyes to digest the reality she'd subjected herself to.

The cells were situated in three tiers, with twenty one cells on each level. Each cell, the size of a large closet, housed two men. *I can't see how they fit two men in these things,* she thought, as she did her thirty-minute walkthrough. The dorm was usually wild with ruckus, but with most of the block gone to eat, the atmosphere was as peaceful as it would get. Officer Givens was midway down the tier when she heard a strange noise.

"Eh! Eh! Eh! Eh! Get it-get it, daddy," a tense voice moaned low.

"Shut up, bitch, before someone hears you and—

"Uh-uh, I *know* I'm not seeing this ... I know not! Not you, come on now, Patterson!" Givens exclaimed, when she found the source of the soft moaning.

On the ground floor, and fourteenth cell, a convict known as Fo'Tray had a slightly muscular, chubby man bent over the table and was humping away. Givens's shrill voice caused both men to jump in surprise.

"Aw naw, Mrs. Givens, it ain't what it looks like! We just wreswrestling, I swear," he exclaimed, out of breath. "See!" he shouted with a goofy expression on his face, before leaning forward and placing Diamond, the he-she, into a headlock. Naked, the position was strange to her, and with her mouth still ajar in a surprised *O-shape*, Givens shook her head in disbelief. She'd always viewed Fo'Tray as a standup guy, and here he was, dick-deep inside another man's rectum. Both men were naked and as sweaty as two fat men in a sauna.

Seeing she wasn't going for it, Fo'Tray slipped out of his position, and with his private portions on full display, he rushed over to the bars with his pointer finger to his lips.

"Shiiiiiish! Shiiiiiish!" His face was pleading as he gestured for her to hold her silence. Givens watched as Diamond covered himself with a sheet. The man had breasts almost as big as hers due to the hormone shots the unit was forced to give the *he-she's* of the incarcerated LBGT community. "Look, man, you can't let this get out, Ms. G, they'll kill me. Listen, I got high and—

"No, *you* listen," she said, cutting him off with a disgusted expression on her face. "I ain't gonna tell nobody your little secret, but you bet not ever- *evvvver* fuck up and call yourself showing out, or I'm gonna expose that ass!" She snaked her neck. "Hey, Diamond, I see you gettin' your freak on, girl!" Givens giggled as the muscular man pushed his slicked-back hair back with his hand. The man didn't have a feminine bone in his body and had the nerve to have titties. Diamond smiled big.

"Oh, girl, you know I be turning these niggas out, I got th—

"Shut up, hoe, you don't speak unless I tell you to!" Fo'Tray checked his punk. Though Diamond looked as if he could whoop his ass, Fo'Tray was the man in their unnatural relationship.

Givens shook her head and pushed on. *Damn shame,* she thought as she completed her check of the first tier. The second row was empty, save for someone in the eighteenth cell. She hadn't made it that far down the tier, but the reflection from a small mirror, the inmates had dubbed *a peep mirror,* caught her eye.

"Commissary on the run, y'all, two row jammin'!" whoever was in that cell shouted. Commissary was usually used as the prison's store for inmates, but when it was broadcasted on the tier, it was code for *a female.*

"Get that mirror off the run before I take it!" Givens shouted. The mirror disappeared as she made it to the cell. *Ugh, I should've known,* she thought, as she scrunched up her nose at the strong smell of weed smoke. "Really, Solo, y'all just gonna disrespect me like this?" She frowned as her eyes bounced from him to his celly. Solo stood at the bars taking deep pulls from a stick (*joint*) while Lil Yank, his celly, stood over a big bowl of K2.

"Where the law at, Solo?" Someone shouted from the third tier.

"Hol up, Fam"—Solo responded, as he stood and faced off with her—look, Ms. Givens, don't go to trippin', you know how this shit go. Let us finish our business, and by the time you do an in and out, we'll be in order. We got you, mane." His voice was slow.

Givens rolled her eyes. "Y'all need to hurry up, and do something about that *smell,* 'cause if my sergeant comes over here and catches y'all, I'm gonna swear I didn't know *and* I'm gonna write y'all asses up," she vowed, before finishing her security check on two row. The third tier was empty as well, but at the twentieth cell... "Man, hell naw! You nasty ass punk! You got me fucked up, Williams, give me yo 'I.D., you funky ass rapist," she shouted.

Standing before her, ass naked and jacking off, a tall muscular cat was in raw form. All he had on was his socks as he stood in the middle of the cell, stroking his dick with a hand glistening with

40

petroleum jelly. From the way his stomach muscles tightened, she could tell he was about to explode.

"Nigga. Give. Me. Your. Damn I.D.!" Givens demanded.

"Hol-up, wait, ma, hold up, this-this the money shot!" He growled before exploding. Nut shot from his nature and splattered inches from the cell's door.

"Damn, why you trippin', Ms. G? You ain't ever tripped like this. I thought we had an understanding," Funk huffed, while trying to catch his breath. CO Givens stared at him as if he had shit on his face.

"Fuck? Understanding! Fool, we ain't *ever* had any type of *understanding* of *me* letting you jack off on me. Surely we don't! See, you dudes are really sick in the head. Just because a woman doesn't speak on it, doesn't mean she likes it! Fuck can you get it in your head that *I* want to see your dick, nigga? I go home *every day*, so what seeing *your* dick gonna do for me?" She hissed, and in an instant, she saw when the man's posture changed. Funk used his towel to cleanse himself as his expression became confrontational.

"Bitch, you're just like all these other hoes who come up in this mu'fucka! You a freak! You know you like to see this shit."

"Oh yeah, okay, cool. Let's see how much I like it. Give me your I.D., I bet your ass won't do it again." CO Givens extended her hand for the I.D.

"Fuck you, bitch, you ain't getting shit! You can't be sometimey and watch the dick, but then switch it up on a nigga when you feel like it. Shid, you don't be saying shit when these other dudes puttin' the dick on you, but—

"*Come on*, Funk, that's hoe shit right there! You dry snitchin', homeboy. Don't be bringin' another man up in yo' convo!" Solo shouted from the second tier.

"Uh-uh, don't sweat it, that's *two* cases! A code twenty for masturbating in public!" She counted off one finger. "*And* a twenty-four point *0* for disobeying a direct order!" CO Givens counted off the second finger. "I'll get your info off the roster!" She fumed before making her way to the last cell.

Gambino had been awakened by their exchange, and while they went back and forth, he slipped from his bunk to take a piss. He slipped his nature through the slit of his boxers and tended to his business.

"Damn, I hate these long pisses," he whispered to himself, before shaking himself off, and—

"Oh, hell naw! *You* too? Y'all must think I'm a hoe or something! Give me your I.D., Ridge!" Givens demanded. Gambino jumped in surprise before staring at lady incredulously. His eyes left her and took in the situation. In his haste to relieve himself, he stood sideways, his personal business exposed.

"Damn!" He spat in frustration. He tucked himself before washing his hands, and only then did he give her his undivided attention. "Hold up, Ms. Lady. What you thought you saw ain't what was goin' down. I was taking a leak and—

" I don't wanna hear it, just give me your I.D.!"

"So, you're just gonna smoke my game based off a misunderstanding? When I see you, I see a grown woman, not some irrational little girl who doesn't listen to reason." Gambino's face was death serious as he took his I.D. off his table and made his way to her. As he did, he noticed her slick eyes take him in and knew under different circumstances she'd be his. Since he'd traded his life, all Gambino did was exercise and read, and with his pale skin being covered in tattoos, he knew his effect.

"Yeah, and I thought you were a real man and not just some horny little boy who can't control his dick in the presence of someone you find attractive," Givens shot, as she copied down his info.

Gambino chuckled as he admired her, his eyes molesting her every curve. Givens was a true red bone, standing five six, and with naturally curly, kinky hair, lady was bossy.

"Attractive? Who told you that? What makes you feel *I* find you attractive, lady? Naww..." He cracked her confidence before turning and making his way over to his locker. He pulled out a *Straight Stuntin* magazine, a photo album, and a stack of Instagram pictures.

Curiously, CO Givens placed his I.D. on the bars before setting her eyes on him.

Gambino spread the pictures out at the end of his bunk before opening the photo album. "See her? All these Instagram flicks? Look, that's a lady friend of mine, she's biracial, Moroccan and Cuban, bad bitch, huh? Hol up." He pointed at the photo album. "This my BM, she's from Trinidad, exotic work," he capped, before closing the album and opening the *Straight Stuntin* Mag. "You see this bitch? Her name is Seiko..."

"Man, what's your point? I don't care about all— Givens attempted.

"My point is, I've seen and see women I'm attracted to *everyday!* That shit don't move me, Ms. Givens. You don't get a reward for being attractive. Even though I've been gone three years, your physical can *never* overpower who I am as a man, gangsta, or as a playa. Your pussy has no value to *me* unless you dedicate it to solely *me*, or unless you got an ATM machine up in that mu'fucka ... and I don't see you walking 'round here with hundred dollar bills popping out your ass crack! So please, *please,* Ms. Lady, don't disrespect me like that again." He gave it to her. The silence was thick between them as the beast studied the beauty. Givens wanted so bad to go in, but—

"Givens, they're coming back from chow, come get the gate!" Officer Branford called from the picket. Givens gave Gambino an *ugh* look before turning and making her way down stairs.

"Say, my dude, what kinda games you playin', you got us both smoked!" Gambino gritted to his next door neighbor. Simon, better known as Funk, was a gangsta in his own rite, and he and Gambino were sometimes cool, but often times at odds. He stuck his mirror through the bars and over toward Gambino's cell so they could see each other.

"Bruh, you was putting that dick on her too? I'm tellin' you, fam, that hoe good!" Funk laughed.

"Man, hell naw, you know I don't rock like that, Funk! Now look, ole girl on some punk shit tryna burn me and all I did was take a piss!" Gambino spat.

The look on Funk's face was a mixture between amusement and confusion. "I know, bruh. I *knew* I shouldn't have used so much grease! That bitch don't like it when the dick all shiny and shit," he retorted. Gambino shook his head in disbelief. *Is this boy serious?* He wondered.

CHAPTER TWO
REFLECTIONS

2014

It was a beautiful day in the city of Houston, Texas. Birds glided through the air and over the heads of two beautiful, Afro-American girls jumping rope in front of their home. Dressed identically with their hair pulled back into pigtails, they giggled, enjoying the luxury of being children.

The neighborhood was a middle-class community that was usually quiet and safe, as to be expected of a suburb, and on that Fourth of July, the neighborhood opted for the sunshine.

Tracy, the girl's mother, stood in the door smiling at the freedom she and her husband had worked so hard to give them.

"Y'all better not leave from in front of this house or I'm gonna give you "the special treatment!" she warned.

"Yes, Ma'am."

"Okay, Mom," they answered simultaneously.

Both knew the special treatment meant an ass whooping and a thirty minute stand in a corner. The white woman smiled at her interracially mixed children as her youngest daughter jump roped.

"Brian and Shay, sitting in a tree, K-I-S-S-I-N-G! First comes love, then comes—

"Alright now, Ms. Thang! Watch your mouth! Neither of you gonna be sitting in anyone's tree, no time soon!" Tracy scolded. Though she was a Caucasian woman, dedicating her heart to a black man had given her some soul. After her doting parents disowned her when they discovered she not only relinquished her love to that black man, but was also with child, she'd been forced into a world beyond her conception— a world where she was considered a traitor for loving a man with too much melanin in his skin ... a world where Jungle Fever was best left in the jungle! Luckily, she'd found a good man, with a good job, and they'd escaped the reality of the ghetto.

"Mommm!" The girl whined after she'd stopped jumping and turned to face her mother. She placed her small hands on her small hips. *"It's just a song, Mom!"* She giggled as Tracy's right brow rose high upon her face.

"Yes, and an inappropriate song nonetheless! Watch your mouth, young lady," she admonished, with a stern expression.

"Yes, Ma'am." The child conceded before Tracy turned and headed into the house. As soon as her back was turned, the child stuck her tongue out at her before returning her attention to the pink and white jump rope. *"First comes love, then they get booty, then—*

"Uh uh! Uh uh, that ain't even the right song, you being nasty! You're not even crossing the rope right! Here, let me show you how to do it," Shay, her eldest sister volunteered.

At sixteen and thirteen years of age, the two girls had never experienced the broken home cycle that eighty-five percent of Afro-American children were subjected to, and outside of spent nights with their cousins in Third Ward, the ghetto was a foreign place to them. Yet— just as it is with any other sibling rivalries, the sisters fought and competed over everything!

"I don't need you to show me how to do it, I do it better than you do anyway! You always think you're better than somebody, I hate you, hunnn!" The thirteen year old rolled her eyes and snaked her neck dramatically. *"I don't wanna use your funky jump rope no way,"* she spat, before tossing the jump rope to the ground and crossing her arms over her chest.

"Girrrrl, I'm about to ...," Shay begun, while taking a step toward her, but before she could get the words out completely, her sister turned and ran towards the house, pigtails flying backward as she fled.

"Daddy-Daddy, Shay is trying to hit me!" She tattled as soon as she entered the house. Their father reclined in his lazy boy, nursing a chilled beer as he watched ESPN. He eye'd his princess curiously as she rushed over and buried her face in his chest. *"Daddy, Shay told me she wasn't gonna let me use her jump rope because I didn't know how to do it correctly,"* she cried her fabrication of the story.

46

Her father was immune to the plays for his aid during the sisters civil wars, so he merely chuckled before his eyes drifted back to the television. *"It'll be okay, babygirl, go tell your mother."* He deflected the authority. Before he could lift his beer to his lips for another swig, the child was already headed for the kitchen.

"Mama, Mama, Shay said she was gonna hit me! She took her jump rope and won't let me play with it, I hate her!" She was in raw form.

Tracy was preparing the meat for her husband to put on the grill when her daughter stormed in. The woman gave the child her attention before using a dish towel to clean her hands.

"What I tell you about 'hate', little girl, and what is this mess you're screaming about your sister?" Tracy gave her a, 'don't-you-lie-either' look. Just like her husband, she knew her babies, but even more, she knew her man! When he was too absorbed in his sports, or the girls merely approached him with questions or situations, he either viewed as trivial or uncomfortable for him to deal with, he directed them to her. Tracy smiled as her daughter wiped invisible tears away from her face.

"She-she's being mean to me, Mama ... she told me I can't jump rope like her," her youngest girl fibbed. A woman knows her seeds, so Tracy lifted a brow in amusement.

"Oh, she did, did she? And 'that' warrants you 'hating' her?" she inquired, before crossing her arms over her chest. The girl looked up at her mother with wide, innocent eyes and nodded, 'yes'.

Tracy burst into laughter. She couldn't help it. Turning toward the fridge, she spoke over her shoulder.

"No, it doesn't, little girl, and I don't want to hear you fix your lips to utter those words again! About nobody! 'Hate' is a bad thing, and people who live with hate in their hearts, die faster than people with love in theirs. You wanna die, child?" she asked, as she opened the freezer and reached inside. *"Do you?"*

"No, Ma'am, I don't hate her, Mama, I just don't 'like 'her," the child cried. Still amused, her mother shook her head. She understood that children only understood 'like 'versus 'dislike', rather

47

than the notion of true love and care. She turned to face her daughter with two red freeze pops in her hand, and with a mischievous smirk on her face, she held them up enticingly.

"So, you don't like your sister or you're just angry with her? If you don't like her, 'your' freeze pop goes to her." She manipulated the lesson she wanted to teach. Her daughter's eyes bounced back and forth between her and the popsicles, until a wide smile stretched across her face.

"No-No, Mama, I looooove my sister! She just makes me mad! I like her, Mama, I promise!" The child retracted her statement. Tracy shook her head in amazement as she laughed. It never ceased to amaze her how a person's mood could be swayed with the offer of a gift. Whether young or old, a kind word or offer of one's pleasure stole the tension from a situation and had the power to turn a sour expression into a broad smile. Tracy handed her daughter both desserts, before reaching down to fix one of the pigtails that had come loose.

"Give your sister one and tell her you love her. You never know when God will call you home, Baby, and you never want to leave those you love on a bad note."

"Okay, Mama!" The child exclaimed before turning and running toward the front door.

"What I tell you about running through this house? Now, slow down before you fall and hurt yourself," Tracy screamed, but the little girl was already making her exit.

"Shay- Shay, Mama gave us—

Scurrrr! The sound of screeching tires interrupted her excitement. She made it just in time to see a fleeing car speeding down the suburban street before making a sharp turn when it reached the corner. As soon as it disappeared from sight, the little girl's vision began to digest the evidence of how crooked life could become.

The pink-and-white jump rope lay astray on the hot asphalt, but that wasn't what caused her little heart to start its gallop. It was the lone, size six, child's sandal that rested on its side that told the tale of how different life would become for her and her family.

"Shay- Shay! Where are you! Why'd they take you?" Her bottom lip began to quiver as her eyes darted left and right in a desperate need to believe that "maybe" what she'd just witnessed was only a figment of her imagination. "I'm sorry... I'm not mad at you anymore, I promise," she sobbed, as the freeze pops slipped from her grasp and tumbled to the hot ground. She ran over to where she and her sister had just had the argument moments earlier and fell. The concrete scraped her knees as she snatched her sisters discarded shoe off the ground— "Nooo, Shay, I'm not mad anymore—please—please come back!" She cried as she began to slap the sandal against the pavement.

"Little girl, have you lost your darn mind? Why are you keeping up all this ruckus? I know you and Shayniece aren't still"—Tracy began as she made her way out of the house with a perturbed expression on her face. Yet, frustration quickly melted into concern as her suspicious gaze swept her surroundings for her eldest daughter. Her eyes fell to the two freeze pops and—

"Please, Shay, come back, I'm not mad, I swear! Mama gave us freeze pops; we have fire crackers too! Please?"

Her baby girl's plea caused her heartbeat to accelerate. At that moment, Tracy's vision captured the single shoe, and she wasted no time racing out to where her daughter sat, on her knees, drowning, in a puddle of her own tears. Tracy fell to her knees before her. The woman's eyes were wide in fear as she studied the child in an attempt at finding a contradiction to what her mental was trying to feed her heart.

"What happened? Where's your sister, huh? Where. Is. She," she cried, as she reached up and gripped the child's shoulders so roughly, the girl flinched in pain. Tracy's panic made her oblivious to the pain she was inflicting, and she began to shake the little girl viciously as if she could shake answers that she couldn't produce out of her.

"Where is she? Yourrr sister," she cried, but the child couldn't answer. Something beyond conception had stolen her innocence. There were twin puddles in her young eyes, but with a wide-eyed determination, she refused to blink and allow them to feed the rivers

that were already running down her face. Tracy could feel her heart crumbling into a thousand pieces. The child was seeing something beyond her. Though she hadn't revealed it, as the car sped away, she'd caught a glimpse of her sister in the backseat, and terror was aflame in Shay's eyes as she was stolen away from the only love and true family she'd ever know.

***

Present Time – 2020

The club seemed alive as Megan Thee Stallion and Cardi B's voices blared from the monstrous speakers. Club *Address* was lit that night and it seemed as if the entire city of Houston had turned out to see Megan and Cardi perform.

♪ *"There's some hoes in this house / There's some hoes in this house / Certified freak, seven days a week / Wet-ass pussy, make that pullout game weak ..."* ♪ Cardi B began her verse to *WAP*.

It was dim throughout the building, but whoever was controlling the lights created magic, and the effect the light show was having on the crowd was vibrant. A flash of green lights would illuminate the room before disappearing to allow a red glow to dominate. For a brief pause, a blue laser-like flash beamed across the room, before being replaced by a golden strobe light.

"Get it gurrrrl, heyyyy, work! Work!" A short, petite cutie shouted as her friend-girl danced. It wasn't long before others took notice of the light skinned diva who had her elbows on her knees as she looked back at it.

"Awww yeah, I see you, babygirl, you just *look* like you got that *WAP*! Real hot-girl shit! Come on up here and show these other hoes how to do that shit!" Megan shouted over the music.

Patrese paused mid-twerk and gazed up at the stage to make sure she wasn't imagining what she thought she'd heard. At five foot nine, weighing a nice hundred forty-five pounds of sexiness, lady was one of those women who appeared slim from the front, but when one was blessed with the vision of all that ass she had, it was automatic to wonder *how* so much ass could be supported by such a thin frame. With a raised brow, Patrese pointed to herself, silently mouthing, *me?* Megan Thee Stallion smiled before nodding her confirmation, but it was her friend, Tabitha, who made her assumptions official.

"I know Patrese Marie Valentine ain't being bashful!" She leaned over so she could be heard over the noise. "Gurrrl, you better get on up there and show out! Loosen up, sis," she encouraged with a playful smack to her butt .

Patrese gave her the side eye. At 26 years old, she wasn't the promiscuous type, and she had only gone out that night because Tabitha, her bestie, had begged her to get out of the house. Although she was an exceptional dancer, her occupation as a social worker made freak-dancing in the middle of a club too irrational. *Oh, lord, what've I gotten myself into?* She wondered as she made her way toward the stage.

"Girl, just get up there and act like you're at home in front of the mirror." She mumbled to herself as she made her way through the crowd. Though the club had been packed to capacity for the past hour, at that moment, it made her claustrophobic. As her eyes scanned the jovial crowd, it seemed as if the entire club had their eyes on her. Patrese encouraged herself to block them out and just do her thing, and as soon as security helped her onto the stage, she'd done just that. To her surprise, there was another woman there they'd chosen from the crowd, and as Patrese studied her, insecurity reared it's ugly head. *Is this some sort of competition? Every part of this girl is enhanced!* She thought as she admired the girl's thickness.

Megan and Cardi had paused their show and outside of the loud cheering of the crowd, the only sounds she could hear was the instrumental to *WAP* and the loud pounding of her heart.

"Real hot-girl shit! I saw you, Bihh, so look, y'all the two that was shutting shit down, so here's what we're gonna do. Whichever one of y'all can twerk the best will get a role in my next video. I—

Before she could finish, the crowd went stupid.

"Heyyyy!" a female shouted.

"Ahhhhhh," another seconded.

"I bet that lil slim booty gonna hurt that," a random dude added to the hype.

Cardi leaned and whispered something to Megan that brought a smile to her face. The two superstars high-fived before Megan Thee Stallion brought the mic back to her lips.

"Cardi got her money on slim booty"—she paused to give Cardi B a playful roll of the eyes—"You slim bitches always thinkin' y'all the shit 'cause y'all got a lil ass now!" She smacked her lips humorously before turning her back to the crowd. The black, leather one-piece she wore had the ass cheeks cut out and allowed the crowd to get a glimpse of how the lime green G-string disappeared between all that ass she had. The DJ brought the instrumental to *WAP* back to the top and without effort, Megan Thee Stallion made her ass cheeks convulse as if they were epileptic.

"AAh! AAAhh! AAhhhh," she shouted her trademark, as her gluteus maximus had an erotic seizure.

The crowd went wild as Cardi slapped her on the ass before talking her talk. "Hop on Top / I wanna ride / I do a Kegel / While it's inside!" She rapped as the chocolate cutie they'd brought on stage with Patrese spread her feet apart and showed her work.

With her feet apart, she was able to turn to the crowd and mimic Megan, but having more ass than the rapper, chocolate's backside seemed to be experiencing an earthquake. She placed her hands on her knees and put an arch in her back before rolling her hips in a dramatic wind. Her ass seemed to pick up momentum as the people cheered her on. When Megan thee Stallion turned to watch, the chocolate held her arms out at her side and began to throw that ass in a circle. The act stirred the crowd into a frenzy.

"Throw that ass in a circle, throw that ass in a circle," they chanted. She began to twerk and make her cheeks bounce in so many different directions, it became a blur of jiggles.

Patrese twisted her lips in that *'umph-whatever-bitch!'* kinda way as she watched the competition. *You got ass, sis, but you not 'that' lit!* She thought as her vision fell to her own attire. The big bird yellow spandex she wore appeared to be melted over her soft skin—from the thick elastic waistband with the *"Pink"* name boldly stitched across it, and all the way down to her ankles. The white heels she wore brought life to the white-and-yellow *"Pink"* shirt she wore. She could feel hundreds of eyes on her, but as if someone was praying for her, calm washed over Patrese. Everything seemed to disappear around her, and she pictured herself standing before the full-length mirror she had at home. Her competition had a light sheen of sweat glistening over her skin as she gave her ass one more pop before facing off with the slimmer woman.

To add to the hype, the DJ changed the temp in the room. The song came on and even Megan Thee Stallion seemed surprised. *Body -ody- ody- ody-ody-ody-ody-ody – Body -ody- ody- ody-ody-ody-ody- ody / Body crazy, curvy, wavy, big titties, lil waist—* her latest twerk song filled the club.

"Heyyyy!" someone shouted.

"Bitch, that's my song," another seconded.

Patrese took a few steps back to get some room, and as curiosity dominated the room, she dropped to her hunches, her ass cheeks down by her calves, and her hands on her knees. In a slight duck walk, she turned her back to the crowd. The yellow tights she wore rode the slopes of her hips, cheeks, and thighs so perfectly, the depths of her ass crack was prominent and the imprint of her kitty lips protruded through the stretchy fabric. She glanced back over her shoulder and gave the crowd a seductive smirk before causing her right butt cheek to jump twice; after it stilled, her left jumped three times.

"Body-ody-ody- ody- ody- ody,"—Megan rapped along as Patrese's backside begun to resemble the waters of a jacuzzi— *"Body crazy curvy, wavy, big titties, lil waist!"*

The fat of Patrese's booty jiggled as she leaned forward and placed her hands on the stage. That ass began to clap as she pulled herself up into a strange pushup position. With her ass in the air, head aimed at the floor, she showed that work! Ass, thighs, and hips vibrated as she twerked. Left- right- up- and down, her backside did more tricks than a daredevil, and when she placed her elbows flat and lifted herself up into a headstand, it was official! *Please don't let me fall,* she silently prayed as she popped that pussy.

"It's over, it's a done deal!" someone shouted, clearly hyped.

" I told y'all, I told y'all, that's sis! I told y'all!" Tabitha was her number one fan. As the song came to an end, Patrese pulled herself down to the ground until she lay flat on her stomach. She pointed at the other woman with a pouting expression on her face before burying her face in the crook of her arm, and with a closed fist, she began playfully hitting the ground like a child throwing a fit. The dance was called *The Crybaby,* and as her cheeks shook with the motion, Patrese added insult to injury.

"Whannn! Whannn," she playfully cried. Megan Thee Stallion and Cardi glanced at each other with knowing smirks, but it was Cardi that set fire to the crowd.

"One time for my slim bitches with a big booty," she shouted into the mic, before turning her back to the crowd. Then she made that ass clap as she stuck her tongue out seductively.

***

"I'm sorry, bruh." Malcom's voice was strained. Gambino frowned, suspicion evident in his gaze. Life took on a slow-motion effect as Malcom raised the pistol.

"Don't do it, fam, I'm tellin' you!" Gambino warned, but the warning fell on deaf ears. To his surprise, Malcom placed the tool to his own temple, his last tear fell from his left eye before – Boom! He blew his brains out. A splash of blood and brain matter stained the side of Joey's face.

"Fuck! What-the-fuck, dude?" the white man cried out in shock. Surprised, his mouth hung agape in an O-shape. He gripped the steering wheel with all his might and stared straight ahead as if, if he kept his vision fixated on the concrete wall ahead of him, it would make the reality they were living not so real. Yet, Malcom's spiritless body crumbling sideways anchored him to a reality no man that lived a crooked life could escape. Malcom's body landed

in a crooked position and to each man's horror, the dead man's head had landed in Joey's lap.

"Tell me this isn't happening, man ... this is not happening!" He seemed to be in shock. He was a professional stickup kid but he was a good man, and unlike the others, he'd never been up close and personal with cold blooded murder, let alone suicide. Slowly, his eyes drifted down to his lap. Malcom's eyes were wide open and soulless. Panic surged through Joey's veins as blood pooled in his lap. Time seemed to pause as he and the dead man had a stare off, and as if someone had pressed the play button, Joey lost his marbles.

"God, Je-sus," he cried, before forcing the door open. He pushed the man's leaking head away as he scurried out of the truck. The sounds of him vomiting echoed off the concrete walls as Gambino's eyes drifted from the corpse to the man beside him. Cat Eyes' facial expression was etched into one of disbelief and though he couldn't see, he could taste the presence of death in the air.

"Gambino, fuck just..." Cat Eyes' words were cut short.

"Shissh," Gambino hissed before reaching over and placing a hand over his mouth. Cat Eyes pried his hand away, but before he could get back to the verbal, Gambino leaned over and placed his lips inches from his partner's ear.

"If you don't wanna spend the rest of your life in a cage, you may wanna shut – the – fuck up!" he gritted, as he held onto his bro's arm so tightly, he felt him flinch under the pressure.

Something was off to him. He knew Malcom wouldn't have spoken about their sins so "uncut" under ordinary circumstances, and the fact that he had, made Gambino sense a snake in the garden. Cat Eyes slapped his hand away but held his silence. He could hear Joey tossing his lunch when Gambino pushed the door open and slid from the truck.

"Dead! He-he fucking killed himself!" Joey could be heard, followed by another splash of the contents of his stomach. For a moment, that's the only sound one could hear until ...

Boca! The gunshot was offensive in the silence of the parking garage, and the absence of sound from Joey's regurgitating told an evil tale of betrayed trust.

Cat Eyes' heart began to pound against his chest when the truck bounced on its springs from Gambino sliding into the driver's seat, but he allowed a brief moment to pass before speaking.

"Sup, my dude, you gonna tell me what's—"

"Shiiiish," Gambino hissed again, with a glare toward the backseat. Though he couldn't see it, Cat Eyes felt the heat from the stare and held his tongue. Out of the six-man crew, he and Gambino had come out of the trenches together and trusted each other with life.

Gambino's gaze drifted back to Malcom's cooling body. The rancid smell of his muscles relaxing and releasing excrement fouled the air, but his gut spoke louder than his sense of smell. He reached over and peeled the bloody coat open before yanking Malcom's wool sweater up toward his chest. And though the dead man's blood was now tainting his hands, it was the least of his worries.

"Fuck." The word slipped from his lips in a harsh whisper. He froze, gently shaking his head as he stared down at the long, thin piece of wire taped lengthwise up dude's stomach and chest, and even without Malcom's words replaying in his head, Gambino knew it was closed curtains for him. As if snapping out of a faraway day dream, he reached over and snatched the wire so savagely, it snapped in half. "Fuck! Fuck! Pussy-ass-nigga," he growled. And in his bloodlust, all he could see was a river of blood. He slipped the still warm .40 from inside his coat and began to pistol-whip the dead man, unmercifully. Blood splashed with each point of contact, and with his head already busted, Malcom's brains and thoughts found their escape.

"What the hell's going on? Somebody tell me something, goddammit!" Cat Eyes' sudden outburst was the calm to the storm. Gambino's dilated eyes went back into focus and slowly fell to the mess he'd made. A light luster of sweat made his face shine in the darkness of the SUV. With an exaggerated release of breath, he flung the dead man away, and watched as the body fell toward the

56

floor of the truck. Gambino fell back against the seat before using his palms to massage his temples.

"Look, family, this pussy-boy has been mic'd up and it's no telling how much he's given up. It's curtains for us, homie, but I think the fuck-nigga was tellin' the truth..." His words trailed off as he stared out at the wall that was illuminated by the headlights. Subconsciously, he knew the body of one of his crew members was lying in a pool of his own blood, a sin committed by his own hand, but in Gambino's dark mental, Joeys weak stomach was the testament of a weak backbone.

"A man with a weak backbone can be easily bent, bro, forgive me, but weakness made you the sacrifice," he whispered, hoping Joey's soul understood his rationality.

"What? Gambino, my dude, I swear on my mama's life, if I could see, I'd punch you in your muthafuckin'—

The sound of Gambino's chuckle cut through the threat, caused Cat Eyes to frown in frustration. "Fuck so funny, bruh, you think my—

"I'm sayin, bro, we made it all the way across the world, took off millions of dollars' worth of rich men's goods, only for me to make it back to American soil and not be able to blow a bag of the loot I risked it all for?" He burst out laughing at the irony, but Cat Eyes didn't find the humor within the truth.

"How you find that shit funny, G? Malcom's rat ass whacked himself, "You just ... Joey ... man..." He couldn't formulate the words, let alone, wrap his mind around the hand life had just dealt them.

"And you, you the blind one! You don't get it, fam?" he asked between bursts of manic laughter. "Get it? Joey's dead, the dead can't hear, he's the deaf. My stupid ass couldn't see that Malcom's fag ass was plottin 'on me the entire time. I'm the dumb, and you, you're the blind! Deaf, dumb, and the blind, dawg." He laughed harder as Cat Eyes shook his head in disbelief. He couldn't understand how his comrade could find the nuts to laugh under the circumstances. He stared absently, until his childhood friend's laughter subsided, and silence filled the truck. "We have to split up, Cat

Eyes, Plan B is officially in effect, fam." Gambino's voice held a tinge of regret. He slid from the truck and made his way to Cat Eyes 'door. His heart cracked in his chest as he became resigned to his fate. Cat Eyes 'heart pounded against his chest when the door opened, and Gambino took him by the arm.

"So, you're about to silence me too, bruh, that's your plan? Whack all possibilities and take off into the sunset with all the shit we risked it all for?" he verbalized, while shaking his head in disappointment. He couldn't see the look of shock Gambino gave him, nor the tears that blinded the man's vision from the power of the accusation.

"Damn, my nigga, that's how you see me? "Me", Cat Eyes?" he asked, wondering how and when he'd become a reptile in the eyes of his family.

Cat Eyes ran his hands over his stubbled face before exhaling a hard whoosh of breath. He turned his head toward his brother in arms, he could "feel" the hurt radiating from him.

"I'm trippin, bruh, my mind is the devil's playground right now. Shit just ... it's just crazy." He fumbled for the words to express what no man could rationalize. "Malcom? How we miss the snake in our grass?" Cat Eyes questioned in disbelief.

"I don't know, nor does it matter at this time, family. Right now, we have to get you safe." Gambino's mental was doing a thousand in the seventy-five.

"What-what? Me? What about you!" Cat Eyes fought for understanding. When he was out and standing beside the truck, Gambino took his phone out and made a call. He was a thinker and always kept a plan for that just-in-case type of situation. His call was answered, but the person on the other end said nothing, only listened.

"Trouble in paradise," Gambino spoke, before ending the call. His eyes digested his man's. Cat Eyes had always been a thorough, stand-up guy, and as they stood in the dim parking garage, he wondered if money was powerful enough to change that?

"I'm gonna board this plane and stick to the script as if I don't know shit done got funky. I'm sure them folks heard what just

58

happened, but shid ... " Gambino's words trailed off as he shrugged his shoulders as if to say 'fuck it'! "As soon as that plane lands on U.S. soil, they're gonna take me down, bruh, but you won't be there for the showdown, Eyes," he revealed. At the same time, the sounds of screeching tires echoed off the walls.

A black-on-black SUV jerked to a stop beside them, and when the rear doors opened, two white men with long hair jumped out. One raced to the passenger's door and pulled it open for the man who slid from the seat. A tall, polished European with cold eyes, he was clad in a black tailored suit with a burgundy turtle neck sweater beneath the suit's jacket. He nodded toward the SUV Gambino and his team had shown up in, and without a word, the two long-haired men stepped to the business.

"You seem to have a knack for creating messes for me to clean up, Monsieur," the European acknowledged. His eyes studied Cat Eyes' bandaged face before drifting to where his cleanup men were lifting Joey's cold body off the pavement, before carrying it to the backseat of the truck. Cat Eyes tensed at the sound of the man's voice and a knowing chuckle escaped Tom Norris's lips.

Tom recalled the night of the charity dinner when Cat Eyes almost eternally closed his curtains, never knowing that he was the mastermind behind the double cross that had become a triple cross. Cat Eyes didn't know that Tom Norris, the same man who had stood beside Rafique Amedeo in his time of death, was the bridge that had led Gambino to Tamia.

At the thought of the woman, Tom cringed. "Did you have to kill the woman as well? She was not a part of our deal." His curiosity slipped from between his lips.

Gambino's suspicious gaze found him in a side-eye glance. Malcom's treachery and willingness to wear the wire had placed his trust in a closed casket. He held his tongue but allowed his eyes to tell the tale. "No witnesses."

Tom merely shrugged indifferently, but his middle-aged face unveiled a hint of regret. "Shame ... the whore had some good snatch, didn't she." He shook his head in pity.

"All that shit is buried with the dead, homie, the bizz is handled and you got the reins to that multimillion-dollar organization, right? That's what this was all about, right, Tom?" Gambino's response was loaded. If the man wore a wire, he'd be charged with accessory and even conspiracy!

Tom Norris's expression held a moment of shock, that melted into an expression of amusement, after registering the tactic. He nodded his understanding, before reaching into the pocket of his coat and coming out with a pack of Clove cigarettes. Extracting one, he placed it between his lips.

As if the thought had just occurred to him, Gambino's eyes shot wildly around the parking garage until he found what he was looking for. Up in the far corners of the walls were cameras pointing directly down at them. "What we gonna do 'bout those?" he inquired.

Tom Norris retrieved his lighter and sparked a flame to the tip of the tobacco stick and used his free hand to shield the flame from the chilled wind as he inhaled. A thick cloud of smoke framed his face as he glanced up at Gambino.

"It's taken care of," he confirmed, with an exhale of the tainted smoke. Gambino frowned in disgust. He hated cigarettes. Fanning the smoke away, he gestured toward Cat Eyes.

"Give us some space, homeboy, we don't have much time and I need to vibe with my brother. Personal shit." It was more so a demand than a request. Tom shrugged his indifference before giving them the space needed. Gambino returned his vision to Cat Eyes, wondering would he ever see him again. "You'll have to catch the next flight out, my guy, and by then, shit should have already hit the fan. All I'm asking is that you keep it a buck wit' me and hold my cut till I send for it ... pay Julio what's owed, and the rest is yours." He came from the hip. Cat Eyes nodded with a look that exposed offense.

"Say, bruh, we've been rockin' since the North and South sides of the city had smoke, what's overstood ain't gotta be explained. Love is shown, not talked, brodie!" He gave it up as they embraced in a gangsta's embrace. Gambino led him to the back of Tom

Norris's awaiting truck, as the cleanup men transferred their things from the casket on wheels the two dead men rested eternally within. After all was said and done, the two trucks were driven away as Gambino stared at their fading taillights. His vision trailed to the puddle of blood that Joey's slain body had left behind.

"Weak ass dude," he spat, before making his way toward the exit. He had a plane to catch and a date with a court he was truly considering holding in the streets!

"Gambino, say, you playin' these games like you ain't hearing me, but..." Funks voice seeped through the lucidness of the dream he'd been having.

Gambino's eyes cracked open, and it took him a moment to convince himself that he was actually still trapped within that prison cell and not back in that cold parking garage in Paris. He exhaled a long breath before tossing the stiff wool blanket away and sitting up on the stiff plastic mattress that was so lumpy, it felt as if he was sleeping on a bed of soft *rocks*. A light sheen of sweat glistened on his skin from struggling in his sleep, and the slight chill drifting through the cell caused his skin to prickle, as the sound of water sloshing in the toilet caught his attention. Pierre, his celly, was a dark skinned man with a pretty boy persona and the two men were as tight as the pants of a fat girl on her way to the club. The steel toilet and sink were connected in one unit, and in that cramped space, it was only a mere three feet from where both men rested their heads.

"Look out, G, I know you hear me calling you, homeboy. Shid, if you don't feel like talkin', just say that shit and I'll slide back, but don't have a nigga callin' yo' name over and over again like I'm yo' bitch or somethin'." Funk's tone held a hint of aggression, and without invitation, he stuck his handheld mirror through the bars and positioned it toward their cell so he could see inside.

"Say, dawg, didn't I just tell you he was sleep? If a mu'fucka ain't answer you the first *six* times you called them, why the fuck would you *keep* callin' their name like you *are* their bitch?" Pierre growled, as he stood and glared into the reflection of the mirror. The two lions glared at each other as the cell became thick with a dangerous tension. Pierre was from the '*H*' and was at the end of paying his dues to the state of Texas. At six foot, the color of dark chocolate, with a very high bald fade on his head the natives of Houston dubbed a *"South side fade,"* the man had a way with women in which only bonafide playas could relate to.

"I wasn't talkin' to you, homie, so you might wanna tame your tongue before shit gets ugly," Funk growled. They all knew Pierre wasn't built for the smoke, but it was written in stone that he'd rep hard if the occasion arose.

"Shid – if that's what you wanna do, when the door rolls, we can—

"Chill, my dude, don't fuck off your parole on some shit you can avoid. You'll be free in three weeks," Gambino intervened, before they reached the point of no return.

Pierre's glare found him before the truth of his words sunk in. *Hoe-ass nigga hatin' 'cause I'm on my way out the door,* he thought, before shaking his head in frustration. He gave Funk a sinister smirk before returning his attention to his laundry, and Gambino slid from the bottom bunk and made his way to the bars.

"Say, fuck you got your mirror in my spot for anyway, bruh? Secondly, I ain't *your bitch*, homie! I ain't gotta answer you *period!* So, don't be trying to flex on my celly like *he* the one out of pocket. Fuck you want anyway?" he growled.

The frown on Funk's face told him that dude wanted to get on some gangsta shit, but he tamed it when he saw that boogeyman staring out from Gambino's pupils. Predators respect predators, and Funk eased the tension. Reaching out, he extended a piece of paper to Gambino, and for a moment, the man merely glanced down at the carbon-like paper. He was heated and felt like Funk kept testing him, but as the seconds ticked away, curiosity defeated his gangsterism.

He accepted the page and began to read:

Case # 20150254125
NAME/TDCJ # James, Nikki #1630417
Time/Date: 12/12/2020 – 3:22 p.m.

Grade: MA
Offense Code: 20.0
Charging Officer: Givens, Co II

On the date and time listed above, and at E2, G1-320 cell, offender, James, Nikki, TDCJ-ID Number 01630417, did masturbate in public. Officer Givens, CO II , did and there demand him to stop and give her his TDCJ I.D. and said offender continued to expose himself and said offender did state, "Take this dick bitch, this the money shot." This did interrupt the operations of the units movement because I was doing my security check. Said offender did refuse to give me his I.D upon request.

Time/Date Offender notified: 12/12/2020 – 9:55 a.m.
Offenders plea- Not Guilty
Offenders statement: She's lying! Officer Givens asked me to masturbate and when I told her no, she got mad and wrote me up. I told her I was trying to make parole, but she said, "Not after I write this case."

Findings: We find the inmate guilty. His disciplinary record and the Officer's report is substantial in our findings.

Punishment
45 days Commissary restriction
45 days cell restriction
Demotion from S4 to L2
390 days good time loss
He read the case before handing it back to Funk. Funk studied him from the reflection in the mirror, but Gambino's facial remained as placid as a pond on a windless night.

"What you want *me* to do 'bout the lady smoking yo' chucks, bruh? Shid, I just read *your* statement. You lied on lady, mane." He chuckled with the words. Funk frowned but the chuckle he returned was like a serpentine to Gambino's ears, and it sounded as if he was hissing like a poisonous snake.

"Fuck? That boy wrote a statement on the hoe? Awww, mane, weenie ass niggas can't take their licks, mane. Keep ya' dick out ya' hand, sucka-ass dude and you won't have to worry 'bout no case!" Pierre spoke his heart. The look on Funk's face was one for the books. He was *hot* hot, but couldn't deny what truth was. He kept his vision on Gambino.

"I'm sayin' though, the hoe got both of our I.D.s that day, but I ain't seen *you* there in the disciplinary line."

"Police-ass, dude, I swear, mane!" Pierre spat.

"Fuck you just say, fuck boy? You *knooooow* you ain't wit' the shit. *I* know you pussy but we gone have to get that when they roll the doors for shift change." Funk took it there.

"You ain't said shit, playboy, that's in stone, on Bounty Hunna Blood!" The challenge was accepted.

Gambino's eyes shot to his celly. Homie ain't ready for the free world… nigga always on some prove something type shit. He thought before returning his gaze to Funk. "Both y'all boys Bloods, so you know it's gone be some smoke 'bout this. My question is why you always on some fuck shit, bruh? You're the drama Queen type, my dude, and you know you out of bounds. You know fam just made parole, why you tryin 'to fuck over him, let bro go home," he reasoned, but it was his next words that became the music gangsta's groove to. "What, you gone squeal 'cause the bitch ain't write me up too?"

"Wha-what?" Funk sputtered. He didn't wanna take it there with Gambino, but prison life was a jungle affair, and like the head of a pride of lions, when one was challenged, no matter if it was to a mere game of basketball, a game of chess, and especially a squabble, the challenge had to be met off top and in raw fashion, or the one challenged would become prey. "You got me fucked up, G! Matter fact, I knew your weak ass ain't ever like me anyway. *You* can get it too!" Funk was far from pussy.

Gambino nodded his agreement, and his hand became a blur as he reached through the bars and slapped the mirror out of Funk's hand. The plastic handle broke off when the mirror skidded across

64

the concrete like a hockey puck on smooth ice. Gambino sealed the deal.

"Let the door be the bell, Fuck boy," he hissed.

***

"Last call for alcohol! Last God-damn-call for alcohol, and then you drunk, funky mu'fuckas got to find somewhere else to go. I ain't sayin' y'all have to go home, but you no-mask wearin', sons-a-b...," the DJ said, as the club wound down.

"Girl, my feeeeet hurrrrrt!" Patrese playfully whined. She and Tabitha were making their way toward the exit when they were intercepted.

"Hold up, hol-up, Queen ... where you in a rush to? The night ain't over yet." The voice was deep like Berry White's and filled with just a *taste* of seduction.

Both women paused and gave the brotha their attention, and as soon as their vision captured the cutie, Patrese and her girl's eyes met in that sneaky-agreement way that only women can make seem like an inside joke. *"Yeah, bihh, he can get it,"* their eyes seemed to say, before refocusing their attention in curiosity.

The stranger smiled, though a bit confused as to why Patrese kept looking beside her, but allowing the woman's sex appeal to override his curiosity, "What's your name, sexy?" he asked with a nod toward Patrese.

Her eyes digested him. The deep waves on his head were freshly tapered and his boyish facial features were cute. Her eyes took in the black, Polo V-neck sweater he wore along with the black skinny jeans. She liked what she saw, but women could always tell the caliber of man they were dealing with by the type of shoes he wore. Her eyes dropped to the black-and-white Retro 11 *J's* on his feet that looked as if he'd *just* pulled them out of the box. *Umph... young, school boy, maybe a little hood in 'em,* she assessed as she nodded her appreciation. However, Patrese wasn't the type to pick men up in the club and give them the cookie—no matter how attractive or paid they were.

"Sexy will do, *buuuuttt...,*" she dragged the word, before nudging Tabitha with her elbow. *I'm* taken, but my girl here is as single as a forty ounce beer! He's cute too, ain't he girl?" She tossed Tabitha to the wolves. Dude smiled at the exaggerated way Tabitha rolled her eyes before returning his smile. He knew Patrese was lying about being taken but he had no complaints with the pass off.

Tabitha's eyes were mischievous. "Well damn, just put all my little business out there, why don't you!" Her stare never wavered as she stepped forward and extended her hand. "It's not my fault the brotha couldn't recognize a good woman when she's standing *right here in his face*," she added, with a smile that revealed her dimples.

"I'm Maxo, or just Max, ma, whichever you prefer." Dude came proper. The chemistry was so real, it belonged in a science lab. He took her hand and pulled Queen closer, already knowing she'd be sliding off into the night with him. His eyes flickered to Patrese, though Tabitha was as official as a court document. The other woman was a perfect blend of Afro American and Latina that gave her an exotic flare. Though she was tall in terms of being a woman, she'd always been slim with a nice booty. Her thighs were tight, and she had just enough titties for a lucky man to get a mouthful.

She noticed the *slick* appreciation in Maxo's stare and made a mental note of it. *Sneaky ass. Men have no respect these days!* Her thoughts contradicted the smile she gave him.

"Maxo, what's good, playboy? Whoaaa, damn, my mans, you were just gonna cuff all *this* and not introduce yo' boy!" A tall, dark, and mutually handsome brotha exclaimed after strolling over and drooping an arm around Maxo's neck. The Greek symbols on his red jacket would've told the tale of his fraternity, even if the face mask he'd worn down around his neck hadn't of had it scrawled across it in bold letters. As his eyes molested Patrese's curves, she could read his erotic thoughts. She gave him a stank face because lady was too grown and had never been the type to be dick pressed.

"Damn, lil mama, what's up with your girl? She butch or just not feeling *me*?" He nodded toward Patrese, but his question was directed to Tabitha.

Patrese shook her head in mock amazement. *Niggas! If a female ain't throwing themselves at the dick, she must be gay! If she's just chillin' and not feeling being bothered, she must be stuck up or unhappy! Ugh!* Her thoughts collided in her mind like waves of the ocean on a turbulent night. She scrunched her nose before allowing her eyes to inform him she wasn't trying to hear it. Completely ignoring him, she turned her vision to her girl.

"Girl, you have fun. Call me tomorrow 'cause I want *all* the juicy tea!" She gave her a mischievous smirk before using her thumb and pinkie to symbolize a phone while bringing it up to her ear.

"Come on, lil mama, my mans was just playin' wit' you, lighten up, damn! Look, our frat is having a party for one of our brothers who's visiting before being deployed again. Nothin' major, but everybody there will be boo'd up, everyone except..." Maxo cut in, allowing his words to trail as he nodded at his boy. "You don't have to do anything you don't wanna do, just escort hi—

"Uh-un, an escort is a hoe with a pretty title and I'm not she. I'm just not feeling it and it has nothing to do with your boy." Patrese cut him off, but playboy was persistent.

"Two hours and you can leave his silly ass there. Come on, beautiful, help the poor guy out. I mean, damn, look at the brotha." He paused as all eyes found Mr. Tall, dark and handsome, his earlier arrogance had evacuated the building and was replaced with a sad, puppy dog expression. He stared at her with wide eyes and his bottom lip poked out like a big ole baby.

"Pleeeeease?" His fraternity brother playfully begged.

"Seeee! How can you turn a brotha like him down?" Maxo instigated. Both women laughed, but when Patrese glanced at her Apple watch, Tabitha knew she'd decline. It was 3:45 a.m., and though she didn't have to work the following day, she yearned for the comforts of her own bed, and more so, to get out of the heels she was wearing.

"*Maybe* some other time, I'm dead tired and—

"Aww come out, girl," Tabitha whined with a cute pout. She took Patrese's hand and pulled her away from the men. "Damn, bitch, why you being a party pooper!" She smacked her lips in frustration.

"O-M-Geeeee, Tab, you *know* I'm not the party girl type! Hell, you had to *beg* me to come out tonight and now you're pushing it!" She glared at her friend. Patrese placed her hands on her slim waist, awaiting the rebuttal she knew was to come.

"I know, girl, I know, but damn, Trese, you're *always* working or cooped up in that damn apartment. You're so uptight it's rare you just let your hair down and kick it with your girl. Just one time, *one* hour, sis, and we'll leave. Look at them and tell me those brothas ain't fine as hell!" She played her hand. She watched the impatience in her friend's posture elevate as her vision trailed to the two men who were smiling as if they just knew she couldn't say no to her bestie. Patrese rolled her eyes once more before fixating her stare on Tabitha.

"Ugh, you're always on the extracurricular. *One* hour, Tab, one, and I'm leaving whether your hot ass tail is with me or not. I'm telling you now, sis, I'm not—

"OK-OK, I get it! One hour!" Tabitha cut her off before pulling her into a brief hug. "Thanks girl, you always coming through."

"Yeah, whatever. Just make sure you use protection with him, with your nasty ass!" Patrese reciprocated the hug with a girlish giggle.

"Really, Patrese? And what makes you think I'm gonna give him some on the *first* night?"

"Bihh, *pulease!* Ever since you and Dre called it quits you've been too *thirsty*. You're fiending for some new dick, I can smell it, bish, your thot ass in heat!" Patrese was beside herself with laughter, and the stank look Tabitha was giving her only added fuel to the fire.

Tabitha wanted to deny the claim but knew her girl was speaking the gospel. She was in dire need of some good dick, and as good as Maxo was looking to her, he could get double servings of the kitty. She shrugged before giving her friend-girl that sneaky smirk. She glanced over at the two men through the gaps of the groups of people who were exiting the club.

"I'll meet y'all at the "Whataburger" off 45 and Little York," someone shouted to their friends.

"Mane, I'm tired of Whataburger," someone responded.

Tabitha's promiscuous gaze returned to her girl. She allowed her eyes to slide up and down her slim frame before wagging a pointed finger down toward the imprint of her paradise.

"Maybe *you* should consider letting Mr. Tall, Dark, and umm... Her words trailed off as her vision drifted to the man of topic. She thought of a word to fit the description of the brotha, and her smirk was conniving as it came to her. "Edible!" She giggled. "Maybe you should let Mr. Tall, Dark, and Edible knock the cobwebs off that kitty. Lord knows she needs to get out and *stretch if* you know what I mean." Her laughter followed her as she made her way over to Maxo and took his hand. As they passed her, Tabitha gave Patrese a slick wink.

"I didn't get your name, beautiful, I'm Trevor." The tall brother slid up beside her and made the proper intro. Patrese gave him a polite smile before heading for the door.

"*Taken*. You can just call me *Taken*. This isn't a date, it's a *favor*, so don't be on any extras, lil daddy," she spoke, as he shook his head in amusement and followed her out of the door.

Damn, he thought, as he watched all that ass jiggle with each step she took. *She frontin'... she gonna let me hit that*, he thought.

CHAPTER THREE
NO LOVE

The tension was as thick as a tub of Murray's hair grease when the cell doors unlocked and rolled open. Everyone had heard the call of that gangsta shit, and just like in every other jungle, ocean, or hood, when the smell of blood was in the air, predators were lured to its aroma.

Funk rushed out of his cell at the same time Gambino was making his exit, and if the man's natural instincts hadn't been up to par, the sharp tip of the homemade knife would've plunged into his face.

"Oh shit, watch out, bro," he shouted to Pierre in surprise. When he ducked, and back peddled to dodge the blow, he crashed into him, but Pierre hadn't recognized the smoke until the devil was already in the terror dome.

The grit on Funk's face was menacing as he swung the *shank* for the second time, but Gambino had already embraced self-preservation. He flattened himself against the wall, just as the tip of the shank had made it within inches of his face and pierced the stone. A small piece chipped off as Funk came in with another quick swing – *swoosh!* The screwdriver-shaped piece of metal cut through the air, and before its wielder could position himself for a third swing – *Bam!* Gambino's fist crashed into his nose. A burst of warm blood exploded into the air as he followed up with a quick jab and powerful cross that caused Funk's knees to buckle.

Without hesitating, Pierre rushed forward and fed him two quick ones that knocked the doomed man back out of the doorway of the cell. The tier was lit with the thirst of blood.

"Whoop that hoe ass nigga, dawg, y'all bet not let up! crush that boy, Gambino!" Tay shouted, as he rushed toward the action. Gambino and Pierre were smoking dude's chucks, and in a desperate moment, Funk took a wild swing with the blade. It tore through Gambino's state issued shirt and sliced through his skin. The jagged wound burned and began to bleed heavily, but that animalistic shit had strong armed his mental, and all he could see was red as he gave it to that boy.

Blood shot out and leaked from the splits on his face, and when Gambino stepped into his next over hand, it slumped dude against the rails that had been built into the concrete to protect people from falling over the tier. From three stories up, the fall would be devastating, and in an instant, the mere squabble had transcended into something more wicked.

"Hol up, dawg, wha-what y'all-y'all doing," Funk stuttered, when a giant of a man, the streets knew as big Compton, rushed over and joined the gangsta's party.

He reached up and grasped Funk's wrist, handicapping the hand that clutched the homemade knife. Funk's eyes shot open as wide as a prostitute's legs at the sight of the big man—Big Compton was originally from Compton, California, and the man was G'd up to his bone marrow. He was known for crushing shit, and as Pierre took hold of the man's other wrist, their intent cried louder than a hungry infant in the Ghetto.

Blood dripped into Funk's eyes as they lifted him from the ground. "Please, man, please don't do me dirty like this! Big Compton, you know I fucks with you, homie," he pleaded, and to his utter relief, an angel appeared.

"Let me through, what are they doing back there? Y'all better move out of my way!" Officer Givens attempted to fight her way through the throng of men who were blocking her path.

"Naw, this ain't got nothin' to do wit' you, Ms. G, go on back down stairs," one of the goons tried to reason, and prevent the worst of the worse from happening. He knew when things got out of hand amongst inmates, it somehow evolved into a chance to take it there with the officers. Yet, in prison, there was a thin line between animal and man – *Smack!* Someone had taken advantage of the situation and slapped her on the ass, causing her to jump in surprise. A slight trickle of laughter could be heard over Funk's cries and his struggle to live.

"Y'all got me fucked up, uh-uh, which one of…" She began to say, but her words died in her throat when she noticed the men begin to encircle her. Out of instinct, she reached down and freed the can of chemical agent from her correctional belt.

"Givens, get the hell away from those animals! I'm calling for backup right now," the officer in the picket shouted, before pulling the walkie-talkie off of his hip. He placed it to his lips and shouted into the radio, "Flash, flash, officer surrounded by inmates! G1 pod, need immediate response! I repeat, officer being surrounded, G1 pod," he shouted into the hand held radio. The tension rose as the inmates gave each other silent looks of communication , they knew when backup got there, there would be no understanding for anyone who wasn't wearing a gray uniform.

Without warning, one of the men turned and ran for the stairs. He wanted no parts of what was to come but assuming he was moving to attack *her*, Givens raised the can of mace and let loose. As she sprayed, she waved her hand in a sweeping arch—she wanted to make sure she got as many of those sons-of-bitches as she could before they did the unthinkable. What she hadn't anticipated was the potency of the chemical and it instantly stole her breath. She began to cough, and only when the can was empty, did she drop it.

"Aww fuck- I- I can't can't breathe!" someone shouted.

"I can't see, dawg, arrgh! Dumb ass bitch sprayed us for nothin'!" another casualty of her reaction shouted.

Givens couldn't see due to the gas in the air, but she could hear the stampede as the fleeing men made their way down the stairs. Yet, not everyone was affected by the gas, a muscle bound, older cat known as Beast was on the lurk, and when he noticed the woman's momentary blindness, devious thoughts of doing dark perversions to her caused his dick to rise. Like a Komodo dragon, he stalked his prey. Unaware, CO Givens used the rail to feel her way down the stairs, but the loud warning from her coworker froze her.

"Givens, watch out," he shouted from the picket, but it was too late. Beast had positioned himself in front of her. Forcing her eyes open against the chemicals in the air, Givens almost had a heart attack from the sight of him. Before she could free the scream that had been clawing its way up her throat, Beast's hand found its way around her neck. At six foot five inches tall, and weighing three hundred pounds, he could've snapped her in half, and the life sentence he was serving made him not give a fuck about the consequences. The woman's eyes grew large and filled with tears as he squeezed her tighter than a child does a teddy bear when the lights were out and they thought the boogeyman was beneath the bed.

"Yeah, I got yo' lil pretty ass n—

Bam! A powerful punch knocked blood free from Beast's bottom lip. Time seemed to stand still as his eyes captured Gambino in a deadly stare. The punch was like a snack to the monster and seeing that it only caused his grip to tighten on his prey, Gambino wondered if it was time to switch it up to his WWE tactics. *Damn, I'm bout to have to chok- slam this big ass dude! Why am I even protecting this woman?* His mental was troubled waters and the sounds of Givens scratching at dude's arm while gagging for air was the only thing that yanked him out of his indecision. *Bam! Bam!* He shot two more *baaaad* mu'fuckas at Beast's exposed face and though the punches split the man's skin, the only other reaction he gave was a wicked smirk.

Uh-oh! Gambino thought in alarm. At that moment, a shrill scream echoed off the concrete walls. "Ahhhhhh... noooo!" Gambino recognized Funk's fading screams until *BOOF!* The man's body slammed against the concrete of the *first tier.* A body flying over three rows did nothing to quiet the call of the beast, his grip loosened as he flung CO Givens to the floor with retarded strength. Though Gambino was all "G", the look in his eyes revealed his consideration. *Mane, if I run, people will think it was just the gas in the air, they'll never think it's because of this big booty bandit cat,* he thought, as a smile spread wide across Beast's face. The big man's eyes dropped to the bloody wound's Gambino clutched tightly in order to staunch the escape of his blood.

"Yeaaaah, I've been waiting on yo' pretty ass to step out of line, lil nigga, *and* you're just like I like em," Beast growled, but paused to lick his chops as if he were a big ass wolf. "Bloody *and* feisty, just like a VIRGIN." His deep voice was filled with malicious intent, but Gambino's thoughts had become homicidal. *Fuck naw, I'll catch another body before this boy turns me into Sally from the alley!* He braced himself, and just when Beast lunged for him – *Boom!* The impact of something slamming into the big man sounded like a train colliding with a wall. Big Compton had watched the altercation and wanted to see how Gambino would stand under the pressure. Luckily, the man didn't fold, 'cause that's all Big Compton's eyes needed to see, so he'd snuck dude with a heavy overhand that rocked him. At six two and two hundred and eighty pounds of muscle, Big Compton was a monster, and though the blow was efficient, Beast, too, was a boogeyman. He quickly recovered and from that point on, each blow traded between the two men sounded like gunshots.

Gambino moved to aid his fellow gangsta, but before he could take another step, a stiff overhand from big Compton broke the man's jaw and crumbled him where he stood. Seeing that the homie had it under control, Gambino shrugged and switched directions. He made his way over to where Givens was climbing to her feet. "You good?" he gritted through the pain of his wounds. She nodded as their eyes connected, she couldn't understand *why* he'd placed his life on the line for *her*. At the TDCJ training academy, they taught the officers that the inmates were manipulative crooks who couldn't be trusted, but as man and woman faced off, Givens wondered so much.

"Get down! Get down *now*, motherfuckers!"

"Get down, on your stomach's with your hands behind your backs!"

"On the floor! Now! Get the hell down!" Numerous voices could be heard from the first tier as backup arrived on the pod.

Givens made her way over to the rail and gazed down. About twenty or so correctional officers rushed onto the pod with gas masks and riot gear on. Yet, it was something more sinister that held Givens' attention— there, lying in a puddle of his own blood, twisted on the pavement, lay Funk, motionless.

"Givens, Givens, you alright? What the hell happened?" Captain Vincent shot off question after question as he ran up the steps with a forty millimeter clutched in his hands, and Givens knew it was used to shoot canisters of tear gas that exploded and released the gas into the air. Four other officers had run up to the landing with him and they immediately got on the bullshit.

Gambino and Big Compton knew the drill and had already lay on their stomachs. Mad that they wouldn't be able to crack any heads, one of the officers reared back and kicked Big Compton in the side.

"Say, cuz, fuck you do that for? I'll break your mu'fu—

"Chill, big bro, don't give these hoes a reason to do what they already *want* to do." Gambino was the voice of reason as he reached over and placed a hand on Big Compton's shoulder to calm him. The big man glared at him, and Gambino saw the lion roaring in the man's pupils. He prayed silently that Big Compton would tame his gangsterism. He knew if he didn't, he'd be obligated to pick up his slack. His blessing was his curse when one of the officers viciously dropped a knee onto the middle of his back and ruffly yanked his arms back to cuff him.

"Don't move, motherfucker, if you do, I'll break your damn neck!" the man growled. As the same *excessive force* was given to Big Compton, Gambino wished they would've set that bitch off rather than be subdued. He gritted his teeth against the pain of his wounds as another officer ran over and dropped his knees down onto his legs.

"What's all this about, my man? It don't take *two* of y'all to cuff me. I'm already down. I'ma let my family know how y'all in here *dry* abusin' your power," Gambino growled, but most correctional officers were as sour as the grapes vineyards make their wine out of.

Bam! The officer punched him in the back of the head with his set of hand cuffs.

"Stop resisting, scumbag!" he spat.

"Wait, hold up!" Givens was stunned. That was her first introduction to the crookedness of the system. *It's us against them,*

76

she recalled one of her coworkers telling her. Her suspicious gaze lifted from the brutality and found Captain Vincent observing it all with an amused smirk on his face. "But-but, they were trying to help *me*, Capt. If it weren't for them, I—

"Enough! Captain Vincent demanded, but his stare was fixated on Givens. The strange thing about it was the accusatory glare he was giving her. *Bitch, really?* she thought. He studied her as if he'd caught her fucking one of the inmates and chuckled before returning his gaze to his four officers. They'd cuffed and gotten the two men to their feet. "Take their asses to lockup and place 'em on *PHD*! Strip 'em, and if either of them gives you the slightest problem…" His words trailed off as he made eye contact with his officers. *Beat their asse,* the stare read.

"I need to go to medical, Captain. I'm leaking," Gambino spoke through clenched teeth. Now that the adrenaline had fled from him, the knife wounds burned like someone had set a fire *inside* him, not to mention the split in the back of his head the handcuffs had created. A thin trail of warm blood leaked down the side of his face as all eyes fell to the bloody holes in his shirt. The tears were jagged and just beyond the torn cotton material, and a slow river of red spilled from his side.

Captain Vincent contemplated ignoring the man's war wounds and just tossing the man in lockup, but when his eyes flickered to CO Givens… *dirty bitch, I know she's fucking one of 'em,* he thought, and knew if Gambino bled to death, she would be the one to turn him in. The corners of his pink lips turned up into another conniving smirk as he fantasized about watching Gambino's stiff body being loaded onto an ambulance – *dead!*

"Who tried to take you out, Ridge? You must've really pissed someone off, huh?" He chuckled. "Who was it so I can lock their ass up?" He asked with mock concern. Gambino gave him a look that would've sliced his throat if looks had the power to kill, but since they didn't, he spat on the ground in contempt. Captain Vincent laughed lightly. He knew he wouldn't get any info out of either of the two men. "Take that one to the infirmary to get him looked at. I want cases on every one of these inmates who was out of place and not in their assigned areas," he relented. The man was a five foot three Caucasian *shit kicker* who had an erotic addiction to the paradise between a *black* woman's legs, but he despised the black man.

"Pussy ass cracka!" Big Compton spat as he was led down the steps. Captain Vincent's smirk didn't waiver as his eyes studied Gambino. He had a *special* dislike for him and his circle of crooks and knew they were the ones supplying the demand of drugs and technology to the unit. *I'm gonna catch you sons-of-bitches and make sure Walker County gets their day in court with each and every one of you sneaky bean eaters and niggers!* His thoughts were poisonous as they led Gambino toward the steps. The wounded man matched his enemy's smirk as if he could read the man's turbulent thoughts. Captain Vincent's smirk morphed into a full-fledged sneer as he stepped forward to block their path. If there was anything he hated more than being outsmarted by an inmate, it was surely the act of a black man manipulating the system and rubbing it in his face.

"You find something funny, Ridge?" His voice held an edge.

"Yeah, I do." Gambino's admission was followed by his eyes trailing from the shorter man's head, down to his feet, and back up again, as if to say: *you're the joke, white boy!*

"Yeah, well, we'll see how comical you find things after we search your cell and find the contraband you have. When was the last time you been on Facebook, the Gram? Hmm?" He smiled as if he'd hit the nail on the head. Gambino gritted his teeth against the pain he felt but forced himself to chuckle.

"If you find *anything* in my cell, white boy, *you* put it there." He gave the captain a superior smirk before—"Arrrr," he cried out, as the ranking officer reached up, took ahold of his wounded side, and squeezed. Blood soaked his fingers as Gambino winced in agony.

"Make sure to let Tay, ole Papa, LeLe, Tracy, Thug, Little K, and that cocky bean eater 100 know I'm coming for all of you shitheads." His name dropping revealed he knew all the movers and shakers in Gambino's circle.

"Captain!" Before she could tame it, Givens spoke out against the action.

"Get him out of here!" Captain Vincent demanded at the same time one of the officers nodded toward Beast.

"What about him, Cap?" he asked, as all eyes drifted to the big man. He'd just stumbled up from his nap.

"E yoke my aw!" Though he was attempting to snitch about his jaw being broken, his words were incomprehensible. "Dey jumped eeeee," he tattled, before bringing a hand to the side of his aching jaw. "Awww!" He cried in pain.

"Shut the hell up, Murphy, and get your ass down to medical to see what they can do for your jaw." Captain Vincent gave him a silent reprieve. Givens frowned in confusion, she was as green as a golf course when it came to the politics of the pen.

"But, Captain, he's the one that—

"Find your way to the major's office, CO, I'm writing *you* up. You had no business up here with these inmates without backup." His words surprised her so much, they rendered her speechless. CO Givens' lips parted into a surprised "O" as the officers led Gambino off, followed by the departure of Captain Vincent and Beast. Little did she know, Beast was merely *one* of the Captain's many in-house snitches. Just like the house nigga sold out his people for the smallest of comforts, so did he. The big man told all he heard and seen merely for his *stay-out-of-lockup-free* card. The penitentiary was no different from the streets, it was merely a contained ghetto ran by underpaid officers.

***

"Awww shit, take it off, take it off, uhhh," one of the frat boys shouted, as he rested his cards down on the table. The two other frat brothas reached across the table and gave each other a pound, as one of the three women at the table reached back and unsnapped her bra. She peeled it off and her perky breasts sprang free, then lady lifted the lacy Victoria Secret top over her head and began to twirl it like the blades of a helicopter.

"Heyyyy," she shouted, before tossing it at the brother closest to her. When it landed over his shoulder, he took it, brought it to his nose, and without breaking the stare-down he was having with the lady, he inhaled deeply.

The afterparty was just as live as the club had been that night, but Patrese sat in a corner, seemingly uninterested as if she'd be happier at a funeral. She was on her own vibe as she played with her phone. Her Instagram and Facebook pages were lit-lit and that's where she had her attention. She briefly glanced up to observe her surroundings and she felt out of place.

Everyone seemed to be flirting and touching on some of *anyone* and no one seemed to be concerned with the Covid pandemic, so she mentally chastised herself for forgetting her mask at home. She shook her head before smacking her lips at the girls at the table because the game of strip poker was obviously going in the men's favor. She watched as one of the men poured a shot of Cîroc into three different shot glasses and passed one to each girl. All three men were down to their boxer briefs, but all three women were stripped to nothing but their Victoria Secret thongs. Patrese shook her head in shame. *Black girl's lost!* she thought. She recognized one of the girls who had attended Sam Houston University with her, and the fact that she was cool with the girl's boyfriend only added to her dislike. *I told you, Deshun, girlfriend is foul!* she mentally spoke to her friend-guy. Returning her attention to the screen of her iPhone 10, she clicked the icon of her Facebook. It opened up to her notifications, but she scrolled until she found the post button:

Friends and stalkers, I have a few questions for the ladies:

Why do we as women disrespect ourselves for the sake of momentary gratification?

1.   If you had a homeboy/friend and you saw his girl out being disrespectful, I mean, outright hoeish ... do you tell him or wait for him to find out from someone else?

2.   At what age does partying and running the streets become old?

80

She posted.

"Hey, there you are, I've been looking for you." Trevor's words were followed by a shy smile. Patrese glanced up from her screen to find him making his way toward her with two glasses in his hands. Extending one to her, he attempted to appear as innocent as possible under her curious stare.

"Oh, so now you want to get me drunk and take advantage of me?" She asked without the slightest indication of the statement being a joke. The absence of a smile caused Trevor to finally give in to his irritation. She'd been stiff arming him all night and seemed to be going out of her way to let him know she wasn't pressed. He exhaled a long whoosh of breath in frustration.

"Damn, Ms. Lady, why you so mean? You've been on the defense all night like you're trying to protect yourself from me, and all I've done is try to be nice to you. What's your thing, ma?" Patrese studied him for a moment. *Cute*, she thought of the pouting face he was giving her; this one's sincere. To his surprise, she reached up and took the cup out of his hand. He studied her as she tilted the glass and tossed the drink down her throat. The burn caused her to frown as she began to pat her chest to calm it.

"Lord, what was that," she cried as the heat subsided.

Trevor chuckled. "That's that grown man shit right there." His response was followed by him mirroring her and taking the drink to the head. He tried to keep a straight face, but the power of the liquor conquered his restraint. He frowned just as hard as she had, and that's what officially broke the ice. Patrese gave in to laughter.

"Yeaah, grown man shit, *riiiiight!*" She almost sung the word.

"Sup, T-Mack? I see you bagged the baddest one in the room!" A short, stocky brotha strode over and interrupted their vibe. He eye'd Patrese with a hungry gaze before giving his frat brother a sneaky glance. They shared a mannishness that Patrese had missed since she was lost in her own thoughts.

Where the hell is Tabitha's fast ass? Who the hell is T-Mack? Is it hot in here or is it just me? Her thoughts seemed to collide with

81

one another like animals in a stampede. She began to fan herself dramatically as her eyes found Trevor. "It's getting hot in here." She murmured. Then, her vision blurred.

***

The temperature had dropped in the city of Houston, but even as the chill of winter swirled around the tall skyscrapers of downtown, Mirage appeared oblivious to its kiss. The day was a dreary gray as if the sun didn't feel like making its appearance, and outside of the casual attire of gray slacks and a black button-down dress shirt, the only protection he wore against the cold was a long black trench coat that was open and fluttering with every gust of wind that heaven blew.

Mirage's long dreadlocks hung loose as he concentrated, being extra careful as he guided the paint brush against the canvas. He was an artist with a raw talent, and though he had a beautiful condo apartment a few blocks away, he enjoyed being surrounded by the giant buildings that made up the skyline of 'the H'.

WOOF! WOOF! Picasso, his hundred and three pound pit bull barked a warning.

Mirage smiled, the dog had been his best friend for the past few years, and he loved the all-white beast. "Easy, boy, easy." He calmed the dog as the patter of small feet caught his attention. Mirage paused the stroke of his paint brush as he listened.

"Hey, what ya' doin?" A child's voice posed the question. Mirage was a bitter man who hated to be disturbed while creating, so when he realized there was no danger, he ignored the boy's question and returned his attention to his creation. "I know you hear me, Mr.," the child declared, before stepping forward and hitting him on the leg. The little boy glared up at him like, yeah, take that! Mirage paused once more as Picasso's guttural growl told him the dog didn't take too kindly to the trivial assault.

"Oh my God- there you are," a woman's panicked voice declared, as she rushed toward them. Picasso bared his sharp teeth, ready to attack.

"At ease, boy, sit," Mirage demanded. The large beast's growl died in his throat as he sat back on his hunches. The dog licked i's chops as its eyes studied mother and child. The woman pulled her Covid mask down.

"I am so-so- sorry! My son tends to just wander off!" She apologized before slapping her son's hand. "What I tell you about this? You don't wander off without mommy!" She admonished the five year old before giving him another pop on the hand. The child instantly began to wail as if he'd just received a beating.

WOOF! Picasso barked as if he wasn't feeling that.

"Maybe you just need to watch him a little better, or maybe instead of pops, you should whoop his little ass. A good ole ass whoopin' ain't ever hurt nobody," Mirage spoke over his shoulder.

The woman frowned from behind him. She wasn't feeling his vibe but before she could give it to him, her vision captured the supplies. Allowing her eyes to take it all in—the paint brushes, the tray with a variety of different color paints smeared on it—the woman curiously peeked over his shoulder. Astonished, she inhaled a sharp intake of breath at the sheer beauty of the piece. Her hand drifted to her mouth in awe...

"Oh-my-God, it's so beautiful," she spoke from behind her fingers. Mirage had yet to turn around to give her the proper attention, but he nodded absently at the compliment. She was one of the select few to have actually seen his work. He was a very private man who had acquired himself a handsome sum of wealth by means he planned to take under the tombstone with him. Though he enjoyed being a loner, deep down inside, he wanted to be loved for *him* and not his wealth. Mirage was a rich man with everything a man could want, but it was like being on an exotic island without a woman to gaze out at the sunset with.

"Thank you," he murmured.

"May I?" the stranger asked. She found it odd that he still hadn't turned to face her, but she was willing to overlook the lack of manners for the sake of beauty she seemed so captivated by. Mirage stepped to the side to give her an undisturbed view, and the woman's jaw dropped. The painting depicted a weathered black man, seemingly chasing after someone, and as the lady took in the entirety of the masterpiece, she saw that what the man was desperately pursing was a fleeing heart. Mirage had drawn legs on the bleeding heart and the hole in the man's chest told the tale of who the heart belonged to.

"What do you see?" Mirage asked in a whisper the lady could barely hear. She stared wide-eyed at the canvas, lost in the beauty of its strangeness.

"It's a man chasing after his-his own *heart*," she stammered, her voice holding a tinge of sadness. Mirage chose the moment to turn and face her, and his gaze kidnapped her breath. She took a step back, again, bringing her hand to her mouth to muffle the shocked scream that was clawing its way up her throat.

"Mommy-mommy, *ouch!*" The little boy cried when his mother reached down and snatched him backwards.

"What the... Her words trailed off, unable to confront what she was seeing.

"The heart is a strange thing to chase, especially when it's your own heart that's running away from you," Mirage whispered, as his dreads swung across his face in a strange web.

***

The room was dark and humid, so dark in fact, Patrese could barely see her own hand when she brought it to her face. To make matters worse, her head was fuzzy, and she could barely focus. The sounds of erotic moans serenaded the room, and she couldn't remember *how* she'd become naked, nor how she'd wound up in a room, sweating as someone fucked her from the back.

"Auuhhh- ummm," she moaned, as he pumped in and out of her essence. She could vaguely feel someone beneath her, suckling her breast. Double penetration. Her mind cried, but her body was as ready and willing as an infant who had spent too much time in its mother's womb.

The man stroking her from behind was balls deep inside her anal as the man beneath her bucked up into her paradise. On all

84

fours, Patrese thrust her head back in unrestrained ecstasy, but she truly couldn't understand how her pleasure was so great. She'd never felt that level of euphoria before, and as her head swam in and out of subconsciousness—"

"Arrrughh!" The brotha behind her growled as he pulled out and began to feverishly jerk his masculinity. Patrese felt his warm seed squirt onto her backside as the man beneath her wrapped his arms around her waist and bucked with a vicious passion.

"Take it! You- nasty- slut," he rasped, as that demon shot from his nut sack and burst through her like a speeding bullet cutting through a glass of water.

Patrese was drenched in sweat as other men replaced the first two, and the process continued until she'd been had by more than ten men. By the time they were finished with her, she could only lay motionless on the bed, sticky with the juice of strangers. Yet, her body was on fire, craving more.

CHAPTER FOUR
SHOOTING HIS SHOT

The Past—2014

The eighteen wheeler coasted down I-35 like a big ship upon still water as its royal-blue paint glistened beneath the glare of the sun. The long cargo trailer connected to it was Pepsi blue and even had the Pepsi emblem painted across its smooth surface. The driver was a gruff Mexican man who sported a five o'clock shadow and wore a tinted pair of Oakley sunglasses. As he feverishly chewed a glob of gum, he navigated the big truck, constantly glancing down to ensure he kept to the speed limit. As legit as it all appeared, the Pepsi logo was just as artificial as the driver of the monstrous truck.

He and his passenger were members of the Gulf Cartel and it had been drilled into them that in the event of the truck being pulled over by law enforcement of any kind, there was no other option except to shoot it out with them. It was a suicide mission without a doubt, but their starving families back home in their native country of Mexico made the gamble between dying or becoming rich, worth the risk.

The inside of the trailer was humid, and though the fear was thick, and the soft cries of the girls echoed throughout the large space, nothing was more prominent than the foul smells of shit and piss that tainted the air. With nowhere else to relieve themselves, the thirty or so girls were forced to do the unthinkable wherever they stood.

Shay was huddled in a corner of the huge container, it had been three days since she'd been snatched from in front of her own home, and she still didn't know the evil intent of the evil men who had kidnapped her.

"I'm only sixteen," she mumbled to herself, before wiping the pooling tears from her eyes. There were girls ranging between the ages of twelve to seventeen who had been captured from all over the United States of 'Amerikkka,' and as the truck coasted along the freeway, She couldn't help but wonder what would become of them.

Little did she know, young children, especially young girls, were kidnapped and forced into white slavery two times out of every other week. Nationally!

"Let- me- out- of- herrrrre!" one of the girls cried, as she pounded her small palms against the wall of the trailer.

"Where are we? Where are they taking us?" another child's cries echoed throughout the darkness.

Shay glanced up at the roof of the container and realized some- one had drilled small holes through it; hundreds of them. They were big enough to allow just enough air to circulate through the space to keep the majority of its cargo alive. Bang! Bang! Bang! Bang! The girl continued to pound. "Pleeeease, help us," she wailed. Her cries were followed by a multitude of sentiments as the other girls cried for home and freedom, and to merely be awakened from the nightmare they'd become swallowed within.

"Helllllp us! Mommy? Dad! Someone-help-us," Yet, another child cried. The rays of sunlight that snuck through the small holes were only enough to cast an eerie glow around certain portions of the trailer. The rest of the space was bathed in darkness as Shay stood silently and strained her eyes to see.

"Godddd my stomach hurts," the light skinned girl beside her moaned. Shay glanced at her and though the girl was half bathed in the shadows, she could make out the dark smudges of dirt that had caked up on her pale skin. The girl clutched her stomach as tears streaked down and through the smudges on her cheeks. Shame was evident in her eyes when she glanced up into Shay's concerned gaze, and when the foul smell of her released bowls permeated throughout their captivity, she cried. Shay's eyes fell to the dirty floor of the trailer just as the girl's urine seeped through the leggings she wore and puddled at her feet. She'd soiled herself in both manners and not wanting to cause her any further embarrassment, Shay hurriedly returned her attention to the speckles of sunlight that seeped through the small holes in the roof.

"Ewww!" a Hispanic girl cried in disgust, before gagging and covering her nose. "You shit yourself!" Her accusing glare only

added to the terrified child's fear, and another trickle of pee soaked through the hot pink spandex she wore.

"Leave her alone!" Shay demanded, before stepping around the embarrassed girl and shielding her from the accusing eyes of the Hispanic girl.

"I no talking to you, so shut—

"She's right," another girl intervened. All eyes diverted to her. She was only seventeen, but like Shay, she was womanly developed for her age. Her eyes bounced back and forth between Shay and the Mexican girl. "We are older than these other girls, and we shouldn't be fighting each other. We should be trying to find our way out of here." She brought rationality to an irrational situation, and though she couldn't see too much, she smiled.

"My name is Ann." She extended her hand to Shay, but the girl's trust was on zero. She merely stared suspiciously as the rest of the girls began to glance at one another, wondering if it was safe to trust. And after what seemed like an eternity, Shay extended her own hand.

"My name is Shay and I'm from Houston, Texas." For the first time in those three days, smiles were genuine.

"My name is Tonya, I'm from Oklahoma. I was taken from the park where me and my friends were playing."

"I'm Trish, and I'm from Rochester, New York. I was taken while I walked home from school."

"Hi- I'm-I'm Tresey, and I'm from California. I- I was stolen out of the car when my mother went inside the store for milk," Tresey, the girl who'd just soiled herself mumbled, as the remaining girls introduced themselves.

In that dark space of stolen life, sisterhoods were forged, but just as it was with any other good thing, someone had to buck the system. Ann turned to the Hispanic girl and extended her hand with an unsure smile on her face.

"Ann," she offered, but the other girl merely rolled her eyes. Her family's upbringing had made her ugly.

The Latina turned to make her way deeper into the confines of the trailer, but the sudden turn of the truck caused her to stumble.

The ride became bumpy and a sense of panic filled the air. They were close to their destination.

***

Patrese's eyes shot open in alarm, and her dream was overshadowed by the rays of sunlight pouring through a nearby window. Disoriented, she allowed her eyes to focus before sitting up in the unfamiliar bed, and as soon as she did, a splitting migraine caused her to bring her hands to her temples.

"Ahhh, my headdd," she cried. Making small circles with her palms to ease the pressure, she didn't register that something was wrong until a slight chill caressed her skin. Patrese couldn't remember anything of the night before, but she knew that no matter what had transpired, there was no reason for her to be naked in a bed that wasn't her own. As if in slow motion, her hands fell away from her head and her eyes drifted down to her exposed breasts. Passion marks and dried semen tainted her skin in so many places, it was hard to see her hue. Confused, she began to rub her hands up and down her arms as if she were cold, and when the dried substance began to flake against her flesh, she paused. Her head slightly tilted to the left as her eyes focused straight ahead into nothingness. Her skin began to prickle as her mind rewound and began to play blurry images of pornographic recollections that were so *rated R,* they'd make an adult-film star blush. Flashes of herself in the doggy style position, silhouettes of multiple strangers mounting her, their warm, sticky release splashing against her skin ... inside her.

Her eyes grew wild. The buildup of the scream that was racing its way through her vocal cords, was similar to that of a cooking volcano before an eruption. Her thoughts spun so dizzily that she couldn't decipher one from the other. Her body began to tremble, to perspire, and before she knew it, she had vomited on herself. After she'd emptied her stomach, the earth-shaking scream that had been coursing through her being, burst out from between her lips at a shrill timbre...

"NOOOOOO! NOOOOOO! Hellllp meeeee! NOOOO!" She cried as she began to scratch at the dried flakes on her skin. She clawed viciously at her arms. Her nails dug so deep, she broke the skin and bled, but no matter how thoroughly she cleaned her skin, it was her mind that needed to be purged.

***

"Price, get ready for disciplinary court, you're the first on our list." The sound of her voice woke Gambino from his nap. He'd just fallen asleep only an hour ago and though his dreams were beckoning him back to slumber, he knew with the noise of the penitentiary, there'd be no returning.

"Ms. Givens, look out, Ms. G, come fuck with me!" someone shouted.

"Damn, that bitch thick-thick! Send her down here to eight cell," another inmate shouted.

"Look out, Lil Yank, who that is down there? Tell 'em I need some toilet paper, dawg. I ain't took a shit since I been back here!" Lock up was alive.

They'd placed Gambino in the hole for the altercation that transpired, and though he had a few cats back there that he thugged with, the man wasn't feeling being knocked out of position for trying to protect himself. Funk had survived his flight over three row, and since he was broken up and unresponsive, the unit warden wanted answers.

"Damn, Ms. Givens, bring yo' sexy ass over here real quick. I promise I just need a few seconds of your time. It's *important,*" someone shouted.

Lock up on the Estelle unit was on A-wing and it was similar to small tombs. Two different cell doors separated each cell from it's entrance, making each offender double secure.

"Boy, what the hell you want? You better not be calling me down here for no foolery!" Gambino heard her say. "Uh-un! I know- I- just- *know*, you didn't call me down here for this weak shit, Johnson, I know not. Your dick is the same size as my little nephews!"

Gambino chuckled at the disbelief in her voice. He hadn't set eyes on lady since things went bad, and he'd been anticipating a chance to encounter. His eye's drifted to the folded piece of paper he'd placed at the head of his bunk. He'd tossed caution to the wind and used his pen to stain a piece of paper with his most forbidden thoughts. His only dilemma was getting it to her.

"Look out, Big Compton, you good down there, big homie?" he shouted, so his voice would carry down the tier.

"I'm Gucci, homie! They down on one row running disciplinary. I'm 'bout to get ready. Say, you got any more of them chicken soups to eat?" Big Compton's question was encrypted, but Gambino overstood it.

"For shit 'sho, I'm 'bout to eat one too, shoot ya' line," he responded, before reaching down into his boxer shorts and pulling a small baggie from beneath his nuts. He smiled at the eight grams of *loud* he'd snuck to lock up with him. Slipping from the bunk, he made his way over to the small sink and poured a few nuggets of the cannabis onto it's ledge before glancing back at the blue *NIV* Bible he'd placed on the head of his bed.

Bowing his head, he whispered a quick prayer: *"God, you know I don't mean no harm, and if I had something else, I wouldn't even fuck with You like this, but shid..."* He paused and shrugged, hoping the OG understood. *"This all I got! I ask Your forgiveness and for Your protection, God. Don't let these people send me to G4 or G5 for this boy, Funk. God, You know this boy sour. You said that no weapon formed against me shall prosper, show me, OG, for only You can Judge me. In the blood of every real nigga I pray- Amen,"* he concluded, before retrieving the Bible. Gambino opened it to the index, shaking his head in shame at how many pages he'd used as rolling papers. Chuckling, he tore just enough of the waxy paper to twist two joints, before tossing the good book back into the bunk.

As he went about his business, he thought of how much of wasted life prison was. Some of the greatest talents were trapped inside those cold stones and some would never be known beyond their prison fame. *I wonder who the first mu'fucka was that thought of smoking out of Bible paper... I bet that boy wanted to get high as bad as a bitch!* He smirked at his thoughts before rolling the first stick and licking it to seal it closed. It was crazy how innovative people became when their backs were to the wall. Gambino glanced down at the three pieces of pencil led and shook his head in amazement. Placing the stick between his lips, he placed a thin piece of toilet paper around the third and longest piece of led. He then tore off a long strip of toilet paper and twisted it until it resembled a wick, and with a slight tap of the third piece of led against the two in the socket- *voila! Fire! He* hurriedly lit the tip of the stick before sticking the wick inside the large holes of the suction vent to minimize the smell of the burning paper. He attempted to suck the soul from the joint on his first inhale, and the potency of the smoke spanked him for the disrespect.

Gambino coughed until his eyes blurred with tears. *This that gas,* he thought, before placing a clenched fist in front of his mouth to muffle the cough. Composing himself; thereafter, his every kiss of the weed was with caution. Making quick work of the joint, he tossed the evidence in the toilet before sending it to the sewer.

SSSSSiiish! The sound of something sliding across the floor got his attention. The Kush had hit him hard, and Gambino was in love with the lazy feeling it gave him. His head was submerged in weed smoke, and it took him a moment to focus. His bloodshot eyes focused on the water bottle that was attached to a long line of torn sheet.

"Get that line, homie, and put that soup on there," Big Compton shouted. Gambino knew that *Soup* was code for the second stick he'd rolled. Compton was speaking code to throw the other inmates off their trail, but everybody wasn't lame.

"Sayyyy, somebody on that *loud*! You niggas break bread or play dead! Come on with it, baby, I got money on deck! Soups, chips, Swiss rolls, cookies? What it's hittin for, Gambino?" someone shouted. Gambino frowned while shaking his head in disbelief. *Niggas don't know how to mind their business... always putting the next man's movement out on the air waves, he thought.*

"Homeboy, fuck you talmbout? You down bad coming on the runway talkin' reckless like that! Cold part 'bout it is, you don't even know what you talkin' about! Fuck off the air waves with all that *dry* snitchin' before you get your jaw broke, homie," Big

Compton spat, and as if someone had hit the mute button, silence fell upon the tier. Compton was feared 'cause he was a savage and repped that *CC Rida* Crip business with his entire heart.

Gambino chuckled as he retrieved the homie's line and pulled it into his cell. He quickly sliced a small hole into the package of a dial soap before sliding the stick under the bar of soap. Tying it to the long strip of torn sheet before tossing it back out onto the walkway.

"I tripped out, family, my fault! I ate the last Soup I had, but here's some soap to wash yo' ass with. Get at me if you need any more hygiene. Pull it!" he shouted.

"It's love, homie, ridaaaa!" Big Compton shouted his favorite mantra.

"Two row jammin', laws on two row!" someone further down the run warned. Not knowing if they were coming for him, Gambino hurriedly tucked his stash before racing over to the baby powder bottle he had. He began patting the bottle, watching as clouds of the powder clouded the air.

"Yeaaah, somebody on that *loud*, holla at ya' boy!" The sound of officer Kennedy's voice calmed the gallop of Gambino's heartbeat. Kennedy was his partner. He was just a young cat from the slums of Waco, Texas, who was trying to do right for his mom's piece of mind, so he'd become a correctional officer. "Ross, you're up next for court, be ready!" he called, as he studied a piece of paper with a list of names on it. He was so engrossed in what he was doing, he walked right by Gambino's cell. Gambino was so high, he'd patted almost half the bottle of powder into the atmosphere before he realized he was doing too much. He laughed before waving his hand through the air to clear it.

"Un-unnnn, you need to do better, Ridge, that's not working." The sound of her voice startled him so much, he jumped in surprise. Givens giggled and shook her head in amusement, and as the particles in the air thinned out, their eyes connected. His bloodshot eyes danced with hers, both of them wondering who'd blink first.

"I wanted to—

"My fault, I— They had spoken at the same time. Givens blushed as Gambino ran his hands down the sides of his face. He exhaled a soft breath before making his way over to the bars.

"Look, lady, it seems like we both have something on our minds, so you get it off yours first and I'll open mine to you after you're finished," he offered, as her eyes fell to the stitches on his side, before quickly lifting back to where their stare was on opposite sides of the battlefield. He recognized the confusion that registered in her features, the uncertainty, and she recognized the resolution in his. His mind was made up and he was venturing into uncharted waters whether she wrote him up or not.

"Nah, I- I was just wondering if you were okay. I saw how you were bleeding the other day, and- and"— She shrugged—"That's all." She'd spoken with measured convo. It was just something about the way he studied her that made her question herself. *Is my hair in place? Do I got a booger in my nose?* Yet, she prayed he wouldn't mistake her cordialness for flirtation. "I still can't believe my coworkers did you like that, I—

"Say, mane, I don't mean to cut you off, but fuck yo' coworkers! These white boys don't give a damn 'bout me or *you*. I can bet my life on it that they wrote *you* up and all you did was try to be a good officer. How far *that* get you, ma? But, I'ma soljah. Since it didn't kill me, God gave me another chance at it." He gave her a crooked smirk. The surprised expression on her face got a chuckle out of him. "What? You don't think street niggas believe in God or something?"

"No-nooo, it's not that… I just didn't take *you* as the type." Her response caused him to give her a peculiar look.

"The *type*… What, the type to talk to God? Shid, if you ask me, it's niggas *like me* who have the strongest faith, 'cause if we didn't have something or *someone* to believe in, we'd cut out our own hearts just so we could ignore that bitch." He absently ran his hand over the war wounds he'd recently incurred.

"Look out, G, let's escort this…" CO Kennedy spoke from behind her, but paused when he saw who she was dialoguing with.

"Gambino? Fam, what you doing back here in lockup?" He was truly off balance. He knew how Gambino carried himself and knew it would take a lot to get him out of character. Gambino glance at CO Givens before his vision returned to CO Kennedy. Kennedy caught the subtle message: *'we don't talk street shit in the presence of ladies.'* He nodded before it dawned on him that he was interrupting something. A sneaky smirk eased onto his face as his eyes bounced back and forth between man and woman.

"Ohhh- I see, I see." He chuckled with a playful glint in his eyes. In every prison across Amerikkka, the men CO's were real suckas. They *hated* to see a female officer being too friendly with an inmate, because though they were free and had more to offer, men had insecurities just as women do. They see what the female CO sees in those inmates. The fitness, the clear skin, the swag, the *ability* to hold a real convo. But whereas the woman CO saw attraction, the male saw a *threat!* It was a male CO's greatest fear to face the embarrassment of their woman's heart being stolen by a crook. Yet, CO Kennedy was one of the *few* true playas employed for the department of corrections. He playfully elbowed Givens.

"Damn, Givens, all this time you've been stiff arming me from getting the kitty cat, all because you got that penitentiary fever, huh? Shid, I ain't mad at ya', my mans here is a real one." He put on for the home team. He chuckled. Givens frowned. Gambino merely studied her reaction.

"Boy, don't play, you know I'm not with none of the extras. I'm just here to get my check and make it back safely to my *husband.*" She gave him a stern expression to punctuate her claim.

CO Kennedy lifted his hands in surrender. He knew how extra lady could get when it came to her job. He backed away chuckling.

"Aiiight- Aiiight, girl, I was just playin' with you, but come on, we have to escort this man to court." He nodded at Gambino before making his way back to the cell he was about to escort. CO Givens rolled her eyes at him before she fixed Gambino with her honey-colored gaze.

" I was only making sure you were alright. This is my job, but I'm not with all the extra stuff. Y'all are human just like—

"Take this." Gambino's demand cut through her spiel.

"Huh?" she inquired, lost to his meaning. Again, that expression of confusion fell over her pretty face. He didn't know if it was the courage of the Kush smoke or merely the natural boldness he'd been born with that had him going for what he craved, but no matter the source of encouragement, he had it on his mind. Though his heart was rapid fire in his chest, he nodded down to where his hands rested on the bars. As soon as her eyes followed the gesture, he lifted his hands to reveal the folded piece of paper. She stared down at it as if it was a one way ticket to jail.

"What's that?" The question was rhetorical, yet, it was all he could do without laughing.

He answered. " It's a *kite*."

"A *kite*? What the hell is a kite and—

"Look, G, a kite is a code term we use for *a note* pertaining to shit we don't want the laws to know, but ..." He raised his hands up as if the police were telling him to freeze. "Before you spazz out, listen to me real quick."

"Boy, I'll write yo' ass—

"Listen, mane, you know what, hold on." He held up a hand before turning and heading for something on his bunk. After retrieving it, he returned to the bars and held it out to her. Givens glanced down at it before her vision recaptured his with question marks dancing in her pupils.

"Why you handing me your I.D.?"

"'Cause you're actin like you're about to arrest my convo and write me up for speaking my mental, shid." He left the rest hanging in the air as he shrugged indifferently. Gambino exhaled the breath he'd been holding.

"I'm coming from the gut with you. I know this your bread and butter, just like I know you got a man at home who *can't* know what he has in you. Your eyes tells me that much. I'm on game, so I know how they poisoned you at that academy where they train y'all at. They teach y'all that we're manipulative ... that we're animals. They taught you it's officers versus the inmates, but how can these people forbid what God said is natural?"

"Boy, you are—

"The Bible said God created woman for man because it's not good for a nigga to be alone. Look around me, mama." He interrupted her resistance and waved his hand around the room to indicate his cell. "This is as alone as it gets, Queen. And yes, I *will* tell you some of *anything* to win you over, *but* ... How can you fault me for doin' it all to obtain what I crave? Even a fallen Angel deserves a chance to fly again, right?" He gave it up as he studied her.

Givens' eye's fell to his side where the evidence of the reality he lived made him appear more of a wounded animal than a man trapped in a million dollars' worth of concrete and iron.

"Just take it and read it. Victoria has kept her secret for decades, I'll keep ours till the grave," he professed, before crossing his finger over his heart in pledge. Her eyes lifted to take him in.

"Givens, come on, girl, before people get the wrong idea," CO Kennedy's voice broke through their spell.

"Hold up, Kennedy, I'm 'bout to write this nigga's ass up!" She surprised not only herself, but Gambino and Kennedy as well.

"What! Why you writing Ridge up, G, he good. Chill!" Kennedy came to his rescue, but her next proclamation fucked the world up.

"Nah, this fool over here jacking his *small* ass dick on me. So disrespectful!" Her eyes took in Gambino's stunned expression. *What! This bitch done lost her marbles!* He thought as she reached for his I.D.

"Bitch, you get your police ass up outta here! If you ain't tryin' to see no dick, stop lookin', this the penitentiary, a *men's* prison! You walkin' 'round here with your pants all up in that ass and think a mu'fucka ain't gone be aroused? Fuck outta here!" one of the inmates down the tier spat.

"Come on, Ms. G, don't come over here trippin.'"

"Gambino, what's good, bro?"

"Aww shit! Gambino down there putting that link on that hoe! She say you got a lil dick, bruh, say it ain't so, fam, say-it-ain't-so!"

The tier exploded with expletives. CO Kennedy held a handcuffed inmate by the arm when he paused by the doorway to Gambino's cell. Givens turned and made her way over to take the inmate's other arm. Kennedy glanced over at Gambino before looking back to her. "You good?"

"Yeah, motherfuckers always trying to test me 'cause I'm a woman."

"Naw, Ridge a good dude, no cap," Kennedy stated as they walked off. Gambino stood as still as a statue. His mental became a spider's web of thoughts as he tried to figure out what happened. A slow smirk spread across his face as his eyes glanced down at the I.D. still in his hand, and when his gaze fell to the bars, he knew that God sometimes had a soft spot for a real nigga. *The kite was gone!*

CHAPTER FIVE
CHANGE GONE COME

"Can you handle this by yourself? I have to go to the little girls room," Givens asked, as she shuffled from foot to foot like a little girl in dire need to tinkle. Kennedy and the inmate they were escorting both looked to her, but it was the inmate who spoke.

"Damn, Ms. G, that thang hot in all them clothes, huh?" He chuckled at his own humor.

It was something about being locked up that brought the freak out of the humblest niggas, but the truth of the matter was, lockup also created a sexual psychosis in brothas that led them to say and do some of the most disrespectful shit.

Givens glared at him as she became as still as frozen ice. "I'm not the one, dude, you want an *attempting* to establish a relationship case, you got the right one, don't play with me," she spat, before diverting her attention to her coworker. "You gonna be alright with him or what?" she asked, before her right leg began to bounce in impatience. Even CO Kennedy took notice of how her thick thigh shook in the gray uniform pants. "Uh, Kennedy, let's not be disrespectful."

She rolled her eyes.

"Huh, girl, what you talkin' about? Ain't nobody worried about you. Gone and take care of your business." He gave her a guilty smile. CO Givens shook her head. *Shame,* she thought, as she turned and headed to tend to her feminine duties. *I bet these niggas looking at my ass,* she thought, as she strutted toward the staff's restroom. Suddenly, she stopped and spun around. "I forgot," she began. Kennedy and the inmate jumped in surprise, caught dead in their moments of lust. Givens sucked her teeth before turning and making her way to the place where she would sell her soul to the devil.

***

Gambino had taken another stick to the face, and he was so blitz, all he could do was stare at the graffiti other inmates had tagged the wall with. In Pre-Hearing Detention (*PHD*), all the inmate was allowed was baby powder, a tooth brush, one toothpaste, a Bible, spoon, bowl, and their fan. This made time slow unless one had someone they knew back there to chop game with.

"Say, Bino, you ain't wrote nothin' lately? I know you got some new real shit for the streets," one of the inmates he knew asked. Everyone on the compound knew Gambino loved music and had dreams of being the next star coming out *the H.*

"Yeah, let me hear that shit you just wrote, lil bro. I'm feelin that B-I," Big Compton fed the fire. Gambino nodded his confirmation as if they could see him before snatching up his pen and spoon to make a beat with. He flipped his mattress back so he could beat on the steel of the bunk, before taking a seat and closing his eyes. He loved the vibe music gave him, and as his hands began to move rhythmically, the pen and spoon became drumsticks in his hands.

"You niggas feel me as I take you down through there. This that real nigga's blues, medicine for the soul type shit. That RIP MO3 and Papa roach shit," he announced, as he began to do a churchy whistle.

It seemed like the entire tier had quieted to hear fam speak the gospel as Gambino spat from his gut:

♪"Got a visit from my mama, say she been dreamin' 'bout the reaper busting my head / say she's been prayin' for me, told her I've been praying too, but must've missed what He said /
For trying to feed the fam, system crucified me, without the thorns on my head / make me wonder what Jesus felt when He begged God to save 'em, nailed to the cross, betrayed as He bled / Prosecutors tryna nail me, not guilty all that I said/ I'm lyin', told 'em before I talk, they can tie me up, drench me in gasoline, and throw a torch in my bed /
Where I'm from, we thug on the ledge of the Devil's island / my young niggas wildin'/ struggle got us surrounded / somethin' like an island / on the corners that I'm grindin', sharks hunt for the profit / eat dinner with the piranhas, swallow the scuba diver while he's divin'/ say money's the root of all evil, so I'm in all black while

I'm slidin'/ got me doing a hundred down the road to riches without lookin' where I'm drivin'/

    Me and my apes on the lurk for the land of honey and *milk*, and I ain't talkin' 'bout *calcium*/ For that bag we'll jump out squeezin' them *bananas,* all led, *no potassium*/

    We starvin'/ me and you niggas ain't the same, I'm a martian / *no Marvin*/ Big ole thirty on the carbon got me clutchin' like a *marksman*/ for real / they whacked my nigga Papa Roach, the money made 'em connivin'/ his blood cried from the concrete, they sped off while he was dyin'/

    Got me wondering if God watchin'/ with Ray Charles vision / some sunglasses, the nigga blinded/ love not one sided/ He should wanna see me better/ I'm not Jesus, if the devil tempted me for forty nights I would've robbed him in that desert /

    Versace, Versace, Versace/ my guys all black, *secret society* / Gang Gang the *illuminati*/ then I skirt off in that Ghost like my soul just left my body ... Bitch!"♪

***

    Givens made sure to lock the door before pulling the folded note from her pocket. "What am I doing? Why'd I accept this from him?" She questioned herself before glancing up at her reflection in the mirror above the sink. It stared back with an expression that was just as confused as her thoughts.

    Unfolding the notebook paper, she wondered how he'd gotten it to fold so compactly.

    Gambino's hand writing was slightly slanted and sloppy, but still, she opened her mind to his words:

Egypt ... Yes, that's 'my' new name for you. It's a play on your middle name. "Alexandria." Alexandria just so happens to not only be where my family is from in Louisiana, but it's also a city of Northern, "Egypt!" I did my homework. Smiles! Look, I wish I could simply say, "Open Sesame," and open your heart to just the idea of what's become so natural for a woman to reject. But I don't think Ali Baba used those words in the movie of Arabian Nights to

103

open the cave of the forty thieves, for the same purpose I want to open the cave of your mind. *Feel me, I don't know all the mysteries there is to know about a woman, but I know enough to know that you've been sleepwalking through life, giving yourself to men, and maybe even women that can't recognize value, so they'll never understand "how" to value what's priceless. You ever seen the fairytale Sleeping Beauty? I hope so, so you understand. See, just like the woman in this fairytale, you've been poisoned. Just for different reasons, and by different people. You've been poisoned to the "idea" of men like me. I bet you may be thinking I'm just like every other nigga that lusts for you. Think if given the chance, I'll fuck over you, make promises I can't keep, and even get you fired. And to be all the way solid, all those "could" be possibilities. Yet, the thing about possibilities is, they're like a sword, it has two potentials. It can either cut you or protect you. It just depends on which side of the blade you're on. Maybe you think I'm just out to use you, and if that's a thought, guess what ... you're 100% correct! I do! Fix your face though. See, people place the wrong definitions after the right words. "Everybody" uses someone! You go home and use your man for his dick ... to make you cum. He uses you to make him feel masculine. You use your clothes and makeup to help you feel sexy, and the attention you get uses you to influence the next woman to seek it. See, it's not the "use" of someone that should make you weary, but the "misuse" that should give you caution. The shit I wanna use you for has the power to transform "a moment in time" into " a lifetime," and if a lifetime is too much for you to give me, I can settle for merely "a piece of your time in life." I know that just like Sleeping Beauty, you've had different men to touch you, love you, and do all they could to wake up within you what fell asleep ... Your heart! Yet ... it refused because only a special kinda nigga can do that. Listen, I know my situation is ugly, but there's beauty in my struggle, ma. You just gotta believe, the impossible is only impossible if you can't see that I'm the impossible. Get it? I'm-possible. Yeah, I tried it! And you know what? For you, I'd try it again, and again, and again, and until trying it again seems too foolish to try it again. All I'm asking is that you allow curiosity to get the best of you. Please, let it. Pweeese? "Begging face" You 're my weakness, lady. Can I be weak for you, ma? Being strong takes too much energy.*

Tryin' to be yours,
- A special kinda nigga-

After concluding the kite, Givens sat on the toilet seat, not to use it, but to think. *What the hell have I gotten myself into?* She wondered. "This is your job, girl!" she whispered to herself. Confliction is the worst thing to have during a moment of decision making. It means that one is in favor of both possibilities but knows only one can be chosen. Crazy part about Givens' situation was that though she'd just reminded herself that Gambino was a threat to her job. The fact that she was a married woman never crossed her mind.

***

With nothing but a bottle of Remy XO as a dinner companion, Mirage dined at his dining room table, absently picking over a Lean Cuisine steak dinner. Though the jeans he wore were torn at the knees and had paint splotches splattered in various places of their material, they were his favorite pair. The way the man lived, one wouldn't know he was a millionaire a couple times over.

The condo he'd purchased on Gray street was located on the outskirts of the Fourth Ward section of the city and was on the top floor, but it was a cluttered mess. Finished, as well as incomplete art, lay some of anywhere there was space, and though he had a keeper that cleaned the condo every two weeks, Mirage's demand of his creations not being touched made her work seem mediocre. Outside of Marisol, his housekeeper, and Mike, his driver, the man was a loner and valued his privacy.

Arrrrff! Arrrrfff! Picasso barked down by his leg. Mirage chuckled before taking the *mystery* meat off the tray of the cuisine dinner and extended it down to the animal. The massive dog instantly chomped down onto the processed meat. *I ain't hungry anyway, Mirage* thought, before reaching for the bottle of Remy and cracking the seal. Twisting the top off, he tilted the bottle to his lips

105

and took a generous gulp before resting the bottle back down. The burn down his throat was a pleasurable pain that he'd grown to love. Just the taste the texture of the Cognac was a euphoria to him.

It was a frigid day in the city of Houston, Texas, and the temperature was said to drop into the mid-forties. Yet, the cold didn't bother him, since winter was his favorite time of year. Mirage was a man of sporadic decisions and being childless and as single as a dollar bill, he had the liberty of living on the edge. He slid from the chair and *slowly* allowed *familiarity* to carry him around his domain until he found what he was looking for. He'd developed an addiction that he hadn't missed partaking of since his pops had died two years earlier, and just like his old man, he'd found that the addiction was an outlet when he'd become submerged in his feelings.

Without much effort, he found the black lacquer coated case in the corner of the living room where he always kept it, and for a moment, he could feel the spirit of his father cursing through it.

His head dropped from the weight of missing his old man, and as his dreadlocks swung wildly about his shoulders and face, he fought the river of tears that cried to be liberated as his mind dropped him into a pool of memories...

It was a gray morning back on that date of December 16, 2000. As a young boy, Mirage was a late sleeper. He'd become so accustomed to his mother storming into his room and forcing him out of bed with one of her old southern palms, he'd began to oversleep purposely. "Boy, a man who sleeps all day is a man who doesn't deserve a good woman or children, because he's gonna love his dreams more than he loves them. Get ya' lazy butt up, now, and don't make me have to tell ya' again," she'd say. Yet, that morning, there was no wakeup call, nor the smell of that southern breakfast that usually wafted throughout the old house on Buck Street in the Fifth Ward. That was unusual, Mirage slipped from the warmth of his bed and stretched.

"Ma must've overslept . . but... He paused when his eyes found the time on the clock. 8:45 A.M! "Naw, mama don't oversleep like this," he whispered, before glancing up at the posters of his favorite

rappers he'd hung on his wall. Fat Pat, Z-Ro, Lil KeKe, Podina, and his idol, Scarface, all seemed to be gazing down at him with that H-Town pride the city was known for. He gave the posters a nod before exiting the room, and the first thing he noticed was the silence. It was too quiet for the Goldsmith's household. His mother "always" had some Anita Baker or Betty Wright on to start her morning, but that morning it was as quiet as a cemetery.

With a frown on his face, Mirage made his way through the house, and as soon as he made it to the living room, his heart began to hammer against his chest. Though no one was there, it was the notes of the saxophone dancing on the wind that gave him pause. Over the years he'd learned his father's thoughts and moods by the melody he played. He followed the deep notes until they led him to the kitchen where he found the back door open. Each note that carried on the wind seemed to have a life of it's own, whispering a wordless song that was saturated with emotion. He stepped out onto the back porch, and that's were he found his father— eyes closed, with a wet trail of salty tears cascading down his face. He held the saxophone as if it was an intimate lover. His slim fingers danced over its keys as if they were a woman's clit, and he was determined to make her cum. He'd never seen his old man cry. The man was a man's man and the sight crushed Mirage. His father showed no sign of noticing his presence, but as Mirage's eyes fell to a lone piece of paper that lay abandoned on the ground, his gut told him that all the answers his heart reached for would be found on it.

Without disturbing his father, he reached down and retrieved the paper. As soon as his eyes recognized his mother's calligraphy, the melody of Sam Cooke's, "Long time Comin," finally registered as the tune his father was making the old instrument cry. His eyes flickered to his father for a brief moment as he caused the sax to cry at a long, fading note, before it dropped back down to a series of notes so clear it was as if he could hear the actual words of the song. Fresh tears were dripping from the man's face and that's what reverted Mirage's attention back to the missive. He could almost hear his mother's voice expressing the words as he read:

Dear Mirage Sr.

I know that a woman should step to her business in person, but, Baby, the love I have for you won't allow me to look you in those gray eyes and hurt you. 'Cause I do love you, sweetheart, it's just that I'm not "in" love with you anymore. Mirage Sr., I've given you twenty long years of my life. I've cooked, cleaned, and birthed you a handsome son, but, Baby, I must live for "me" now. I'm tired of Fifth Ward, I deserve better than this shithole of a house.

I know you and our boy will hate me for this, but maybe one day you both will understand that love is more than just holdin' on, sometimes it's about letting go. I'm moving far away, Mirage Sr., so it's no use to come looking for me. I found a new love, one that sees me as more than just mama, or the woman that sits in a house all day and slaves over a stove.

You're a good man, Mirage Senior, and you're gonna meet a beautiful woman that's gonna love you soooo deeply that you'll forget about little ole me. But know this, as surely as the church's doors open on every good Sunday monin', I won't ever forget about you, Mirage Sr. I'm leaving a piece of my heart here with you . . . hold on to it for me, ya' hear.

Sincerely yours, Joann

Mirage's vision lifted from the piece of paper, and as if just then realizing that his son was standing there, Mirage Senior's watery gray eyes cracked open. As they shared a reality of pain too deep to speak on, the father played that saxophone as if it had the power to bring love back to them. Sam Cooke's melody danced in the air as man and boy were forced to understand that love was only as strong as its possessor.

The sound of the elevator doors opening snatched Mirage back to the present. They'd opened out to the roof of the building, somehow, as he'd reflected on his life, he'd subconsciously boarded the elevator. There was nothing out there but the generators that served as a backup to the building's main power source, and the main source that fed the AC and heat to the complex.

No one really had reason to venture up that far, but Mirage had found a safe haven of sorts up there on that tarred roof, so he'd paid the owner a pretty penny to keep others from up there. He'd placed a futon and paint supplies up there so he could go out and get lost in his mind on the nights or days that his soul cried. A gust of chilled wind engulfed him, but he welcomed its embrace. Barefooted, all he wore against the cold was the tattered old jeans and a button-down dress shirt that he'd left unbuttoned and open to allow the wind to kiss his bare chest. He carried the small, lacquered suitcase as Picasso trotted leisurely a few feet ahead of him.

Arrrrff! Arrrff! The dog barked and caused Mirage to pause a few feet away from the inner wall of the building. He took slow-measured steps until the tips of his toes touched the wall which rose up to about mid stomach.

The sounds of the city greeted him as he gazed out toward the Skyline of downtown Houston. Seventeen stories below, cars sped by. As the cold wind carried the aromas of fast food, a light tinge of cigarette smoke, car exhaust, and other fragrances of the city, Mirage rested the case down on the dusty roof. He gently laid it flat on its side before kneeling down and unclasping the gold latches. The case opened with ease, and though the sun had dropped low, on the verge of calling it a night, the golden saxophone seemed to glow against the red velvet it was encased within.

As Mirage pulled it free of it's captivity, he already knew the melody he would play. Erecting himself with the sax clutched with the gentleness of a mother holding an infant fresh out the womb, he studied it before fitting the mouth piece to it.

The liquor was making love to his system and had him warm within the icy winds of the late evening, and as the ends of his opened shirt began to flutter in the wind, he brought the hard plastic tip to his lips. His eyes drifted close as the orange sun dropped a little lower, almost as if silhouetting him, and he began to play that same melody his father loved to play when his mind was clouded and his heart heavy. Though the saxophone couldn't sing, the words of Sam Cooke's, "A Change Gone Come," played in the breeze ways of his mental…

♪It's been a looooong, a long time comin, and I knoooow, a change gone come/ oh yes it is/ It's been toooo hard livin, and I'm afraid to die/ Ohhh, I don't know what's up there, beyond the skyyy/ It's been a lonnngg, A loooong time comin, and I knoooww, A change gone come/ oh yes it is...♪

PART TWO
The Girl
and the
Million Roaches

All her life, the girl lived beneath the strict rules and scrutiny of her mother and father. She hated their stone aged perceptions and couldn't wait until she was old enough to move away on her own. She began to work every odd job she could to save up the money for just that occasion, and her mother hated it.

"A woman shouldn't have to work, that's the man's duty, a lady takes care of home and stays sexy for her man," she would drill into the girl, but the girl had a different perspective.

She wanted her own shit! She wanted to make her own decisions. She wanted to be sexy for "herself", and one day in the spring, that day finally came. She'd graduated high school and was of age to leave the nest. Her mother and father pleaded with her to stay, they'd even attempted to scare her with the stories of how bad life could get, but she wasn't to be deterred.

For weeks, she searched for an apartment suitable for her small budget, but each one she liked seemed to be overpriced or too far away from the college she wanted to attend. She'd almost given up hope, until, one day, she stumbled upon a cute little one bedroom apartment on a side of town she was unfamiliar with.

The housing projects was quiet at that time of morning, and the city had kept the exterior of the building up to par.

"I'll take it," she exclaimed to the landlord, as she handed over her deposit.

Days later, she had what she'd always craved—a place of her own and freedom to do as she pleased. Though they had been totally against her decision, especially since she'd chosen the projects, her parents helped her decorate the apartment and make it a home. The girl loved it, even after she'd traded the burbs for the Ghetto. That is, until one morning she rose to cook breakfast and found a million roaches crawling throughout the kitchen.

"Oh my God!" She cringed. She'd never much seen a roach, let alone, so many. Yet, she wasn't to be ran out of her dream home by no damn roaches! That day, she went to the store and purchased a few cans of Raid roach spray, and every other form of roach reliever she could find. "I'm gonna kill these damn roaches if it's the last thing I do," she vowed to herself.

When she returned home, amidst the hoodlums and bad ass kids running to and from throughout the projects, she noticed an elderly lady sitting on the bench in front of the building. In fact, she'd noticed the woman sitting in that same spot every day since she'd moved there, but the girl never gave it a second thought as she made her way to her apartment.

As soon as she entered, the first thing she noticed was that those damn roaches had taken a vacation from the kitchen and were now doing the damnest things in the living room. Some were on the coffee table, and she even noticed two of them on the couch fucking. She'd had enough! The girl dropped her bags and went to work with those cans of Raid as if she was the exterminator herself. By the time she finished, she was drenched in sweat, but there were what seemed to be a million roaches dead in various places. She burst into a gleeful laughter

"Gotcha," She exclaimed.

After cleaning up and showering, the girl fell into a peaceful sleep that night, and when she woke up the next morning, she decided to cook herself a nice breakfast.

She climbed out the bed and made her way toward the kitchen, singing all the while. "It's gonna be a good morning," she told herself, as she hit the lights in the kitchen.

"Arrrghh!" she cried, as soon as light flooded the small space. What seemed like a million roaches milled about as if "she" were invading their space. The girl's shoulders sagged in defeat. "Why won't y'all just-just go away!" she cried, before stomping her feet in frustration.

To her surprise, a nice sized roach that strode along the counter with his arm around a female roach sneered at her.

"Biiiiitch, please! We were here before you got here, and we're gonna be here when you tear yo' ass," he spat.

The girl was shocked at the disrespect and placed her hands on her hips in a sassy manner.

"Un-unnn, you nasty, dusty roach, okay, I get it! I'm just a woman, it's too many of y'all, and you wayy too fast, but just give me a second and I'm gonna have something for y'alls disrespectful asses," she declared, before spinning on her heels and racing for the phone.

"Yeah, whatever, you snobbish bitch, actin' like you ain't ever seen a roach before! We have just as much right to be here as you. Don't we, sugar?" the roach asked his female companion.

"You sho' right, baby!" she seconded, with a wave of her antennas.

"That's right, now let me take you out and get us some of this cereal she keeps on top of this fridgerator," the male roach spoke. The girl had called the exterminator and was told they'd be there in twenty minutes. She waited impatiently until the knock at the door startled her and caused her to rush to it. She flung the door open.

"Oh thank God you made it," she exclaimed before explaining the situation to the elder white man.

After listening to her plight, the man was convinced that he had the solution to her problem.

"Well, Ma'am, I think we're gonna have to bomb your apartment to rid you of this ugly problem. Do you have a place you can go for about two days?" he proposed. The girl hated the idea but knew that her parents would welcome her with open arms. She nodded her answer and fifteen minutes later she was at her parents' home.

The entire three days she spent there they begged her to stay, to no avail. She returned to her apartment to find what seemed to be a million roaches, dead throughout the place.

"Yes!" she shouted, jumping up and down like an excited little girl. She hurriedly cleaned up the place before showering and

113

heading for bed. She slept peacefully. When she woke up the next morning, she slipped from the bed with a suspicious feeling.

"What if those damn roaches are back ... what will I do?" she asked herself, as she made her way to the kitchen.

With a held breath, she flipped on the light, and to her surprise, the kitchen was just as spotless as she'd left it the night before. She smiled smugly. "Got they asses!" She celebrated with a sexy little dance before making her way to the cubbard. She had a sudden taste for a cup of orange juice, but as soon as she opened the cabinet door, to her utter horror, it seemed to be a million roaches crawling over and around her dishware.

"You dirty bitch, we're like Bay Bay's kids, we don't die, we multiply!" one of them shouted, before she slammed the door and stormed out of the apartment.

She rushed out of the building, and not knowing what else to do, she ran over and flung herself down onto the bench in front of the projects. She cried and cried until –

"What's the matter, Chile." The voice was elderly, matured by time. Surprised, that anyone was out at that time of morning, the girl's gaze lifted to find the elderly lady she'd seen sitting out on that project bench since the day she'd moved into those ratchet government housings. The girl sniveled before wiping her eyes.

"Who- who are you?"

"I'm just me, Sugar, now why don't you tell an old lady what has those ugly tears rolling down your pretty face." The elder woman smiled a gentle smile that made the girl feel as if she'd known her, her entire life. The girl relaxed with an exhale of exasperation.

" I've waited my entire life to get my own place, and to get from beneath my parents' watchful eye. Just to have my own, ya' know? "But ..."

The girl paused as her eyes watered. "Now that I've accomplished that goal, I'm being run out by a million roaches. I've tried everything! Nothing seems to work. I kill them and a million more appear! I'm soooo through," she admitted defeat with a drop of her head. The elder woman's smile never waned as she gazed out at the birds that landed a few feet away from them, in search of food. "See, baby, your problem isn't as stressful as it seems. See, this here building is just like the raising of a little girl into a particular kind of woman. Just like that of a building, that little girl is raised upon a certain type of foundation, Honey, and that foundation, rather built upon uneven soil, structured in an area of a moral-less culture, or if it's created as perfect as can be, will be built upon. Yet! You can't build a castle upon a foundation meant for a shack, Baby." The woman's voice was soul sista raspy. She patted the girl's knee affectionately. "And just like that little girl, the building behind us was once a beautiful exterior. The paint was fresh and it's potential was endless, but, Suga, it's never the "exterior" that has the potential to hurt you." The woman waved a hand back towards the deteriorating building. "Some of the ugliest people and places are some of the most beautiful choices. It's what's "inside" those people and places that counts the most. Those roaches that has you so blue won't ever leave here, baby, because they're "inside" the walls!" She smiled before folding her hands down in her lap and glancing at the girl. "What I'm sayin', Suga, is that it's not the roaches you should be wasting your tears on 'cause that's a problem "you" can't solve. Just like when that little girl is being molded, this building, it's the things people, life, put "inside" them that created the ugliness that hurts people. The solution to your problem is simple, Chile, but the problem with the young women of this era is that when they recognize a situation has rotted on the inside, they stay and in the end, become just as rotten as the situation they're in. You have to leave and start anew, Baby, that's the only way you'll rid yourself of those roaches. You can't move to the hood and expect suburban life conditions," the elder woman jeweled before patting the girl's knee.

"Leave and find somewhere that's just as pretty on the "inside" as it is on the outside." She smirked before her vision lifted just in time to capture the flock of birds take flight.

The girl's watery gaze fell to the ground as her mental raced. She'd never thought of things in that manner. With a smile on her face she glanced up to thank the woman for the new perspective.

"Thank you sooooo," she began, but her words trailed off as she stared in bewilderment at the place the old lady had just been sitting.

"Damn, ma, you're too young to be losin' your mind like that. You talkin' to yourself?" someone shouted, as they passed, heading for the building. The girl ignored him as she sat, and stared-astonished. The woman had vanished, and there in the place she'd just sat, crawled a big, brown, cock roach. She stared, speechless, as it crawled slow, wiggling its two long antennas before it disappeared between the cracks in the bench.

The girl and the million roaches: A parable by Renta.

CHAPTER SIX
CROOKED LOVE

"Hello ..."

"Heeyyy, baby, how's your trip been thus far?" Oshaya asked. There was a deep exhale on the other end of the phone. She was sure he could hear Mary J. Blige as it played softly in the background.

"It's been a day, but there's only a few more kinks to work out and hopefully I'll be able to get back to the states. These people of Sri Lanka are kinda *different*," he chuckled. "I'll be home soon, sweetheart."

"I miss you, Nigil," She whined into the receiver.

"I miss you too, baby, and when I get back, I'll make it up to you."

"Promise?" she purred with a seductive smile that he couldn't see.

"I promise, sweety, but listen, they're calling me in for a conference with some very important people, hopefully we can wrap this thing up. The agency has tracked our target here, and if I'm able to bring him to justice, it'll be a milestone for my career and they'll finally make me Administrator, so I'll call you as soon as I'm free."

"Well, okay, *I guess!*" Oshaya made light of the dismissal. "I just miss you, dammit! I love you, Nigil, hurry home to me, okay?"

"Will do, honey, will do. Love you back," he reciprocated, before the line went dead.

Oshaya pulled the phone from her ear and stared at the dimming screen with her nose scrunched up. After a few seconds, she tossed the iPhone beside her on the couch. Reaching over, she retrieved the chilled glass of white wine she'd placed on one of the end tables.

♪*I was your lover and your secretary, working every day of the weeeeeek / was at the job when no one else was there, helping you get onnnnn your feet / eleven years, I've sacrificed, and you can just leave me at the drop of dime / swallowed my fears, stood by yourrrr side / I should've left yo ass a thousand times ...* ♪

Mary J. Blige's soulful voice filled the room.

♪*I'm not gone cry, I'm not gone cry, I'm not gone shed no tears / nooo I'm not gone cry, it's not the time / 'cause you're not worth my tears/ I know there are no guarantees, guarantees, in love you take your chances...* ♪

She sung as Oshaya took a ladylike sip from her glass. The music played softly from the surround sound system as she sat with her feet tucked beneath her and tried to convince her heart to remain silent. *Girl, ain't no need to get all bent out of shape, you knew he was a dog before you saw this.* She willed her mind to whisper to her spirit. "So, this how it feels, huh?" She asked no one in particular, but the older white man who sat across from her on the snow-white sectional leaned forward and placed his elbows on his knees. He nodded solemnly as he watched her reach down and take up the stack of pictures he'd given her. She absently took another sip from her glass as she studied them, and the man couldn't help but to notice the perfect prints of her lips that her nude lipstick left on the rim of them.

"I'm afraid so, Ma'am, it's a heart breaking job, but hey," he said, followed by a shrugged. "That's detective work." The private detective acknowledged. Oshaya absently nodded her agreement. For months, Nigil, her husband, had been claiming to be out of the country working a high profile case for the FBI, but Oshaya's intuition just couldn't believe it. So, she'd hired Ashford and Associates, a private detective company one of her girlfriends recommended.

"Don't call me that." The sudden snap in her voice caused the detective's eyes to grow wide with surprise.

"Excuse me?" he asked, his face contorted in confusion.

"*Ma'am*, don't call me *ma'am*, it's a title slave owners forced my people to use in reference to their superiority. My name will do." She drew her line. The detective nodded his understanding.

Oshaya's eyes became slits as they fell to the pictures, witnessing the man she'd vowed to spend the rest of her life with, the man who vowed forever at making her happy, the same man, captured in still-life adultery. Each photo cracked a different part of her heart.

In the images, Nigil was captured in moments of intimacy with an attractive, blond-haired Caucasian woman. Passionate kisses, him holding an umbrella over their heads on a rainy day, and the most earth shattering image being, one taken from the other side of a curtainless window pane.

Rain drops dripped down the glass and just beyond it's surface. Oshaya could see the blond-haired woman caught within the thralls of ecstasy as she rode her lover. Her upper body, nipples erect, head thrust back, blonde hair spilling down her back, and her pink lips slightly ajar in passion, all captured in raw film.

Her breath caught in her throat at the sight of the dark arm around the woman's waist. It was just another token of evidence she'd use in court when she divorced his dog ass. The gold and brown Arnold and Son time piece on his wrist was a gift she'd given him for his thirty sixth birthday. She shook her head in shame.

"Great work, Detective, you should've chosen photography for your profession, or maybe you can just add it to your resume," she acknowledged, before downing the rest of her glass in a single gulp. "Our business is concluded I believe, and if you don't mind, I'd like to be alone with my thoughts, please." She spoke without taking her eyes away from the pictures of infidelity. The detective gave a morose smile, understanding heartbreak.

Climbing to his feet, he extended his hand, but when Oshaya's misty vision studied it as if it were vile, the man nodded. He'd grown accustomed to the brashness of broken love and had learned not to take natural reactions personal.

"Of course, and if you ever need help in this area again, Ashford and Associates will be of service. In that envelope, along with the photos, you'll find the address to his mistress, as well as her other contacts," he informed her, as she stood and walked him to the door.

Oshaya gave him a weak smile as she held the door open, and out of respect for her pain, the man diverted his attention from her. He could see her pretty eyes held, but barely contained, the quiet storm that converged.

"Yes, and thank you once again, Detective Irish, your service is well noted." She commended him as he made his exit. She watched the man make his way to the F-150 and climb up into the driver's seat, and even after the truck had disappeared from sight, she stood in the doorway of her four-bedroom home, gazing out at the beautifully manicured lawns of the affluent neighborhood.

"I've come a long way," she whispered, "a long way," she reiterated, before turning and making her way inside.

♪*No, I'm not gonna cry no, it's not the time / cause you're not worth my tears…* ♪

Mary J. sung, but Oshaya wasn't as strong as those lyrics. Though she knew Nigil wasn't worth her tears, she was only a woman … she couldn't seem to stop her heart from loving him. So, as she made her way to the suede sofa, she cried. A silent cry where tears dripped down her pretty face, but the only sounds that followed were the snivels and quick inhales to keep her nose from dripping. She leaned forward and poured herself another glass of White Zinfandel, watching as the rosé *wine* sloshed in the glass before retrieving the photos. Her heart was a deserted island as she brought the glass to her lips.

Studying the pictures, somewhere deep down inside, Oshaya *wanted* to lie to herself. *Wanted* to believe there was some sort of mistake. The woman wanted to believe that there was a man somewhere near who resembled her man so closely, there could've been a mistaken identity. Yet, there was no mistaking the faces of pleasure she'd become so accustomed to that, if she'd closed her eyes, she could picture each mask of ecstasy her husband made at the apex of his explosion. Though he hadn't touched her in months, she could picture vividly, his sweat … the way his eyes rolled to the back of his head when his self-control was betraying him … it all played within her mind until her thoughts became her enemy and allowed another woman into the room of her mental.

As Oshaya envisioned making love to her husband, she watched in horror as her very own face morphed into that of the other woman … a white woman!

It sounded as if her heart shattered, and just as she lifted a hand to her chest to determine the damage, it dawned on her that the shattering sound hadn't come from her heart at all. Her gaze slowly lifted from the pictures until it found the shreds of glass and clear fermented drink, seemingly melting down the far wall. At that moment she realized that she'd hurled the glass at an innocent victim since the wall hadn't caused her pain. Her breath quickened. *I'm hyperventilating,* she thought, as she began to gently pat her chest. Tears leaked from her eyes as her heartbeat slowed its gallop. She reached to bring the glass to her lips before she realized she'd just flung it against the wall.

♪ *Homegirl, she wasn't disrespectful / in fact / she was a hundred percent sure / and how could I argue with her, holdin' a baby with eyes like yours / she said it's your child / and that really messed me up /How could you deny, your own flesh and blood...*♪

The song had changed to another one of Mary J's classics. Oshaya flung the stack of pictures into the air and watched them flutter down, before pulling one of the big colorful throw pillows from the couch and hugging it to her bosom as tight as she could. She cried a deep cry as the pictures, the evidence of a no good ass man, floated around the room like feathers from a busted pillow.

***

"Ridge, get ready for visit, we'll be back in twenty minutes!" the officer shouted from the first tier.

"You too Lawson, get ready for visit!" It was an early Saturday morning that found Gambino with his headphones on, bopping his head to Polo G's, *Super Star*. He didn't hear the announcement, but Pierre did. They'd both been let out of lockup after Big Compton

121

stood before the disciplinary captain and took the rap for it all. Though it was eating Gambino alive, he would repay his mans in due time for doing what many wouldn't.

"My nigga, you're in position to do for the team, so ain't no need for you to crash and burn! Just don't let the sacrifice be in vain, we all we got- Riiiidaaaa!" He remembered the gangsta's response when he'd asked him why he'd taken the fall for them.

"Gambino, look out, G!" He vaguely heard Pierre's call over the music pumping through the headphones. Frowning as Pierre's long legs swung over the top bunk, Gambino slipped the headphones off.

"Sup, Gangsta?"

"They just called us for Viso, we got twenty minutes," Pierre informed, jumping down. Taking his toiletries to the sink to get ready, the man was eager to see his people.

"Me *and* you?" Gambino wanted to clarify. Pierre nodded his confirmation as he brushed his diamonds. He kept the top and bottom, six top, six bottom, invisible set, gold-and-diamond teeth on level ten with the shine.

"Who bummin' B, you?" he spoke, with a mouthful of toothpaste.

" I don't know, maybe my Queen, or my punk ass BM, I think it's moms though—I ain't heard from Monay's whack ass in months." He shook his head in frustration. He loved the mother of his seed, but since they'd given him that sixty calendars, she'd proved the old adage true: *"Out of sight, out of mind."* In the end, Gambino had the understanding of a real nigga. He knew lady was a bad bitch with a mean sex drive, not to mention loyalty was a foreign language to her. *Shoulda had a real bitch!* He mentally spanked himself.

After Pierre had finished his business, Gambino took the durag, made out of an old tee shirt, off his head. Gazing in the mirror at his freshly cut hair, he turned his head to the right so he could inspect his tapered cut. His hair was brushed into a diagonal wave pattern the penitentiary was known for, but Gambino's grade of hair was what gave his shit a different look. His hair only had four of five waves that were so big, they started from the back of his head, and into his Steve Harvey's edge up. Well, when Steve *had* an edge up.

"You never know, my dude, but you can bet this, when I touch down on the other side of this gate, I'm gone pull up on ya' BM, she foul for how she givin' it up, bruh," Pierre spoke as he slid the two piece, white prison uniform from underneath his mattress. The mattress had flattened it into a crease as sharp as one the cleaners would've done.

Gambino shrugged his shoulders. *Can't make no hoe be loyal, if she gonna ride she gonna ride, if she gonna fuck, she gonna fuck,* he thought, indifferently, as he brushed his teeth. His younger brother and mother were all he had left, and he was cool with that, but ... *Damn, Cat Eyes, you was 'pose to be my bro . . . I bet it all on you, my dude,* he thought, as he clenched his eyes shut against the betrayal.

Since he'd gotten bammed and sentenced, he hadn't heard from the man he'd taken the fall for. Cat Eyes seemed to have vanished into thin air, and no one seemed to have heard from him. *I'm outta there, mane,* he thought, as he reflected on all the loot Cat Eyes had stung him for. Every time he thought of the betrayal he prayed. Prayed that God gave him the chance to whack that boy.

***

3 hours later...

"Yeah, babe, what's up? I just told you I had a very important meet ..." Nigil's words trailed off as he registered her crying.

"You promised ... you, you promised me you wouldn't do this shit again, Nigil. I hate your no-good, dog ass! I hate you!" Oshaya screamed into the phone. She couldn't remember when she'd gotten in the car and made the trip. All she could remember was a faxed piece of paper floating into her lap when she tossed the stack of pictures into the air. She'd gazed down on it and the detective's words played in her mind. *"In that envelope, along with the photos, you'll find the address to his mistress' home as well as her contacts.*" True enough, the faxed paper contained the woman's cell number, as well as the address in Sugarland Texas, Oshaya had driven to.

"Wha-what the hell are you talking about, Oshaya? Why are you—

"Fuck you, you dog! I'm filing for divorce, Nigil, and you can do whatever you want to try and stop me, but it's over. I'm soooo tired of this-this…" She shrugged as if he could see her. As the song changed into one of Monica's hits, Oshaya shook her head in shame. She was too through. "Loving you hurts too bad, I'm done. I'm soooo done, Nigil. When you get through playing house with your little *bitch* and make your way to 8911 Rumblingwood Courts, the locks will be changed, Honey, and if you try the norm, the police will be waiting on your ass. I'm tired of your dog ass! I hate you!" she shouted into the phone as if it were the device that had stolen her peace.

Nigil was stunned to silence as he listened to her cry, and as if he'd just registered the music playing in the background, he listened intently. *♪At nights I couldn't sleep, you let the sun beat you home/ I ask myself over again, what am I doing wronnng/ To make you stay out all night, and not think to call- what does she have oveeer me, to make you not wanna call hommme…♪* Monica's, *So Gone,* classic played softly on her Pandora.

"Baby, what are you tal—

Click! The line going dead severed his question. Tossing the phone into the passenger's seat, Oshaya moved almost on autopilot as she slid from the car and began frantically searching the ground. The music spilled out of the car as her eyes fell to a nice sized circle of rocks the woman used to decorate the circumference of her mailbox.

♪Drive by her house late at night, in an unmarked car, wondering what she has overrrr meeee, to make you break my hearrrrt…♪ Monica sung as Oshaya reached down and scooped up the biggest stone she could find. Nigil's smoke gray, Ford, Shelby Baja Raptor truck was parked in the driveway of his mistress' home as if it didn't have a parking spot reserved for it not even fifteen

124

miles away at their home. *Where it belonged!* With twin rivers dripping down her face, Oshaya strode with a purpose until she found herself standing in front of the beautiful truck.

♪*Youuuuu make meeee feeeel /I'm so gone- soooo gone/ listen boy I'm a rowdy chick, sometimes I like to fight cause my mouth too slick/ Boy why you doing me like I ain't worth shit/ make me wanna ride by ya' house and sit/ kick down ya' door and smack ya' chick, just to show ya' Monica not havin' it...*♪

Monica's lyrics fed her fire and with both hands, Oshaya lifted the rock over her head, reared back, and with all her might, flung the stone toward the windshield of the truck. It cut through the air and crashed into the tinted glass. Small flecks of glass shot into the air as the windshield caved in and spider webbed with a dramatic effect.

Urrp! Wurrrp! Wurrrr, Wurrr! The truck's alarm began to cry as the woman casually made her way back to her Lexus and slid into the driver's seat. As soon as she secured the car door, the front door to the house was jerked open and her husband ran out with a dangerous frown on his face. His eyes took in the damage to his new truck before drifting to Oshaya's ink-black Lex. The passenger's window lowered as she eased from the curb of the house he considered *Sri Lanka!* Nigil's stare registered shock then confusion, to find his wife there, yet and still, the angry grimace Oshaya had become so accustomed to, found it's way to the surface.

"Bitch, have you lost your everlasting mind! My truck? Look at my truck!" She could hear him shouting as if standing in the doorway of another woman's home, in nothing but his boxer briefs, was as normal as the Covid virus had become. "Ohhh, bitch, I'm gonna...," he began in a proposed threat, but halted when the blond-haired white woman, the same pale-skinned woman from the pictures, rushed out with a concerned expression on her face. Her bright-blue eyes trailed from his glaring stare to the ruined glass of the truck, and finally to Oshaya's creeping car.

As Pandora's channel switched to Beyonce's *Me, Myself, and I* , Oshaya slipped on a pair of dark, bubble-eye sunglasses in an attempt to hide her baptized eyes from their undeserving visions.

She gave the Caucasian woman a friendly smile before waving with her fingers. *Better be glad I didn't burn this bitch down,* she thought, before pressing her foot down on the gas pedal with Beyonce singing to her soul. ♪*Me, Myself, I – that's all I got in the end, that's what I found out/ and it ain't no need to cry, I took a vow cause now on Imma be my own best friend...*♪

***

The room was filled with chatter as they entered the contact visit area and handed their I.D. cards to the guards. She glanced down at them.

"Lawson, table six," the CO directed Pierre with a head nod. Both he and Gambino's eyes trailed to his visitor. Pierre had been rocking with the short, thick chick since they'd met on the *P.O.F.* dating app two years earlier and she'd been down by law. Brittany waved at him with a big smile on her face before nodding toward the snacks she'd ordered and had situated on his side of the table. Pierre and Gambino's eyes met in an understanding between playas before giving each other dap. Pierre stepped as if he had a pair of Now-N-Lator gators on his feet as he made his way over to her. Gambino observed until lady stood and hugged her mans as if she'd been waiting to do so her entire life.

Pierre's hands fell and squeezed all that ass lady had behind her. "Ridge, table three," the guard snapped him out of his observation.

Gambino's attention snapped toward the officer with a sly smirk on his face. The CO giggled before rolling her eyes at him. "Boy, you too much, you better hurry up and get to *your* girl before you start some mess up in here."

His vision drifted to the table she was referring to and to his surprise, Monay, his BM was giving him the evil eye. Gambino chuckled as his eyes shot back to the lady officer.

Umph," she mumbled.

"Never that, love, real niggas don't lust for their potna's bitch no matter how pretty she may be."

"Oh, yeah," lady questioned with a raised brow and sneaky smirk. "So, what were you lookin' at, your man's ass or *his* girls?" she proposed with a – *yeah-nigga-I-got- ya'-ass-now* expression. Gambino's eyes trailed from her head to her feet and back up again. "I *knooow* you're not being disrespectful, Ms. Timmons. You been my potna since you been workin' here, let's not become enemies 'cause you don't know how to dialogue with a real nigga. There's nothin' 'bout the male physical that attracts me and nor does my dude's girl's ass. I was watching my mans put on for the playas. Just like *you* saw what happened so did these suckas who gone go back and gossip 'bout a nigga," he opened up before nodding at his Baby mother. "Just like this punk bitch right here, even the whack dudes that don't fuck with me gotta give it up. Look at her, she equipped for a pimp, so if I walk over there and stick my tongue down her throat, niggas won't think of how many dicks she's sucked before she came up her *playin'* wifey, they'll only lust for the bad bitch and hate 'cause they ain't got her." Gambino gave CO Timmons a suspicious gaze.

"Don't be one of those kinds of people, ma. You do look like you don't mind playing with the—

"Boy!" Timmons began with an offended look. She and Gambino were close. When her and her dude were going through the extra shit, it was Gambino who advised her and listened. She shook her head as he laughed and tossed his hands up in surrender.

"Iiiiight, I'm out." He chuckled before heading for the table. He eye'd Monay for only a few seconds before his eyes found one of his reasons for living.

"Daddy!" Khloe, his little girl shouted, before jumping from her seat and rushing over to him. He leaned down and scooped her up into his arms.

"Heyyy, Daddy's baby," he whispered, while kissing her nose. Khloe was the spitting image of him and the girl was only five years old. Outside of her mother's caramel skin tone and thick hair, the child had inherited Gambino's creole DNA.

"Daddy," she exclaimed with a cute eagerness, "Nana came too, but she had to use the little girl's room," she revealed. Then with a slight frown on her pretty face, she said, "Daddy, why it's called the little girl's room if *big* girls *and* boys use it too?" she asked, with an innocent shrug and lifted her hands in the air as if to say, *what gives!* Gambino laughed before kissing the top of her head.

"Good question, Baby, let me think on it," he answered truthfully, before his vision lifted to his child's mother.

Monay had slipped from her seat and stood as if she were anticipating a hug of her own, but when he took his seat without acknowledging her, Gambino had to fight the urge not to laugh at the dejected expression that briefly overrode lady's sex appeal. Monay sucked her teeth with a roll of her eyes before reclaiming her seat, and the father of her child couldn't help but notice her sex appeal. The white, skin-tight skinny jeans she'd worn had rips at the knees and looked as if someone had taken their time and intricately painted the material onto her bottom half. The Valentines, red-and-pink J's on her feet matched the red, stretch, long sleeved shirt she'd worn. *Titties on fleek, check!* He mentally appraised her. Lady caught his lustful gander and again, sucked her teeth.

"Man, whatever!" she spat, before folding her arms across her chest, pouting.

"Daddy, why you not kiss mommy too?" Khloe asked, with a confused innocence dancing in her eyes. Gambino leaned down and showered his princess with loud kisses as he tickled her.

"Cause, daddy's kisses are all for you, Babygirl!" His response caused Monay to sneer as she glared at him. She'd caught the slug and wasn't feeling dude's vibes.

"Awww, that's so adorable," an elderly , white lady cooed from the table beside theirs .

"Bitch, mind your business, ain't nobody asked for your nosey ass opinion! You should be more concerned with the way you come out your house, over there looking like you borrowed Donald Trump's toupee! Men wear toupees, women wear wigs, boo boo," Monay added a roll of her eyes with her ratchetness. After giving the woman *the hand*, the Caucasian woman's eyes grew wide as she began to pat the top of her wig, wondering if she'd put it on wrong.

"Why... I've ... *never!*" She turned ghostly white with embarrassment, shocked by Monay's rudeness.

"You should've *neverrrr* worn that man's toupee, *that's* what ya' white ass should've never done. Girl bye!" Monay waved her off. She found Gambino's amused gaze as he shook his head in shame. *Same hood bitch as always!* He thought.

"So, you big mad or lil mad, 'cause I can give two fucks, Bino," She fumed before leaning back in her seat and crossing her left leg over her right. He took in the way her wavy hair hung passed her shoulders. He admired how the gold framed designer, clear lensed glasses she wore gave life to her pretty eyes. And as her beauty swallowed him, Gambino wondered if it was the reason he'd ran raw dick in her and shot her in the womb with his seed.

"You can take the bitch out the tray, but can't take the tray out the bitch, mane," he spat, in reference to her Third Ward upbringing.

"Daddy, that's a bad word!" Khloe reprimanded him. His eyes flickered to her, and his frustration melted.

"My fault, Babygirl, look." He nodded toward CO Timmons. "Go over there and ask that lady for one of those coloring books so you can color me something." He waited until she slid out of her seat and did as he'd requested before reclaiming Monay with his gaze. "Dig this, Ms. Lady, I'm neither big nor small mad, 'cause I've learned that when it comes to you, I'd be foolish to put it all on the line, 'cause *I* know beyond all that glamor"—He paused to form a gun with his thumb, pointer finger, and middle finger, and aiming it at her pretty face, he allowed it to trail down her neck, passed her breast, stomach, skinnies, and finally down to the J's on her feet— "You're like a hyped up stock that teases the kid into investing just a lil bit more each time, then you crash and cost me everythang I believe in," he spat with a knowing nod. Gambino's eyes were hard, and his voice was as solid as marble imported from Greece, but the truth was, the man was fronting. He'd merely slid on that mask that every other man whose pride had been crushed, slipped on to deflect prying eyes from their wounds. *Yet,* behind his mask, he wished killing his heart was that easy.

Monay rolled her eyes. She loved him and wanted to be the type of woman he prayed for, but when he was free, Gambino introduced lady to three constants that *sometimes* overrode the power of love. *"When a nigga keeps his dick in his gal on the constant, he creates in her a habit ... a habit that will one day crush his heart if he's ever taken out of the picture, because she won't hesitate to allow the next playa to strike a pose. Gambino, the three constants that create bad habits in a man's bitch are dangerous to niggas like us. Giving her good dick on the regular, creates an addiction to that feeling of a nut. If you constantly blowing the bag on her and not motivating her to get her own, what you think she's gonna do if you go broke or your piece gets taken off the board? She's gonna seek that same stability from a different sponsor, which leads to the third constant, playboy! You gotta know your bitch, Bro. You can't constantly allow her to get away with small shit! Enough crumbs can make a cake, my dude, and in due time, lady will commit the ultimate, and that's for shit sure!"* His mental had rocked him backwards in time, to a conversation Tay had had with him.

"Gambino, oh, so you're just gonna ignore me, huh? I don't know why I came up here to see yo' dog ass!" Monay's rant yanked him back to the present. As he focused, his vision captured something just beyond where Monay sat and it fucked his heart up.

His mother had just exited the restroom and was making her way toward the table. As he observed her, he almost didn't recognize the beautiful woman who'd raised him on her own. Heroine had stolen so much from his queen and in turn, second handedly robbed him as well.

"Me either," Gambino finally responded to Monay just as his mother reached the table.

"Heyyyy, baby, you not gonna give ya' mama a hug?" She smiled a stained smile as she opened her arms invitingly. He wasted no time slipping out of his chair and giving her his *love*. He held her tight in his embrace to let her know his love surpassed her high.

"Boyyyy, you're gonna crush me," she cried mirthfully, as he squeezed her frail body and rocked side to side. He laughed before releasing her. "Let me look at you. You're so handsome, Bino, lookin' just like ya' no good ass daddy," she beamed, her yellowing teeth on display as she appraised her eldest son. "How they treating you in here, they feedin' you okay?" She cupped his face.

"I'm Gucci, Ma, stop worryin' so much, mane. You know you raised a soljah." His response received a raised brow from her.

"Gucci? Like the clothes? Boy, that must be some craziness you young folk done came up with to sound hip. Gucci? Humph! Well, I'll sayyyy." She was tickled as she took her seat. Gambino followed suit as, Ms. June, his mother's vision drifted to Monay. The glare the girl was giving Gambino was enough to know she was as hot as a tea kettle, and her bouncing leg was a telltale sign Ms. June had walked into some *BS*. Her eyes floated to her grandbaby at the empty table next to them, scribbling in a coloring book, and that was her cue to excuse herself. "On second thought," she said, and smiled as she rose out of her seat, "think I'll go get you a few snacks. What you want boy? You better be happy Monay brought some quarters, 'cause I'm broke as a joke, baby." She tried to help Monay.

"Just get me some chocolate, a Sprite, and some hot Cheetos, Mama. Quit actin' like this your first time up here and like you've forgotten what I like." He chuckled.

"Boy, I've been remembering your birthdays and doctor's appointments for twenty-eight years. I deserve to forget some shit." She glanced at Monay and shook her head in shame. She'd warned him about lady, but all that ass and good sex had Gambino's mind gone. She made sure he saw *the look* she gave him before going to pay for his snacks.

"So, where you been? You been so busy you couldn't even take a few minutes to check in wit' me? At least to screw my head on tight about my seed?" He placed his pride to the side. Monay sucked her teeth as she glared at him.

"Damn, Gambino, I'm sayin', nigga, it's hard out here. I know you been hearing how Covid got people out here homeless! I lost my job, *and* I haven't received no stimulus check. It ain't all about you, Gambino. You dudes always running the streets, runnin' yo' dick up in God only knows who, and when things go bad, y'all expect a bitch to just sit around and be just as locked up as—

"Look out, you fag ass bitch, I ain't sweatin' how you do you. Naw, the problem ain't the dude, it's *both* the man and woman. See, when you was able to spend up my fetti and get the dick on demand, you portrayed to be this down-by-law type chic, but now I'm out-of-pocket, you fancy." He cut her off with a frown on his face. Gambino dropped his head as he shook it side to side. *This girl is finito! After this, she comin' off my list, dawg!* His thoughts were final when he glanced back up into her designer lenses. "No pressure, mama, just make sure my lil one good, that's all I ask," he proposed.

"Oh, I got Khloe Denise Ridge, you don't have to worry 'bout that, but what about *us*, Gambino? What, you don't love *me* anymore?" she asked, before leaning forward, placing her left elbow on the table, and resting her chin in her palm. They eye'd each other—him wondering how he'd fallen victim—her wondering why he couldn't understand her plight. Gambino exhaled with a crooked smirk on his face.

"You wanna know what's crazy, ma?" he asked as their eyes wrestled.

"What, bae?"

"A nigga never knows how deep love really runs until he's so far into it, he finds himself standin' in the middle of nowhere, and can't find his way out." He gave it up. Monay's eyes became suspicious as she listened. "What's even crazier is it took me meetin' a bitch like you to realize that it's not love that failed me, it was *my* decision on giving mine to a female who ain't worth more than a nut and a Happy Meal that got me lookin' at love crooked." Gambino sat back in his seat as his mother returned.

"I got the stuff you wanted, but boy, don't you know this stuff higher than it is in the free world!" She complained as she took her seat.

Monay shot up from her seat with water in her eyes. "You ain't shit, dude, and you through, we done," she declared, as if she'd been a model wife.

Gambino snickered. "Bitch, ain't nobody got no glue on yo '
feet, why you still standing there?" He glared up at her. Monay
turned and headed for Khloe.

"Come on, Khloe, let's go."

"But, Mama, I color for Daddy and—

"Bring-yo-ass-ON!" Monay cut her off, as she gripped her
small wrist.

"Monay, don't make me break your face 'bout puttin' your
hands on my baby," Gambino growled. Monay paused as she
dragged her daughter kicking and screaming toward the exit.

"Oh, boo, you may as well get a good look 'cause you won't
see her no more," she spat, before making her exit.

"Daddyyyy! Daddyyy! No, Mama, can I tell Daddy I love—
His daughter was saying on their way out. Gambino was half way
to his feet when his Queen reached across the table and touched his
hand. She shook her head as if to say *no*.

"Let her go, baby, I'll talk to her 'cause she was wrong to bring
that child into y'all's mess. That's not what a real woman does," she
spoke thoughtfully, as Gambino gritted his teeth and reclaimed his
seat. The woman knew her son and knew that it wasn't all Monay's
fault.

"What did I miss… what'd you do to that girl, Gambino Dior
Ridge?" She called his entire government. Gambino finally forced
his eyes away from the exit his baby girl had been dragged through.
When his moms was locked in his sight, he again shook his head in
thought.

"Nothin, Mama. I just shoulda had a real bitch."

"Boy, what the hell you," she'd began, before Gambino
exploded in laughter. He'd just overheard the white woman when
she'd leaned close to her son and asked him a strange question.

"Is my wig on backwards, Blake?" Monay's words had
bothered her. At the sound of Gambino's laughter, the son's eyes
shot to him. Gambino patted the air in a calming motion as he tried
to tame his laughter.

"Naw, you have to excuse ole girl, she wasn't talmbout much,
but ... just- umm- just, kinda twist your hair to the left a little," he

told the white woman, "yo' shit kinda- kinda lopsided, Ms." He tried to help.

"Oh, my God, Gambino!" His mother's mouth fell open as the older Caucasian woman shot from her seat and darted for the restroom.

CHAPTER SEVEN
HAVE SOME RESPECT

"Well, Mrs., all the locks have been changed and here are your new keys." The locksmith extended the brass keys to Oshaya. She gave him a friendly smile as she reached down into her purse for his payment. The man was a deep-chocolate hued brotha, and as he turned his back to her to give her some privacy, he allowed his eyes to take in the beauty of the subdivision. The golf course's green, manicured lawns, coupled with the quietness of the area, seemed to arouse his interest and his eyes found Oshaya in a raised brow inquisition.

"Seems like the type of neighborhood good folks can leave their doors unlocked in and not have to fret about larceny or other evils. Nothin' like the grimier parts of the city I've had to change the locks in," he verbalized.

A moment of silence followed as her own vision took in the red-brick homes surrounding hers, and just a few houses down, a middle-aged Caucasian woman wearing a large floppy hat was tending to her garden. The yellow lady's slipper orchids and beautiful, purple tulips were a beautiful contrast to the bright green grass, and as if sensing admirers, the woman glanced up and over to where Oshaya stood. She offered a brilliant smile before waving a yellow, rubber gloved hand. Oshaya reciprocated the wave before her eyes drifted back to the locksmith.

"Sometimes, the threat a woman has to protect herself from lies right next to her in her bed, and a *familiar* threat can sometimes be confused with a familiar *love*." She spoke her heart before nodding down toward the changed locks. "A woman must master timing, 'cause every threat has the potential to destroy confidence in herself," she whispered, before extending the man's payment to him. He nodded a solemn expression as he accepted and reached down to retrieve his bag of tools to leave. He gave Oshaya a gentleman's nod before heading for his truck, but just as she was closing the door, he paused.

"Hey, lady?" he called to her. Curiosity was a kidnapper and Oshaya skeptically became its hostage. She raised an arched brow while studying him through the partially cracked door. "Why not just leave? Changed locks can only do so much?" His question was valid. A bitter smile curved her lips as she wondered the same thing.

"A woman must also know what she's entitled to and fight for it, the ending of every war comes with spoils." She waved toward the house. "And you're right, changing these locks can only do so much, but that's only because it's the locks *of the heart* that need to be changed. It just takes a different kind of locksmith for that type of work," Oshaya spoke before taking a deep breath. The locksmith watched the door close before hearing the new locks click into place. Oshaya tried to shut the door in time, but he'd witnessed the lone tear that streaked down her shadowed face before the door closed. He shook his head, saddened. *Damn, lady, a house isn't worth those tears...* he thought, as he made his way to his truck.

***

2014: The Past ...

"Where are we?" one of the young girls whispered, as they were ushered into a huge barn that sat out in the middle of ghost-town nowhere. The barn was situated on miles of desolate land on the border of Brownsville, Texas, and Matamoros, Mexico, where the Gulf Cartel was said to dominate with a brutal governing.

There was loud shouting coming from up ahead, a language Shay wasn't familiar with, but she was smart enough to detect the hostility in it. They want us to rush in here so no one will see us, she thought as a Hispanic man carrying a dangerous looking assault rifle stepped forward and shoved her forward.

As soon as she passed through the threshold, it seemed as if they'd entered another world. There were large metal bins stationed throughout the large open area and the soapy water which filled them gave a smell of disinfectants so powerful, it made her stomach knot.

136

"*Para! Alto!*" *Someone shouted, and if it hadn't been for the soft touch against her arm, she wouldn't have understood. She jerked her arm back in surprise as she turned to confront the unknown and came eye to eye with the pretty Latina girl who was raised against the culture of Black people. The girl's eyes were wide in fear as she quickly took in their predicament before reclaiming Shay with her gaze.*

"*Listen*"—*she hurriedly stepped closer to Shay as if to not be overheard* —"*my name is Alane Ortiz and I was taken from softball practice in my hometown of Phoenix, Arizona. I help you understand Spanish, I'm Hispanic,*" *she whispered, as Shay studied her skeptically.*

"*Para! Para!*" *a gruff voice demanded for the second time. The line halted at the same time Alane gently touched Shay's arm.*

"*He says for us to stop,*" *she interpreted. Shay gave her a brief nod of thanks before reaching forward to tap the girl in front of her. Tresey paused to give her a quick look.*

"*Stop,*" *Shay whispered.*

Up ahead, a tall, dark skinned Hispanic man was barking orders in rapid Spanish. He was very muscular, with hair the shade of a raven's wings. He wore a forest- green tee shirt which stretched so tightly over his arms and chest, it threatened to rip down the middle if he moved the wrong way. And the legs of his army fatigue pants were stuffed down into the lips of a pair of Army boots which were so worn and weather beaten, the leather cracked.

"*Quitate Toda Tu ropa-Toda!*" *he demanded.*

Shay instantly glanced at Alane, who had a shocked expression on her face. "*He says for us to take our clothes off. All of them,*" *she whispered. The room was filled with soft cries as the other men, dressed identical to the first, began roughly manhandling the girl's who hadn't understood.*

"*Devistete-Ahorita!*"

"*Devistete!*" *they demanded.*

Alane's pretty eyes watered as she watched one of them sling a girl to the dirty ground before savagely kicking her in the face. "Devistete!" he growled.

Alane quickly kicked off her shoes. "They- they want us to get undressed, now!" she warned quickly.

Shay didn't understand, and the look of confusion on her face told the tale. "Get undressed! Why? Why would they want that? I don't get—

"Calla'te!" the big man shouted, as he quickly approached them with menace in his glare. That's when she noticed, not only the tattoo of the venomous, King Cobra that slithered around his arm, but also the butt of the monstrous pistol he'd stuffed down the front of his pants.

"Shiiiish!" Alane hushed them, before placing a slender finger to her lips in a silencing motion. "He says to shut up!" She whispered urgently, before pulling her pink tee shirt over her head and tossing it to the ground. She stood trembling in a pair of stained jeans and a sports bra. The man stopped at Tresey and glared down at her with eyes so cold, if they had the power to, they would've frozen her into a block of ice.

"Devistete- Ahorita!" he spat vehemently. Tresey didn't understand and her ignorance cost her a slight payment of blood. The man reared his hand back as far as it would go, and he back handed her with brute force. The child crumbled to the ground, balling up into the fetal position, and cried for a life stolen.

"Tu No desobedescas la Palabra De la serpiente De cascavel! Quitate Toda tu Ropa!" he growled in rapid Spanish. The room was filled with weeping as Alane translated the man's fury into English.

"He says that we shouldn't disobey an order from the serpent." She gasped in horror. Her eyes watered as she glanced at the thick, black Cobra snake la serpiente had inked. It ran from his bicep, curved down and around his elbow and forearm, and ended at his wrist, where the wide flaps of its head opened up in a striking pose. "His name is La Serpiente; meaning, the Serpent. My family told us tales of this evil man. They say he steals bad little girls and does terrible things to them." Tears escaped from her eyes as she recalled the mythical tales she'd heard of the man. Until then, Alane always thought La Serpiente was merely the made up monster her father created to keep her from sneaking out. She watched in horror as he reared his size thirteen boot. And just before bringing it down onto Tresey's skull, Shay did the unthinkable. She rushed forward and blocked his intent.

"She don't understand you, why'd you hit her, you bastard," she screamed, as she clenched her small hands at her sides. Shay glared up at him through chestnut-colored eyes as the man known to the underworld as De la Serpiente's dark gaze swallowed her. He lowered his foot to the ground and gave her a wicked smile before slowly stepping closer to her. She trembled as a gush of warm urine escaped her and ran down her left leg. Ever the predator, De la Serpiente's vision slowly drifted from her face, and down to where the warm liquid had pooled around her feet. His smile broadened when his eyes lifted to recapture the girl's face. Tears ran like water down a slide, and it was all he could do not to grope himself from the intense desire which ignited within him, as he licked his lips. Raising a calloused hand, he ran a knuckle over the salty trail that dripped from her left eye.

"Que` hermosura- yo tendre Que` probar Tu panochita, hmm?" he whispered tenderly, before placing his knuckle in his mouth and making a loud sucking noise, as if the taste of her tears were the most exquisite taste since imported wine. Shay's eyes quickly flickered to Alane, who had a petrified expression on her face, yet, she still translated.

"He- he says, such beauty- he- wants to sample your..." Her words trailed as she turned her palms heavenward and shrugged her slender shoulders as if saying the last word was a sin she didn't wanna commit.

"Pussy" was the word she couldn't formulate, but when she nodded down toward her femininity, Shay overstood the vulgarity of the notion. Her watery glare reclaimed la rattle snake in defiant stubbornness.

"I'm not scared of you, dude!" she shouted.

"Noooo, Shay, he's gonna hurt you!" Tresey cried from the dirty ground.

"Silencia!" la rattle snake demanded silence.

"Leave them alone!" Alane declared.

At that moment, De la Serpiente decided to make an example out of one in order to get the respect of all. He moved for Alane, but Shay's small fists connecting with his chest, then his face, surprised him. Before she knew it, all the frustration, all the melancholy, fear, the hate she'd allow to infect her heart, exploded from her with each swing.

"Let- us- go! I hate you," she cried with her eyes squeezed shut. The surprise didn't last long. De la Serpiente` had never met such defiance, yet, just beyond the anger that surged through him, arousal was dominant. The blow he delivered was powerful but restrained due to the fact he wanted to preserve Shay's beauty for himself. At sixteen years of age, Shay resembled a younger version of Stacy Dash with red tint to her skin. The girl was beautiful, and her young body had the developments of a woman ten years older.

"Ahhhh!" she cried, as her hands flew to her bloodied lips. She had no time to appraise the damage because the vile man's hands were as fast as his namesake as he struck out and clamped one around her throat. His fingers had the hug of an anaconda, and as they squeezed her neck, Shay's eyes bulged to twice their size as she scratched at his hands.

"Can't- breathe! Ple-ase?" she rasped, as spots began to pop before her vision. The villain merely smirked a wickedness that revealed his intent, until a door at the back of the barn opened and seven polished looking teenaged girls entered. Behind them, a beautiful, mocha skinned Hispanic woman entered. Her electric-green colored eyes were a shocking contrast to her sun kissed skin as she took in the scene.

"Dejala Ir!!!" she demanded with a firm, but soft voice. La Serpent's eye flickered to her in a quick ping-ponging motion before recapturing Shay with a venomous spite. When the man ran his tongue over his lips for the third time that day, Shay saw how deep he'd ventured into the rattle snake persona. The front of his tongue *was split down the middle to resemble the tongue of an actual snake. She shivered when his fingers slipped from her throat, and as soon as she was able to suck in a breath of fresh air, she placed both hands to her throat as she gulped down lungfuls of it.*

Tresey's barely audible whimpering caused her to forget her minor introduction to La Serpent's anger, and she rushed over and fell to her knees beside the girl.

"Tresey, Tresey, are you okay?" she asked, as her eyes frantically studied the other girl. And after a brief moment, she understood it was more of the fear than the pain that the man inflicted that kept the child balled up in the fetal position like a baby still in its mother's womb. "Tresey, it's- it's okay. You have to get up before they hurt you again." She almost pleaded when she noticed the younger girl was crippled by fear.

Tresey's small body trembled so much, Shay could feel it vibrate up her arm, but as mercy would have it, she detected the fear in her new friend's voice. Tresey peeked from between the fingers she'd had covering her face and only after she saw the reassurance in Shay's eyes did she uncurl herself and throw herself into Shay's arms as if that's where she'd find a refuge. The two girls held each other tightly, but it was to be short lived.

"Enough!" A firm, feminine voice cut through their moment.

"She wants for you to get up," Alane spoke. Both girls eye'd the beautiful woman who'd entered behind the teenaged girls from the back of the barn. She stood a mere five foot four inches in heels, but her aura made her seem six foot ten.

La Rosa Peligrosa was a very powerful woman who had climbed up the ranks of the Gulf Cartel by way of sheer ruthlessness. She was once the wife of one of the heads of deadly faction until the day she became fed up with his drunken abuse. Her husband was found dead on arrival; a sharp butcher knife stuck from the back of his head, and both of his hands were missing. Someone had propped him up at his dining room table with a feast fit for a king laid out before him. Across the table where his beautiful wife would've sat, was a vase of black roses, hence her earned moniker. Since that faithful night, she, nor the man's hands had been found, but her exploits in the underworld were whispered about through the country.

Shay rushed to her feet before reaching to help Tresey up, and that's when she noticed the blood. Tresey's lips and teeth were smeared with it. The woman appraised both girls, but her vision seemed addicted to Shay's beauty. Shay eye'd her with mutual appraisement and was captivated by the woman's appearance. The dark-purple Thom Browne pant suit she wore complimented her slender frame and brought life to the sharp, pointed stiletto heels she stood in. Her long hair was pulled back into a tight ponytail that she'd fashionably slung over her right shoulder. She stood poised as she watched them, but her vision soon drifted to her general. De la Serpiente's cold eyes didn't hold a trace of fear, yet, even the king of the jungle must salute a powerful lioness. He did so literally. La Rosa Peligrosa gave him a loving smirk.

"I know my dear commander isn't having trouble getting these poor Nin`as chiquitas undressed?" she inquired in a broken, accented English. The big man looked affronted, disrespected. He spat on the ground as if the mere suggestion left a sour taste in his mouth. How could she think such a thing was possible? He wondered.

"No, girls are like horses, they mas be broken. I no trouble." His jagged English surprised his captives. La Rosa Peligrosa nodded before waving her manicured hand flippantly toward the girls.

"So why no undressed?" She was curious. The General's shrug was enough to tell her what his pride wouldn't. La Rosa Peligrosa casually made her way over to were la serpent and the girls stood, and glared at the young women. Some wept, some stared at the ground, seemingly in a daze, while others studied her, attempting to gauge if she was a savior or foe. She smiled sweetly at them.

"Get undressed please, you mas be properly cleaned," she informed. "These girls will help clean you." She waved the seven girls she brought.

"Who are you? What do you want from us?" Alane cried.

La Rosa Peligrosa's eyes seemed to bleed to an almost glowing Jade.

"Who-who arrrreeee youuuu!" a slightly chubby girl beside Alane seconded. At that moment, *La Rosa Peligrosa's* hands became a blur when she reached over and snatched the cold steel from the serpent's waistline and with one fluid motion, aimed between the young girl's eyes. *Boca!* The gun burped and knocked the child's noddle across Alane's shoulder and face in a thick, red splash. Life took on a slow motion effect as the young girl's body crumbled to the ground.

"Oh my Goddddd!" someone cried.

Tresey vomited on herself at the same time the other girls let out petrified screams. Shay stared down at the slain girl with her mouth ajar. The child had fallen crookedly, eyes wide, with a thick trail leaking from the right corner of her mouth.

"My name is *La Rosa Peligrosa,*" the woman introduced herself. Alane sucked in a deep breath in shock.

"Noooo, can't be yo-you're real?" Her eyes were as large as wagon wheels when the words of disbelief escaped her lips.

"'Tis' woman's name is Deadly Rose, I know of her. My papa says she kills people by putting poison on black roses," she trembled, relaying this to the other girls. *La Rosa Peligrosa* studied the young Hispanic with keen interest before offering a soft smile and a confirming nod.

"But tu can just call me Rosa, or Mother, because for the next few years, I'll be tu mother." The woman studied the crest fallen expressions of each girl as their eyes bounced back and forth between her and the corpse at their feet. "Now, get de fok out the clothes or die!" she demanded but held her smile. Though weeping was a dominant sound in the large room, every girl complied.

"See, *De la Serpiente*`, these are good girls, no problem`ma!" she declared, as her pretty eyes swallowed the man who had been an asset to her reign of terror throughout Mexico and most of the midwestern states of the U.S. of A. His sharp eyes fell to the murdered child before looking back up into hers.

"Si, I agree," he whispered.

"Patrese, are you okay, baby?" The voice seeped into her subconscious. Patrese cracked her eyes open just a bit, but slumber called her back.

***

Present time: December 22, 2020

"Come on, baby, I fucked up, ok? I know that. I- I'm sorry, Queen. I swear to *God* that bitch don't mean nothing to me, I- I—

"That's not the first time you've told me that, Nigil. What about the other woman, *Tony*, who I caught you giving your dick to last year? Huh? You swore on *your dead father's grave* not to do it again. Or," Oshaya cut him off, before holding up two fingers, "or what about the time I caught you getting your *little* johnson sucked on? What about *that* time, Mr. I-Love-You-And-I'm-Not-Gonna-Do-It-Anymore? You swoooore on ya' mammy you would keep your *community* dick where it belongs, in wedlock! I'm starting to believe, if it was up to you, every person you love would be dead and in the ground just like ya' nothin'-ass daddy. I swear on my mama! I swear on my granny! Hell, that's probably how ya' daddy died in the first place," she spat, before sipping from the chilled glass of wine she nursed. She glared at him from the other side of the small, square-shaped windows they'd had installed in the foyer. Tears dripped from her husband's eyes as he pleaded, and since she'd never witnessed a single tear fall from his orbes, it caught her by surprise, but lady stood firm.

Nigil had shown up a half an hour earlier to find the doors locked and the new locks rejecting his key. The sun had been hidden behind a wall of dark clouds and remembering the news anchor's prediction of rain caused Oshaya to glance up toward the heavens before resettling her vision on that dog of a husband of hers.

"You think I *want* to be like this? You think I *want* to cheat on you, Oshaya, huh? I'm human. I fuck up just like everyone else. Just like *you*. Remember that time I caught you and dude flirting on Facebook? We worked our—

"Really, Nigil?" She deaded that. "My fucking cousin! Omar is my cousin! There was no flirting, sex, nothin' inappropriate. Un-un,

144

don't- do-me!" She shook her head in disgust. *Why men just can't man up and accept when they're dead ass wrong! Always on some "you too" type stuff!"* She thought. "Just, just go, Nigil. You've done nothing but lie, cheat, and cheat some more since we've been together, and when you're caught, you put your filthy ass hands on me like *I'm* the one committing adultery. Those days are long gone." She gave a bitter laugh before sipping from her glass. "You can carry yourself back to your side bitch 'cause love don't live here anymore," she declared, and as an afterthought, wine glass midway back to her lips, Oshaya paused. "a *white* girl, Nigil? What, I'm *that* boring in bed that you've contracted Jungle Fever?" Oshaya spat, with a bitter shake of her head, before lifting the glass to her full lips and draining the cup. A solitaire tear cut a jagged trail down her face when she re-offered him her attention. "Why though? I'm *everything* to you, Nigil—I cook, clean, give you me in *every* way you like it, I- I suck your…" Her words seemed to evaporate into thin air, and as she gave another bitter shake of her head, her eyes fell toward his private area. When her eyes lifted to his, she gave a bitter laugh that held many subtle meanings. Nigil placed his palms against the glass like a prisoner on the other side of the division glass and let his tears speak for him.

"Baby, pleeeease, let's just sit down and talk. Oshaya, if I lose you, I lose my reasons, my reasons for everything. You've been by my side before I had a dime! I don't give a damn about the money in our joint accounts, this house, none of it, Oshaya, because without *you*"— he put emphasis on the last word while staring into her eyes. The expression on his handsome face was tormented as tears continued to cascade down his ebony face. He stepped forward and gently placed his forehead against the glass, and as if God felt his pain, a light drizzle began to fall. Oshaya glanced skyward with a quizzical expression and when her vision returned, it seemed as if she could capture *every* drop of heaven's tears that fell and soaked into Nigil's gray suit coat. He shrugged as if to say, *what you want me to do?* To Oshaya's surprise, he turned and made his way to the four stone steps that led up to the porch and took a seat. Oshaya watched as the rain began to fall a bit harder and baptize him.

At that moment, the strangest thing happened, the lyrics to Lauren Hill's *Ex Factor* classic began to play in her head...

♪ *I know what we gotta doooo / You let go, and I'll let go toooo/ 'cause no one has hurt me more than youuuu / and no one ever will / no matter how hard I try*♪

Oshaya's vision became submerged in twin oceans as she lifted her head to the heavens. *God, why can't I just let this man goooo!* She silently prayed before her eyes drifted shut. The tears escaped from the corners of her eyes as her hands betrayed her will power. Nigil rushed to his feet at the sound of the locks turning in the door, and as soon as it opened, he rushed forward and pulled his woman into his arms. She cried hard, so hard in fact, she didn't recognize the tenseness in his body. When they disentangled, the devil invaded the room. *Bam!*

Oshaya doubled over from the powerful punch to her midsection. "Bitch, you ... knooooow I'm 'bout to beat that ass, right?" Nigil hissed through clenched teeth. He slipped out of his suit jacket, but at the same time she was able to suck enough air back into her lungs, and she tried to turn and run. "Un-un, bitch, you," Nigil growled before striking out and punching lady in the back of the head. She fell forward, dazed. In a quick motion, he unbuckled his belt and snatched it out of the loops of his pants.

"Got me fucked up with one of these punk ass fools you work with," he raged, as she attempted to scurry away. *Whap! Whap!* The first two lashes were brutal and Oshaya hurriedly flipped over onto her back, cringing in pain as she hurried backward, scraping her palms as she attempted to stay clear of his wrath.

"Nooo, Nigil, you said you wouldn't doooo thissss again," she cried. *Whap! Whap!* The next two slashes of the leather belt slapped her across the stomach. *Whap!* Her shoulder- *Whap!* Her thigh.

"Ple-*please*, stop, Nigil, pleeease!" she cried. Tears bathe her pretty face. "You're a liar! I hate you, I hate you, I hattte you!" she shouted, but the man she'd fallen weak for was determined to teach her a lesson.

146

Whap! "You." *Whap! Whap!* "Gonna." *Whap!* "Have. Some." *Whap! Whap! Whap!* "Respect!" He punctuated each word with a harder swing of the belt.

Ski Mask Money

CHAPTER EIGHT
A REAL NIGGA'S BLUES

"Last call for commissary," the CO shouted.

"Look out, Gambino, get me a butter pecan or butter crunch pint, fam, I got you out the house!" Tay shouted, as he made his way off the cell block. Gambino merely nodded his affirmation, and when he reached the hallway, he put the pint on his list. He could see the commissary from where he stood, and when he saw that it was only three people in the line, he picked up the pace. *Shid, one minute it'll be empty, and the next time I look around, this bitch will be fuller than a pregnant woman's belly!* he thought, as he returned his gaze to the food he planned to purchase.

As soon as he reached his destination and took his place in line, the cell block, next to the one he resided, released a shot of their inmates for commissary. The convicts rushed toward the line, each vying for the closest spot to the front. Gambino shook his head in amusement, it never failed. *Commissary is necessary!* he mused. The three men before him quickly made their purchases and he made it to the window and handed his I.D. to the commissary lady.

"Excuse us, Ridge, can we go first, we ain't tryin' to get too much," a sweet voice called from behind him. He glanced over his shoulder to find two young female guards he knew. CO Bibbs and CO Smithers were just two felines from the hood of Huntsville, Texas, who had found an easy way to get paid.

Smithers was dark and built like a box of crayons, but as cool as a spring breeze, and Bibbs was short, petite, and flirtatious. She gave him a seductive smile with the request. Gambino knew they were both *in the game*, and had convicts whose struggles they'd embraced, and he respected any and *every* woman who understood a real nigga's plight.

" I ain't trippin," He offered before stepping back.

"Uh-un, girl, let me get the next one real quick. Last time he wrote me up for running out of mint sticks before I ran his card!" Ms. Ferguson, the commissary lady shook her head. All eyes shot to the old man behind Gambino. He glared at them from through the thick lenses of his state issued bifocals.

"And Ridge," Ms. Ferguson got their attention. She slid Gambino's I.D. back to him. "Boy, you know you ain't have no money on here, maybe it hasn't processed yet." Her words crushed Gambino's pride. The silence that followed was thick as the cats behind him glanced at each other with that *better-him-than-me* expression. Someone even snickered, but it was the two women behind him who fucked with his mental.

"Ridge, I know not, you broke?" Bibbs stated the obvious. CO Smithers giggled, but out of respect for lil Black, the convict she was breaking bread with, he held his tongue. Yet, the disappointment hurt. Not everyone had the blessing of having loved ones to hold them down behind the wall, and for the ones less fortunate, the reality of broken love was as cold as a polar bears ass cheeks during an Alaskan winter's night. The half cooked food prison serves was given in rations, and just as it was in the free world, when a person's stomach was touching their backs, it brought out the animal in a mu'fucka. Some gave into guerrilla tactics and *took* from the weak, and others would lose their way, falling victim to carnal behavior ... using the excuse of an empty stomach to justify fucking another man.

Gambino? He was bred different, a man with an upside down heart. He turned to glare at the men who seemed to find his struggle amusing, and though some returned the threatening stare down, he made sure to memorize each face for a later time. *We'll see what's up,* he thought as he turned and made his way back to his assigned housing area. *This shit won't ever happen again! On Fifth Ward Texas,* he mentally declared, as the picket officer popped the gate to let him on the cell block. The section was loud and rowdy when he stepped in, commissary day always seemed like a holiday in that mu'fucka.

"You going to the dayroom or your cell, Ridge?" CO Timmons asked as her eyes fell to the empty commissary bags in his hands. Gambino despised the pity in her gaze. He nodded toward the cell without the verbal. He headed up without glancing back, but Tay had noted his empty handed return, and knew his dude had faced off with disappointment at the window.

"Timmons, you're letting that inmate go in the cell?" the CO in the picket asked with a hint of disdain. He took his job too serious and believed the only way to help rehabilitate a man was to make him feel inferior. CO Brown was a famed scumbag on the Estelle Unit and was known to bring his problems from home to work. CO Timmons rolled her eyes at him. She hated officers who treated the convicts less than men.

"Just roll the door, Brown, damn!" she spat. The man mumbled under his breath but relented. As soon as he trudged up the steps leading to the third tier, two convicts strolled up to the bars of the dayroom and beckoned to Timmons.

"Look out, T, let me fuck with you real quick," Tay requested. Timmons' vision drifted from him to the slim brotha beside him. Papa was a real playa who had a unique way of vibing with women, and only the elite of the prison underworld knew he was one of the main players orchestrating complex infiltrations of narcotics into the belly of the monster. Papa was a humble boss who kept his circle small, and at forty years of age, he'd mastered a perspective that the grandest chess player would envy. Timmons had a suspicious expression on her face when her vision boomeranged back to Tay. Ten years younger than the man he considered a mentor, she knew he had a tongue of smooth convo, and he was as slick as baby oil.

"What y'all want, Tay? I ain't got no time for no bullsh—

"T, mane, I ain't tryin' to hear all that. Look, all I'm asking is for five minutes to see if bro is good and we'll be back in the dayroom before you even remember we left. Timmons, *you* know I wouldn't even ask if I wouldn't have seen my dude's heart cracked like that. I know how that shit feels, to expect something and get broken love instead. Come on, ma, five minutes," he cut her off with pleading eyes.

Timmons glanced toward the stairs Gambino had just climbed before her gaze drifted to the picket. He'd returned and had his attention focused down the hall in someone else's business!

"Mannn," she said unsure, but slid the key into the dayroom's door nonetheless, "five minutes, Tay and Price!" She looked to Papa because she knew Tay would try his luck. Papa merely nodded his acknowledgement as she twisted the key and let them out. Both men ran up the three flights of stairs and made their way to Gambino's cell. When they'd reached their destination, they found Gambino mildly sweating as he pushed out his fifth set of fifty pushups.

"Sup, brodie, you good?" Tay initiated the verbal. Gambino finished out his set before climbing to his feet and nodding his acknowledgment.

"Sup, my guys?" he vibed, before dapping both men through the bars.

"Family, you know if you need something, or just want it, we got you. We won't even speak on the food and hygiene, you know that shit will—

"What's overstood ain't gotta be explained, fam, but y'all know I got a locker full of food *and* I'm a playa, nigga my hygiene gone stay lit even if my stomach is growlin'," he cut Tay off. "Naw, the problem is shit ain't 'pose to go down like this *period!* My account should *never* be on zero, dawg. I'm just tired of being lied to, bro. I kept it too real out there," he spoke his heart.

Papa's chuckle brought both men's attention to him. He allowed his vision to bounce back and forth between them, allowing each man to see what lurked in his pupils. Though his heart was closed shut, he had a special kinda love for the two younger men. "You young niggas got the game fucked up! See, y'all think that just 'cause a mu'fucka loves you, they won't hurt you, but when a nigga loves somethin' the way men like us do, becoming vulnerable is automatic! That's why you gotta be very careful who you give this shit to..." He paused to tap a fist to his chest. "'Cause some people will try their best to understand it, others will get yo' 'shit, and though they don't mean no harm, will just be living life and forget they got your heart in their hands and drop that mu'fucka a few times.

Some people are just intrigued by the heart of a real nigga, and the shit they'll find in it will blow their minds, but never forget this lil daddy…" Papa paused to reach through the bars and tap the side of Gambino's chest where his heart was said to be. "You don't get no trophy for being no real nigga, so when a mu'fucka cracks your heart, you can't rely on what you did to not deserve that pain. Fam, we live under the laws of *no love*, where love is only loving the ones who will hold its hands and dance in the rain. Lil bro, we're all tired of being lied to, shid, I've been lied to my *entire* life, but still want to be loved by somebody. I got a question, fam"—he paused before leaning forward, face inches from the cell's bars— "how you a street nigga, but get fucked up when street shit happens to you?" Papa lifted his hands in the air as if to say *'I don't get it!'* Gambino felt his vibrations and could even two step to that real talk radio he was kicking, but it was his heart that didn't *want* to understand.

" I get that, Papa, mane, I'm just sayin', bro, ain't no way I 'pose to be on my dick in here. Bruh, y'all may not believe it, but I secured that bag, I took care of my business out there!" He gritted as his thoughts of Cat Eyes' betrayal threatened to drown him. Papa gave him a bitter smile before reaching in and pointing at the tattoo Gambino had inked in large cursive letters across his chest: *Die a real nigga!*

"Many men do, but *I* don't pity the fool, lil bro. The streets teaches us that a mu'fucka who ain't ever been loyal, *can't* betray you. A bitch who don't know *how* to love, *can't* love you, and if *you* ain't teach a mu'fucka *how* to love *you, you can't* fault 'em for loving you incorrectly," he emphasized each word by jabbing his finger in his palm. "Bro, being solid gonna come with some shit that's hard to swallow, but through the tears, the years, and heart cracks, you gonna have to digest that shit." Papa tapped his knuckles against the man's chest. "If you gone die a real nigga, you may as well prepare for a lot of disappointments.

Them people we left out there lives don't stop 'cause we're on lock, my nigga, and you ain't gonna ever master love or loyalty if ya' lil feelings get hurt every time shit turn sour. You need to feel this pain. You gotta allow time to reveal what a person's mouth won't. Love comes wit' conditions, fam, so stick yo' chest out and boss up. You don't want them people to lie when they put the words in your obituary. Niggas sayin' you was the kinda guy you truly wasn't. If they have to do that, yo' whole life was a lie," Papa came from the hip, before glancing up at the digital clock on the table in Gambino's cell. He extended his hand to Gambino. "Lady only gave us five minutes to fuck with you, so we'll pull up on you in the turning lane. Hold ya' head, my "G", it don't rain long. In a few days I'll have something that's gonna change the game for us." His love was evident as they dapped and Papa turned for the stairs.

" Tell T I'll be down in a minute, tell her bro cryin' and shit and I'm building with him." Tay's request got a chuckle out of him.

"What! Bruh, don't tell lady no shit like that, tell her *he's* crying, and I'm consoling *him*," Gambino corrected with a nod toward Tay.

Papa was beside himself with laughter as he left them to it. Tay took a seat on the floor outside the cell and glanced up at Gambino with a raised brow, watching as he took a seat on the bottom bunk.

"Big bro spoke the gospel, dawg. When them folks gave me this forty-five agg, I was sick, mane. Then, to put the nails in my casket, by the time I looked up, all the money, all the hoes, all them niggas I use to thug with, all of it had turned on me." He shrugged indifferently, but his eyes revealed what his pride concealed. "Gotta learn to sleep with demons, my dude. It's part of what we signed up for."

Gambino studied him for a second before slipping from the bottom bunk and making his way over to his locker. He reached in and pulled a green photo album down before making his way back to the edge of the bunk and reclaiming his seat.

"Check this out," he proposed, while extending the book he'd trapped frozen moments of his life within. Tay took it and opened it to the first page. There were three photos that opened up the tale of Gambino's journey. Tay could tell that each picture had been taken on different days. "This is my potna Lil James, the lil bitch got that sack and he still a baby! You see all them candy-apple green cars with the 84s on 'em?" Gambino asked after pointing to the first flick. Tay nodded as he observed the picture. It depicted about ten cars in a line. All ten were painted a glossy green and the rims were a style native to the city of Syrup. 83s and 84s were classics that Houston, Texas, made a culture. The 83s originally came on the 1983 Buick Rivera, and the 84s, the 1984 Cadillac Biarritz, but Houstonian's made the protruding, chrome rims a universal style. In the biggest city in Texas, you could find 83s and 84s on some of *any* kind of cars.

"This is called a *slab* line in the H, homie. Different hoods slide through on different colors but *all* slabs *gotta* be dressed up with dem swangas on 'em!" Gambino sounded excited to speak on his city's culture. Tay frowned in confusion at the man's lingo.

"Slab? Swangas? Nigga, I'm out the metroplex, we ride *inches* on Laks, Chevies, and Foreigns! The only time I *ever* saw *these* rims is in my uncle's backyard. He kept his dog tied to 'em. Fuck is *swangas? Slabs?"* he asked, still studying the picture. Gambino wasn't feeling his vibe. To his ears, it sounded like hate.

"Saaaaayy, mane, watch how you handle my city, bro. Nigga, *the H* got the whole world sippin' drank! We're the hottest city right now, on me, bro!" he bragged, while chopping a hand through the air as if he were demonstrating a karate chop. Tay laughed. He respected city pride.

"Swangas, that's what those rims are, and a slab is a car a niggas blow bags on. See how those trunks popped open with all the lights?" Gambino schooled, while pointing at the second picture. It was an image of about eight burnt-orange painted cars, glistening with their swangas poking. The trunks were opened on each car and the inside of each trunk had a neon light enhanced phrase glowing from it. *That bag got you mad- Wit' yo lookin' ass- slippin' thru the city, lookin' pretty-* were some of the phrases that glowed from their respective trunks. "Yeah, slab stands for *slow, loud and bangin'!* You gotta come with it, bro, boys comin' down on gorillas now." Gambino gave the history as Tay turned the page. The next page caused his lips to curve into a smile as his eyes drifted from the page to Gambino.

"Fam, you was on it like that? How much is this?" he asked, with a shocked expression on his face. Gambino chuckled.

"That ain't nothin' but a light weight two." He shrugged as if it wasn't shit.

"Two? As in two what, bro?"

"Two hunny buns, bro bro, what you mean, *two what!*" Gambino shot with a confused expression on his face. He studied his dude as Tay shook his head, lost to the terminology.

"*Hunny bun!* Fuck?" he mumbled, and that's when it dawned on Gambino.

"Say, Tay, how long you been gone, bro?"

"Bruh, I been gone since '04, that's seventeen years! I stay up on the newest lingo and trends, but I ain't ever heard a *hunny bun!* That shit sounds *suspicious*, bruh!" They shared a laugh as both sets of eyes fell to the pictures. Two of the pictures were of Gambino. The first picture was of him standing next to another dude. Both he and the man were heavily jeweled, and in the background two foreign cars were parked side by side like a pair of shoes.

"A *hunny bun* is a hundred bands, family." Gambino laughed. "*Seventeen years* though? *Damn*, what you do, rob the president?" He shook his head in disbelief.

"Naw, dawg, I got a punk ass aggravated robbery case and a dope case. Fam, I ain't even shoot nobody *and* I walked away empty handed, but a court appointed lawyer ain't shit but a prosecutor's puppet. I didn't know shit 'bout law when they took me to trial, and by the time it was all said and done, them crackas gave me forty five years and shot me up the river!" Tay's story touched his soul.

"Pussy ass system, my guy, damn," Gambino spat, before leaning forward and pointing at the picture. "This me and my nigga Bo Eddie, bro official and gone dirt somethin'! That's my Benz, but the Masi his," he confirmed, before pointing at the second picture that had caught Tay's attention in the first place. "This me at one of the spots I had out there, and..." His words trailed off as his eyes feasted on the second man in the image. His silence brought Tay's vision to him in curiosity. The evil grimace on the man's face told a story of treachery, a tainted bond amongst men.

Tay glanced back down at the photo. It was an image capturing Gambino and a paled skin brotha with electrifying gray eyes. The

Ski Mask Money

pale skinned man appeared to be sitting on a raggedy sofa and behind him, Gambino emptied a duffle bag filled to the brim with money over the man's head. As Tay held the photo album closer to his face for a closer observation, he could see the dead faces the U.S treasury had printed on the bills. *Nothin but Grants and Franklins!* he thought.

Gambino smiled. "I'd stumbled upon a mean lick that put my entire clique on, Tay. You ever seen a million dollars, family? I mean really held it. Counted it with your own two hands, my nigga?" His voice had taken on a dark timbre as his eyes lifted to behold his man's. Tay studied him before shaking his head, no.

"Naw, bruh, the most I've ever touched that was *mine*, and at one time, is bout sixty-two bandos. I got bammed when I was just turnin' nineteen, and I was a dope boy that robbed twice in my life. The second time I crapped out," he confirmed, as he studied the picture. Both men in the image were smiling, and if judging from the picture, the bond between the two was as strong as Superman.

"What you boys hit and who is dude with the funny eyes?" Tay was curious of what the man in the photo could've done to create a murder scene in his homie's eyes. Gambino gave a bitter chuckle before leaning backwards and resting his back against the chipped wall. When Tay glanced up to see why silence had become their new conversation, he frowned at the far away expression on Gambino's face —his eyes had become distant as he stared into nothingness.

"I've done some major shit in my twenty-nine years of thuggin', Tay. I've touched two other continents, and took down some big boy capers, my nigga. Let me tell you a quick tale of the nail that sealed my coffin closed and buried me with this *60* behind these walls. The day I fed a serpent and he bit me in return..."

Renta

CHAPTER NINE
JAWS OF LIFE
Gambino

The Past – 2017

Most people don't know I graduated from the University of Houston with my bachelor's degree in Computer Tech and Performing Arts. I've always loved to act, to come out my body and impersonate other identities. And it was there, at that University, where I met three men who would change my life—for better, "and" for the worst.

Malcom was the first black man I'd ever met that made being intelligent seem "cool." He was a man who could find his way out of strange situations. The man had a knack for spotting beautiful escape routes. Dude had an eye for the cracks in a wall, and he'd later become the go-to-man to get me and our team out of some ugly, no-way-out situations.

Joey was the typical, very serious, white guy. He never smiled and the man had a very nasty habit of smoking a cigarette every few minutes. Yet, my mans had a talent for finding some of the most elaborate takedowns. There was nothin' mundane about the Juggs bro found. Casinos, churches, diamond heists, whatever! He somehow found out the layouts, attendees, security, as well as the times of the events, and he soon became our takedown planner.

Our guy to lead us to the pot of gold. Julio? Mannn! Julio was a solid Hispanic cat who was born into the savageness of the Zetas Cartel. His pops was said to be the cousin of La Barbie, the infamous Zetas leader who turned rat when it was time to face off with the consequences of his actions. Julio's mother wanted more than just 'the life' so she made him promise to do a year of college before entering a life of crime. He did, and it was in the same school which was meant to save him, that Joey made him a mastermind of electronics. The man could tap into any system and break through any firewall in any computer software. There, in that theater of the U of H, we became a team of bandits who would do shit that you only saw on TV! If I remember, fam, it was a Thursday morning, with a warm spring breeze and soft clouds, when we met up in the theater building to rehearse. We were working on a drama play I'd written, and it was a masterpiece. As Joey dramatized his part, I studied him, determined to be better. When the time came for me to do my thing, I swooped onto the stage, dressed in all black, and blew their mu'fuckin minds! My brothers in art were so taken aback that everything came to a halt. The men stared at me in awe, shocked speechless! They gawked at my face... The face that wasn't mine. Well, not the face they'd grown familiar with. I'd used cosmetic and pigmentation paints that were created solely to darken or lighten one's skin color. I had also used the substance of drama wax to alter my facial. I'd created the appearance of an elder white man and I knew there wasn't a glitch or a single ... smear... in ... my detail. If I hadn't told them it was me, they would've never saw through my disguise. Yet, it was Joey who couldn't take his eyes from me. After practice, we retreated to the back, and it was there that I couldn't ignore ole Joey boy's gaze any longer.

"Sup, white guy, why you keep staring at me like you wanna kiss me or some shit?" I asked, while using alcohol wipes to cleanse the paint from my face. Dude continued to study me until he came to some sort of resolution. He nodded to himself before asking the craziest question.

"Hey, Gambino, have you ever dreamed of being rich, man? I mean, like filthy fucking rich, dude?" The question gave me pause as I glanced up at his reflection in the mirror I stood in front of.

"Fuck kinda question is that, bruh. I'm a nigga out the slums of the nickel, all I know is struggle. Shid, fuckin' right I dream of ballin'! I got dreams of being a king!" I spoke truth. Joey glanced around the room at the other two men. Julio and Malcom had curious expressions on their faces as they studied him. His long hair fell over his shoulders and gave him more of a rockstar's vibe than a school boy image.

"What about you two? Ever dream of doing something big, man? I'm speaking, like real big! Something that will allow you to sit on your asses for the rest of your lives? Fucking rich, man!" he exclaimed, before spreading his arms out wide, as if they were

wings and he would take flight at any moment. Malcom chuckled at the absurdity of the rhetorical question before returning to his mission of getting dressed, but Joey's next words stunned us all.

"Mal, I know you're originally from Mississippi, and though you made it here on a scholarship, you're struggling with the cost of living here in the Lone Star state. Somewhere along the way, you learned a very special talent of escaping out of strange situations. That's fucking kick ass, dude!"

"Man, what the fuck kind of secret agent shit you on, homeboy, who the fuck are you?"

"Give me a chance to explain, man," Joey cut Malcom's rant short, but the frown on Malcom's face was evidence enough he wasn't felling the shit.

"You better have a real good reason to know what you know about me, white boy, or I'm gonna be all up in your shit!" Malcom declared, but Joey ignored him as his vision found Julio.

"Julio, I know you're just here to appease your mother's worrying nature, but what's more interesting is the fact that after you get just one year of higher learning, you'll become your father's puppet in the Zeta's Cartel and probably get yourself killed by a rival.

"Say, homes, you know nothing! Nada, puta! Fuck you! What, you some sort of policia? You a pig, ese?" the young Hispanic spat in disgust, before taking a step toward Joey with dangerous intent in his glare. I held his arm to stop him mid-stride, and though he paused, his dark browns fell to my hand before his gaze lifted to capture mine. We had a stare down, me having to allow him to see the dark side of me that rested dormant just beyond my pupils. After a moment, he relaxed and spat on the floor. "I'm no ones puppet, vato, no one's," he declared.

My eyes found Joey. "Let's see what the white boy has to say," I reasoned before smirking. "And me? What you know 'bout me, white boy?"

Joey chuckled before running his hand through his long hair. "You, Gambino, are another kind of animal entirely. You're a killer who's too smart for the slums of the Fifth Ward section of the city you seem so proud of. You speak three different languages for Christ's sake, man!" he praised, almost in disbelief. You're also a robber who takes down mostly drug dealers, and just recently, you and your childhood friend killed a m—

Bam!

Before he could complete the sentence I'd went dead into his mu'fuckin mouth with all five knuckles. The punch put dude on his ass, and blood instantly stained his lips and teeth.

"You spyin' on us, cracka! Huh? I'll rock yo' stupid ass to—

"Can't you dumb, sons-of-bitches see! Huh?" He cut me off with a hiss. He glared at me from the floor as he used the back of his hand to wipe the blood from his lips. His vision drifted to Julio, then Malcom, before recapturing me. "If I have access to this type of intel, how much more do you think I can get intimate details of? Fuck, man, we're fucking strangers, but you're smart enough to see the bigger picture. I can get vital info on some big shit, dude, like gigantic! Can't you guys see the dollar signs?" he spat, with a disbelieving shake of his head as if he couldn't believe how dumb we were.

"Fuck you talkin' about, fool, all 'I' see is a white dude with too many intimate details on our lives. What about y'all?" Malcom looked from me to Julio. Julio, again, spat on the floor as he glared down at Joey.

"Miro un hombre muerto!" he hissed in Spanish, but I was the only one who overstood him. I smirked at the puzzled expression on Joey's face.

"He says he sees a dead man," I translated, but the death date would have to wait. My mental was reeling from dude's knowledge of us. Everything he'd said of me was absolute, and if what he'd spoken of the other two was just as accurate, I could see his worth. But, I nodded my head as I gave into curiosity. "I can see the bankroll rather than your funeral. Speak your mind white man." I gave room for chance before extending my hand to help him up. Joey studied my hand skeptically but relented after a brief hesitation. Once to his feet, he strolled over to the costume rack and used a shirt to clean his mouth.

Ski Mask Money

"I've been dating this girl who loves to pillow talk after we've had kinky sex, and the girl can talk! Her family is fucking stacked, man, lots of old money, dude. So, I did a little digging and I found some really good shit, man. Like, things that lead to a pot of gold!" he exclaimed.

"The hell that has to do with us?" Malcom asked, verbalizing all of our sentiments. But it was the look in his eyes that allowed me to realize there was more to dude than merely a geeky ass black dude trying to get his way through college. Hunger! I recognized it because I'd had it in my vision all my life. The question was directed to Joey, but my laughter brought all attention to me as I wagged a pointed finger at the white man.

"You's a slick muthafuckaaa!" I dragged the word as it all came together in my mental. Malcom and Julio had looks of confusion on their faces, but Joey-ole, Joey boy, he smiled like a shark before its teeth clamped down on unsuspecting prey as he nodded his confirmation! I laughed hard.

"It was 'you'! You're the one who switched my classes, whiteboy!"

"Ain't this a bitch!" Malcom's expression was one of pure shock as the words slipped from his lips, and it confirmed my suspicions.

" It was 'you' who changed my shit, asshole! I 'never' chose theater. I just figured the admin fucked up and placed me in here, but..." His words trailed off as all eyes ricocheted to Joey. He gave a sneaky-bloodied smile before shrugging and nodding at Julio whose expression was just as dumbstruck.

"Just a quick few taps on a laptop can change a man's entire existence," he chuckled with the words. *"Listen, Gambino, with your brains and expertise with disguises"*— he paused to glance at Malcom—*"Mal, with your knack of getting out of sticky situations?"*—he paused once more while nodding his head, as if all his planning were coming into fruition. His vision then drifted to Julio—*"and with your connections and means to obtain necessary equipment, we could be rich in..."* His dialogue died, but he punctuated his point with a snap of his fingers.

"What chu speak of ese, what we need to do?" Julio wanted to know.

"Shid." Malcom smirked as if he'd already signed his name on the dotted line. "Whatever it is, if it can put some money in our pockets, I'm in."

"What up?" He became food to the shark without even knowing the intimate details. Joey smirked as his vision captured Julio.

"The first thing we need is a few minor, but essential tools. You think you can get them?" He inquired with a raised brow.

"What kind of tools, ese, be specific?" Our dude wanted to know, but rather than answering, Joey held up a finger, pausing the conversation as his gaze reclaimed me.

"You in or out, G, we can't pull this off without you. I may be the brains behind the scenes, but you're our natural leader, and..." He paused his manipulative assuage of my ego. I smirked to let him know I saw the tactic. "The disguises and plays you create can actually be an asset. What you say, man, you wanna be rich?" He gave his spiel, and I won't lie, he touched that street nigga in me. I studied dude intently, knowing that "no one" sought another without intent, so I wanted to gauge to see if his were of God or the devil? I was at a standstill until the struggles of the times tainted my mind. My struggling mother. My little brother Dunte. My niggas. It all collided in my head like rams locking horns.

"I'll only rock with you under "one" condition, homeboy," I offered. Joey lifted his hands in the air as if to say 'what else could you want'.

"Dude, you can't get a bigger cut than anyone else, we're all—

"Bruh, I'm not asking for no bigger cut!" I cut that bullshit short.

"Then-what?"

"I'll only lock in if I can bring a cat I trust wit' my life on board, he's—

"Ohhh, the Albino skinned guy with the funny colored eyes, huh? Excellent!" The white man fucked my head up with the description of my bro Cat Eyes. How he know, bro? I wondered. How much could dude know about us? I wondered. Clearing my

throat, I nodded, confirming that I was in. Joey's eyes went back to Julio.

"Now that we're all on board, how about the tools we'll need?"

" I asked you, vato, what sort of tools you speak of?" Julio questioned, with a hint of annoyance.

"You ever heard of the jaws of life, Julio?" Joey smirked.

CHAPTER TEN
THE TAKE DOWN

3 weeks later

The modern contemporary, two story dream house was a beautiful structure, built upon fifteen acres of land, and positioned deep on the countryside of Pearland, Texas. It was protected by a ten foot, wrought iron security gate that had cameras mounted on each of its posts. If touched, one would experience a shock so powerful, in comparison, the electric chair would seem like a grandmother's favorite rocking chair.

"*Susan, make sure to remember your appointment with the OBGYN, it's at three. Cathren, remind her will ya', honey,*" *their mother shouted from the doorway of the house. The sisters gave each other a knowing look as they continued to walk, never looking back to show they'd heard her.*

"*Susan, make sure to remember your appointment. Susan, your nails are too long. It's not ladylike. Susan, Susan, blah, blah, blaahhhh,*" *Susan, the eldest girl mocked their mother, before opening her mouth wide, and playfully sticking her finger in and acting as if she were attempting to regurgitate. Her younger sister giggled.*

"*Did you hear me, Susan? Don't be so juvenile! It's not a good example for your sister,*" *their mother admonished, with a roll of her eyes. The sun had barely risen, and a flock of birds flew overhead as they made their way down the driveway.*

"*OK, Mom, I won't forget! See you later, love ya',*" *Susan shouted over her shoulder.*

"*Bye, Mom, see you later!*" *Cathren seconded, with a brief wave. Their mother merely leaned against the doorsill, before crossing her arms over her breast. She watched her girls make their way down the driveway, as the two men standing outside the luxury AMG Benz, stood waiting with the back doors of the vehicle opened. Both men were trained personnel her husband hired to ensure the safety of their children. As the woman eye'd the group of four, she* whispered a prayer for her girls. Both were young beauties who had inherited their all-American features from her, but it was her eldest daughter, Susan, who worried her so.

The girl was only nineteen and in her second year of college, but she was already as promiscuous as a trailer park white woman on a Friday night. The woman frowned at Susan's excessive makeup since it was entirely too much for her taste. Shaking her head in disdain, she watched the two men close the back doors after the girls were secure. As soon as she was safe from her mother's scrutiny, Susan rolled her eyes.

"She can be just toooo extra! Geesh! Like, I'm nineteen! Like, really? Ugh! I can't wait until dad takes off his leash and allows me to get my own apartment."

"Yeah, she can be a bit too much, like, ugh!" Cathren seconded. She idolized her older sister but wasn't as wild.

The sudden activity in the backseat caused the driver to glance up in the rearview mirror, curiously.

"Uhh, Ms. Mitchell, I-I don't think that's such a-a good idea," he stammered, when he saw what was transpiring.

Susan had pulled her wool sweater over her head and completely off. She smirked at his stunned expression as she sat in nothing but her long skirt, clog heels, and a black, lacy bra that covered her grapefruit-sized breasts. She smiled mischievously before cupping them suggestively .

"Does my father pay you to sneak peeks at my titts or to keep us safe to and from our destinations?" She spoke sweetly with a flutter of her eyelids.

The driver decided to hold his silence as he focused on the road. Cathren giggled as her sister stuck her tongue out in jest. Susan pulled her backpack off the floor and hurriedly unzipped it. Pulling a blood-red top out of the bag, she slipped it over her head and down over her chest. The turtle necked sweater stopped mid-stomach, allowing a glimpse of the diamond studded belly ring her parents knew nothing of. The girl then shimmied the long, Catholic style, school uniform dress down her long legs until it pooled at her feet, before pulling a black mini from the bag and slipping it on.

After exchanging the clogs for a sexy pair of heels, she tousled her blond hair to give it a wild look.

"Mom would kill you if she found out you were dressing like a slut to go to school. You know what she says 'image, Susan! A woman's image is everything!'" Cathren exploded into laughter while mocking their mother. She wished she had the courage to defy her parents, but she'd always been the more conservative one. Only two years younger than her sister, she wasn't boy crazy or too concerned with keeping up with the trends of the era.

"Mom is just an old hag, but have you seen my new boy toy? Joe is soooo adorable, Cat," Susan said, and gushed before leaning over to whisper so the two men up front couldn't hear her, "and he has a massive cock!" She giggled. "A wildcat in the bed!" she declared, as her sister rolled her eyes with a scrunch of her nose.

"Yeah, like you need another one of those," she mumbled, as her eyes trailed to the passing countryside. "Seems kind of crazy, dangerous if you ask me," she replied as an afterthought. If only she could've known how close to the truth she was, she would've demanded the car be turned around and skipped that day of school.

***

The stolen F-250 was custom made with a bully dog programmer that allowed its driver to turn up the truck's horse power. As it sped down the winding country road at a blinding hundred thirty miles per hour, Malcom was truly enjoying it's power. He mashed the pedal with an exhilarating smile on his dark face. He felt free as he cut loose with no regard for authority. Tupac's, "Ambitions of a Rida," blasted from the speakers as he puffed on a Newport Short. He exhaled the tainted smoke as he glanced down at all the protective gear he'd wone, and as his vision returned to the road, he whispered a quick prayer...

"God, please don't hate me for what I'm doing. You know I wouldn't do it if my balls wasn't nailed to the ground." By the time he said Amen, he spotted the black Benz up ahead. Smashing the snub of the cigarette against the dashboard, he mentally willed the *truck forward, but even the Ford Shelby Super Snake had to pump its juice to vie with the AMG Benz. "Well, let's see what this pretty mu'fucka can do," he said aloud, and challenged himself when he noticed the AMG pick up speed.*

He glanced up into the rearview mirror with a smirk. The Shelby, Super Snake Mustang and fire-red Hell Cat that trailed him were effortlessly keeping with his pace, and noticing the chase was on, Cat Eyes expertly swerved the Cat into the next lane without regard for oncoming traffic.

Julio gripped the wheel of the blue Mustang as he swung to the other side of the truck, and by that time, Malcom had closed the gap between them and the Benz. He had to ease off the gas in an attempt to cut into the next lane and maneuver the truck in front of the car, but seeing his intent, the driver of the foreign car swung the Benz to block the attempt. The move pissed Malcom off. The steering wheel vibrated in his hands as he tapped the gas. The truck growled in response.

"Aiiight, you wanna do this the hard way, huh?" He gritted his teeth as he gripped the wheel tighter. Mashing the gas, rather than attempting to cut around them again, Malcom surprised everyone when he rammed the bumper of the foreign. "We can play nice or flip these two bitches! I neeeeed this money," he declared, as if the occupants of the car could hear him.

The crunch of metal was defining as the Benz swerved erratically, causing black smoke to rise from its back wheels as they fought for traction. "Yeah! This ain't TV, bitch, yeah!" Malcom shouted in triumph but had to reclaim his focus when the Benz shot ahead a few feet. The road became a snaking path with sharp curves, and he knew just up ahead it would become a 'T' where one could only turn left or right, or they'd plow headlong into the line of aged oak trees and thick overgrowth.

On both sides of the road, wheat fields stretched as far as one could see, and it caused Malcom to smile evilly at their diabolical plan that began playing out within his mental. He mashed the gas, and the growl of the monstrous motor sounded like the roar of ten angry lions. With an angry jerk of the wheel, the truck swerved to the left lane. "Got yo' ass!" he shouted.

***

"OH MY GOD! OH-MY GODDDAAAH!" Susan cried, as she fanned herself as if she were hot and hyperventilating. Cathren stared in horror as the big truck swerved to her side of the car. Just before it passed, her and my boy made eye contact.

"Oh my!" The words slipped from between her lips as her mouth fell open in a shocked O-shape. Malcom's face was concealed behind a black, Friday the 13th hockey mask and he had the hood of his hoodie pulled up over his head as if the mask wasn't enough to keep his identity secret. To Cathren's astonishment, he nodded to her as if to say, 'good day, ma'am.' But it was the determination in his stare that told the girl that my dude had something sinister planned for her and her people.

I watched it all from the backseat of that red Hellcat, and believe me when I tell you, from the scope of the AK designed Drako, I could see it all! I watched Malcom yank that big truck so far to the left, he was driving partially on the road and partially on the dirt where the asphalt ended. At that moment, I lifted the hand held radio to my lips and sealed the fate of the people in that Benz.

"That road up ahead only leads two ways, fam, left or right! The left will take 'em into the city, and the right will lead 'em in a wide circle back toward the house. We gotta stop 'em here. Malcom, cut off the left and do your do! Julio, cut off the right side, and we'll lead 'em into Malcom's trap."

"Overstood!" Malcom responded.

"O'rale, Homes!" Julio seconded. The blue Mustang he drove shot forward and cut a smokey trail through the red dirt on the shoulder of the road. I watched as the metallic blue F-250 shot ahead of the Benz, but instead of pulling in front of it, the truck cut a sharp trail through the wheat field and plowed earth. The move cut the man's mission short by twenty paces, and at that moment, shit got real!

"Pull up beside them, Cat Eyes! Get me close enough to show my work, my guy," I instructed, before reaching forward and snatching my mask off the passenger's seat. *The stitches holding the leather together were jagged and made it resemble the mask Leather Face wore in the movie "Texas Chainsaw Massacre." As I slipped it on, I felt like I'd morphed into another person, a monster! I could feel the torque of the powerful car as Cat Eyes pulled it leveled to the Benz. The man in the passenger seat seemed to be speaking rapidly on his cell phone when I eased the window down and balanced the barrel of that stick on the window sill. There was a young girl I recognized as Cathren, and her eyes grew as large as dinner plates when she noted the muzzle of that death deliverer, but what I had planned wasn't meant for her—her atonement would come from a different form of the reaper. I angled the weapon toward the front of that car. I knew the gun would jerk from the power of its vomit, and I didn't want its fiery regurgitation to hit any other target but the passenger.*

TTTAAhh! TAAAAtttA! The burst exploded from the lips of the assault rifle and as the 7.62s cut through the metal of the Benz, I fell in love with the wicked dance dude's body jerked into as I hit 'em up.

***

"Dammit, I'm telling you we're outnumbered! There's three vehicles in pursuit and we're on—

TTTTAhh! That stick talk silenced the man forever.

"Oh God! Ohh Goddd," both girls cried as the man's body jerked in his seat. It appeared as if he were lunging toward the driver's seat, but the seatbelt held him secure in place.

"Fuck! Fuck! Girls, get down! Get – the – fuck –down!" The driver of the Benz raged with spittle flying from his mouth. He was attempting to keep his calm even though his friend's blood was splattered all over the front seat.

BAM! The sound of metal against metal was loud as sparks shot from the driver's seat. Julio had slammed his car into theirs. Skurrrr! The wheels fought for traction as the driver's eyes were

*filled with the possibility that, that day may be his last. When his
eyes darted towards me, I smiled wickedly on some other shit, giving
him the finger as I tapped Cat Eyes' shoulder. "Ease off the gas and
fall back, family," I instructed. And as the Benz eased ahead of us,
I laughed at the look of confusion on the man's face. Human nature
was so predictable, and that's exactly why calculation was so
effective.*

*The Benz was on a head-on course, and it was only a few feet
away from slumming into the ancient oak trees just up ahead. But
at the last possible second, the driver jerked the wheel savagely to
the left– Skurrrr! BOOM! The back end slammed against the trunk
of one of the trees so hard, the back bumper flew off and the trunk
popped open. Even though Cat Eyes had pulled to a stop in the
middle of the road, I could hear the cries of the girls in the back
seat.*

*Skurrrrrt! The tires of Julio's Mustang kicked up a cloud of red
dust as it fishtailed, and somehow wounded up catty cornered to the
back of the Benz. I climbed over, and into the passenger seat,
settling in as the tension built. With Julio at its rear, the Challenger
blocking its path in the opposite direction, and the F-250 half a yard
up the road, the Benz was trapped within the center of a deadly
triangle and either way he chose to go, evil intent would greet him.*

*Me and Cat Eyes sat, lost in fascination as the Hemi V8's power
caused the car to tremble as the motor growled.*

*"Which way you think he'll go?" Cat Eyes asked. "I think he'll
go right."*

*"Naw," I disagreed, with the shake of my head, "I think he'll
go left, right into the spider's web."*

*"Bet two hundred! White folks got better sense than that," he
wagered. My eyes drifted from the idling Benz and captured the guy
I'd rose out of the slums with.*

*"You sound like a lame, fuck race gotta do with intelligence!
You think Trump had a good idea when he told people to drink hand
sanitizer? Fuck outta here. That's a bet to you, hustla." We locked
the two hundred in with a quick dap of our hands.*

***

"Pleeeease, get us away from here, Paul, oh my God, oh my God, oh-my-God, please don't let us die!" Susan was so flustered, all she could do was hug herself as she rocked back and forth in her seat. Her tears had ruined her mascara, causing her tear streaked face to be stained with smears of black. *"Jesus, I swear I'll never suck another cock until I'm married, and that-that time I snuck out and did Josh in the backseat of his Lexus, I'm—*

"Shut the fuck up!" Paul, the driver, shouted before pounding the steering wheel with the flat of his palm. *"Let me think!"* he spat, as his eyes traveled to his longtime friend, who was now a corpse lying horizontally in the passenger's seat. *"Jesus! Oh, fuck, Chuck, I messed up big time. I should've driven better."* He spoke more to himself as his vision drifted to the rearview mirror.

The blue Shelby Super Snake had him cut off, but left a small space he might've been able to squeeze the Sedan through, but on second thought? His eyes studied the two girls in the backseat. Susan, the eldest seemed to be in shock, mumbling incoherently to herself, no doubt asking forgiveness for her slutty lifestyle. Cathren, on the other hand, was gazing out of the back window, and when she turned back in the seat to face him, her eyes bore into his.

"Are we gonna die, Paul?" Her question was what snapped him out of his stand still; he shook his head no.

"Not if I have anything to do with it, sweety, no, not today, we're not," he declared, before jerking the gear shift into drive and focusing his vision. *"God help us all,"* he whispered, before stomping his foot down onto the gas and snatching the wheel to the left.

The wheels left burnt marks on the asphalt as the car jerked forward. Up ahead, Malcom smiled in anticipation when he saw the car jerk erratically in his direction. He knew the driver intended to give the appearance of a head-on collision. Gambino had prepared him for the irrationality of a trapped animal.

Malcom knew at the last minute, the driver would jerk the wheel and attempt to go around him. He glanced down at all the padding he wore before making the sign of the cross over his chest and *prayed for one more day to live. He waited until the Benz was right up on him before smashing his foot down on the pedal. The 5.0 engine, coupled with the bully dog programmer's juice, caused the truck to tremble with power before rocketing forward.*

The driver of the Benz stared in bewilderment at the truck's sudden departure. The cloud of smoke its tires created against the street was so dense, it became hard for Paul to see more than five feet in front of him. Yet, he didn't let up off the gas, and as soon as the car cleared of the cloud of burnt rubber smoke, he realized too late the foolishness of his rash decision. Time slowed down as he watched in horror. Malcom had stomped down on the brake, causing the truck to fishtail. Paul tried his damnedest to stop the car before the inevitable occurred, but lady luck turned her back on him. BOOM!

It crashed head-on into the back of the monstrous truck and shot jagged pieces of glass and metal into the air, as the Benz lifted into the air at the same time Malcom's masked face slammed into the steering wheel. Blood exploded from his nostrils as his head rebounded just in time for his dazed vision to capture the totaled Benz flipping over, and over, and over again across the asphalt.

"Fuck!" he spat, before yanking the mask off and shaking his head viciously to clear it of the disorientation. He ran a sleeved arm over his bloodied nose as his vision cleared. And as soon as he was sure he was in one piece, the man slammed his fist against the steering wheel. Twice!

"Yeah! Yeeeeeah, mu'fucka!" He celebrated.

"12 on the move, forty minutes tops you'll have company!" Joey's voice came through on the radios. Cat Eyes and Julio 10.4'ed him before aiming the two muscle cars toward the smoking Benz. The foreign rested on its top, upside down. Smoke rose from it like steam from the nostrils of a dragon as Julio and Cat Eyes' vehicles skid to a halt a few feet away from the carnage.

The doors flew open on the Hellcat and Cat Eyes and me jumped out with them sticks on us. The Drako hung loosely by my right leg, but Cat Eyes was on his extra shit, so he aimed a pretty AR 15 at the upside down Benz as he peeped at it through the scope of the weapon. Julio jumped out of the Mustang clutching a Desert Eagle and as we made our way toward the car. I silently prayed that the impact of the collision hadn't injured the efficiency of the tool we'd had installed in the back of the F-250. I lifted my hand and waved Malcom forward as I studied the Benz. The wheels were still rolling on that mu'fucka when our boy backed the truck up toward the totaled car.

It took us some effort, but we got the dented tailgate pulled down. And after resting their tools on the ground, Cat Eyes and Julio reached in the bed of the truck and hefted the jaws of life out. I watched them jog over to the backseat of the Benz and jam the pincerlike mechanism into the body of the car. And just as I was about to hit the lever that would feed power to the hydraulic enhanced tool, common sense reared its pretty face.

"Hold on, famo," I shouted. Both men glanced back at me with curious expressions on their faces. I jogged over and reached down to the door handle. I gave both my boys an amused expression before pulling the door open. Though it was dented in and took a little muscle to do it, the door not only popped open, but fell off it's hinges entirely. We shared a chuckle as Cat Eyes shrugged his shoulders.

"Smart guy, but why you couldn't just let us have our 'TV' moment, fool?" He laughed as they dropped the jaws of life. With no time to waste, Julio dropped low and gazed into the backseat. The look of disappointment on his face told a crooked tale, and before he could verbalize it, I knew the gamble we'd taken hadn't spun in our favor.

"Fuck, Vato!" he spat with a disappointed look on his face. I dropped to my hunches and peered into the confines of the car and came face to face with the dead-eye'd stare of a blue eye'd white girl. Her head was twisted in an exorcist inspired angle, and three bloody trails of blood dripped across her pretty face.

"Cathren," the word slipped from my lips as I recognized the youngest daughter. I shook my head in frustration. We'd killed our lottery ticket. But just as I was about to state the obvious, the heavens smiled down on a gangsta.

"*Ahhh, my-my head.*" *A feminine voice whispered from the other side of the car. My eyes shot up at the same time another surprise made its presence.*

"*Fuck! What happened?*" *Paul, the driver of the Benz rasped.*

Me and Cat Eyes shared a knowing look. He nodded before Julio tossed him the chrome DE to put that work in with. Cat Eyes made his way to the other side of the totaled car and after a second's pause... Boom! Boom! The explosions from the big gun was monstrous. The slow exhale of breath was barely audible, but it was enough to let me know bruh had dome-called the driver.

"*Get the hell away from there! The boys in blue are speeding in your direction,*" *Joey's shrill voice spoke from the walkie talkie on my hip.*

"*Get that bitch and let's mash, fam, time for the finale,*" *I spoke over my shoulder, before heading for the car.* "*And, Cat Eyes, I want my two hundred... white folks got more sense than that, huh?*" *I asked with laughter in my voice but paused in thought before getting behind the wheel of the still growling car.* "*On second thought, get the other girl as well,*" *I instructed. Both my dudes glanced at each other peculiarly, but it was Julio who voiced their thoughts.*

"*But the other girl is dead, Vato, what good is she to us?*"

"*We don't want her father to know that yet, plus*"—*I paused to jump behind the wheel before speaking from the opened window*—"*I got plans for lady... I'm gonna kill her twice,*" *I vowed.*

177

Renta

CHAPTER ELEVEN
THE PAYOFF

An hour later

"Mayor, excuse me." His assistant poked her head into the large conference room. *"I don't mean to disturb you, but you have an important call on line three,"* she informed, with an apologetic expression on her face. Kyle Mitchell, the Mayor of Houston, looked up at her from where he and a group of ten others sat at a long table, discussing the city's coffers. He had a slight frown on his face as he studied her, and she could tell from the tension in the air that she'd just interrupted a heated debate.

"Patti, didn't I ask that you hold all calls until this meeting was over?" The Mayor's tone held a sharpness that caused the woman to cringe.

"Well, I tried, Mayor Mitchell, but the call is of importance."

"It damned well better be to interrupt such a meeting. Your job depends on it," he retorted, before taking a sip of water from the glass beside him. *"Excuse me, ladies, and gentlemen."* He inclined his head toward the assembly of people. When he made it to the polished hall, the words his assistant whispered motivated his pace.

"It's the Governor."

"Well, why didn't you just say that," the man demanded, and whether out of curiosity or surprise, he sped to the nearest phone.

"He's on line three," Patti whispered, as he picked up the phone. But when Mayor Mitchell clicked onto the line, rather than the Governor of Texas, he found a lunatic from the slums of Fifth Ward.

"Governor, sorry to keep you waiting. I was in a very prestigious meeting and—

"If you want to see either of your precious daughters again, you need to follow these instructions." I cut his explanation in half. Even from the other side of the phone, I could imagine the expression of confusion etched into the man's facial.

"Excuse me? Wha-what the hell are you talking about! Who is this? Is this some kind of sick—

"Joke?" I bulldogged his inquiry. Chuckling, I spun my web. "Pick up your cellphone, Mayor Mitchell, and you'll see for sure that the devil has no time for comedy," I suggested, before ending the call. From an untraceable Galaxy phone I'd copped from Walmart, I nodded for Joey to make the call. He logged into Susan's Facebook messenger account and scrolled to the family's group chat section. The girl had readily told us it was the way her and her family spent quality time when separate. The call went unanswered for a few seconds before the mother's face appeared in the first box of the four chat screens.

"Oh my God, Susan, where are you! Your sister? You had us worried sick! The police arrived saying Paul and...," the woman was saying, before her words trailed off. A look of utter horror contorted her all-time American features as her hands shot up to cover her mouth. "Oh my lord!" She exclaimed from between shaking fingers. I knew she'd finally noticed her eldest daughter tied, naked, in the wooden chair, with me, clad in all black and the leather face mask concealing my facial.

"Mother, hellllllp me! Pleeeease, Mom, don't let them kill me, ple-please," Susan cried. Mascara melted down her pretty cheeks as I aimed the cannon at her noggin. And at that moment, the mayor clicked on, and his face appeared next to his wife with a beet-red look of furry in his features. As soon as he witnessed his precious princess' predicament, he seemed to howl his pain.

"Who the hell are you people, what- how- Mother Mary, nooo-not- my- Princess." His heart cracked.

"Listen, homie, as I was sayin' the devil ain't no comedian. Now, let's get to the issue. I want that million in untraceable hunnids. Don't get slick either, white boy... I don't want any tracers or dye packs. Put the loot in an all-black, large duffle, and take it to NRG Stadium, but not the actual stadium— the center beside it. There will be a play hosted there called, 'The Six Thieves and One Fool'. Get you a pair of tickets and you and the wife come and enjoy the show— two days from now.

"When will I get my kids back? I want my daughters back! If there's one strand of hair out of place I will—

BOCA! The explosion of the tool in my hand got the man all choked up, and as he swallowed his threats, Joey shifted the camera, and it was there, sitting beside their eldest daughter, and bound just as tightly that they bared witness to, the ways of the jungle.

"Nooo! Not my Cathren, not my baby! Please- noooo," the mother cried, her pain chilling. Though the girl was already DOA before I'd domed her, the effect my actions had on her clueless parents was enough to ensure there'd be no more games or tough talk.

"MOMMM, please do as they ask, Dad," Susan cried at the top of her lungs, before vomiting on herself.

"That's one less mouth you'll have to feed, and if you don't meet our demands, you'll never know the feeling of having grandchildren. Don't fuck wit' me!" I spat. Tears poured down ole Mitchell's face as he digested the fact that nightmares do come true.

"Why did you do that? She-she was only eighteen ... she didn't deserve this. She—

"Collateral damage with point intended. Now, fuck all the chit chat, I have a better idea. Purchase 'one' ticket for your wife, but you enter the building from the back door. There will be someone waiting to escort you to where the money is to be left. Two days, my dude."

"When do we get our daughters? Oh, God, our daughter, our poooor ba-byyyy!" The mother doubled over as if the pain had made its way from her heart and donkey kicked her in the stomach. Kyle Mitchell's beet-red face was baptized in his own tears.

"When do we get our daughters, you son-of-a-bitch! Both of them!" His question was warranted but I wasn't feeling the son-of-a-bitch part. I chuckled before running the barrel of the tool through Susan's blond hair. She shivered while mumbling a silent prayer that only became audible when she whispered the word 'Amen'.

"Don't fret, Ms. Lady, good ole father will do the right thang, won't you, dad?" I smiled from behind the mask as my eyes drifted to the small screen.

"Fuck you! I'll have you sentenced to life in a fed—

"8:30 p.m., NRG Center, Mr. Mitchell, back door. Have my money as I've asked and if I see, hear, or feel that you've alerted the police, I'll begin to send you pieces of your daughter, piece-by-fuckin'-piece." The words escaped my lips in a hiss. "By the way, have any one of you good people ever heard of the live play "The Six Thieves and One Fool?" I smirked. "It's not Broadway or even the great Tyler Perry, but it's epic if I must say so myself."

***

Present Time- 2020

Oshaya entered Andrea Styles hair salon in fashion. She knew if there was gossip to be heard from her old neighborhood or just the streets period, she'd get all the juicy tea there at Andrea's.

"Heyyy, girrl, very chic, I like, I liiike," her hair stylist and owner of the establishment, Andrea, who everyone called Juicy, announced with a mischievous smirk on her pretty face. Oshaya glanced down at her attire for the day. The golden hued, sleeveless turtle neck sweater she wore gave life to the leopard spotted spandex tights. Her thighs and ass gave the pants just the right amount of stretch which allowed the leopard print to pop out at one who was attempting to sneak a peek, and the leopard-spotted heels offset the black man's suit coat she wore to complete the look.

"Thank you, Juicy, you know I try, girl," she acknowledged, before waving with her fingers at the other four beauticians. "Hey, JuJu, Carla, Monay, Sissy." Monay sucked her teeth at the greeting and kept right on attending her client's hair. She had no particular reason not to like Oshaya. She was merely a hateful bitch who felt like she was the baddest bitch in the room and if anyone threatened the title, she felt lowkey inferior.

"Don't be ugly, Monay." Juicy rolled her eyes.

"Hatin' bitch, like, really though?" Sissy glared at her, pausing on the silk press she was applying to her client's hair.

"Ouch, damn, Sissy, watch what you're doing before you burn my damn hair off," the sista in her chair snapped, when the heat from the presser became uncomfortable. Sissy jumped in surprise.

"Oh, my bad, Terika," Sissy apologized, before correcting her carelessness. "Ain't like you got too much more damn hair to burn off anyway," she mumbled. Juicy's jaw dropped in surprise, and at the same time Carla's eyes grew as large as golf balls.

"Ouuuu." Monay became messy Bessie.

"What did you just say?" Terika snapped with a snake of her neck. She was Third Ward official and as ratchet as they came, but her dude kept her on fleek. Sissy was so frustrated with Monay's hatefulness; she'd *unintentionally* spoken aloud.

"Damn, bihh, you can't take a joke anymore... why so sensitive?" She smiled sweetly with in attempt to clean up the blunder.

Terika studied her with slits for eyes. "Bitch, you wasn't playin', don't be talkin about my hair like *your* shit justa falling down to your ass or something. Underneath all them bundles, you ain't got nothin 'but *a whisp* more than me," Terica spat, before turning back forward in her chair and crossing her arms over her breasts. Sissy rolled her eyes dramatically. Juicy shook her head in amusement, and with a smirk on her pretty face, she nodded toward Carla, but spoke to Oshaya.

"Girl, gone over there and let Carla give you a rinse and prep. I'll be ready for you in about ten minutes." Oshaya seemed hesitant and Juicy noticed it. She studied her girl, and as if an internal navigational system was leading her eyes, they settled on the oversized, leopard print sunglasses on Oshaya's face. They all had known the girl for about a year plus, but only Juicy and Sissy had an *outside* relationship with her.

"Umph, I don't know why y'all giving all these secret ass looks like it ain't national news the bitch's dude keeps her with a black eye or something," Monay added her two cents without invite.

"Bitch, I'm really getting tired of you, like…" Oshaya was too through. Unconsciously, she snatched the glasses off her face. Everybody in the room reared back with shocked expressions on their faces.

"Gurrrl!" They seemed to all shout at the same time.

JuJu smacked his lips. "Baaaaby, put ya' glasses back on." He was a feminine man who was seen as one of the girls, and unlike most men, he fit the bill. Juicy's expression was saddened as silence was replaced with Oshaya's truths.

"I don't wanna hear it, Juicy." She held up her palm before making her way over to the sink where Carla stood waiting. "And bitch"—she paused to glare at Monay— don't act like your freak ass has immunity from a black eye, 'cause if I'm not mistaken, not too long ago, it was *you* comin' up in this mu'fucka looking like a pretty *raccoon!*" she spat.

"Umhmm, tryin' to tell you. Now the bitch actin' like she above a black eye or two. Gurrrl, bye!" Sissy added, before twisting her lips and nodding in agreement.

"Really though, Sissy?" Monay took a step away from her client and placed her hands on her shapely hips.

"I'm just sayin', Monay. You dry be on some hatin' shit sometimes," Sissy spoke her peace.

Monay sucked her teeth. "Bitch, all I'm sayin' is *you* need to stop actin' like *you* ain't in a toxic relationship. You done stepped yo' ass out the house with a split lip and walkin' 'round lookin' like you had a big ball of chewing tobacco in your mouth. Don't be frontin'." She snaked her neck sassily.

"Yeah, and I bet that motherfucker was walkin' around with a matching love tap too, shid!" Sissy declared.

"You go, girl!" her client praised with a snap of her fingers.

"Umph!" Monay wasn't on the wave. She used her hand to flip her curly ponytail over her right shoulder, before giving Sissy a mischievous smirk. "See how much good *that* did. The nigga was *just* at the club wit' his boys, letting the next bitch make that ass clap all on his stuff." She clapped her hands three times. "She was all up on him like—

"Bitch!" Sissy dropped her comb and curler, and with that drama playing in her stare, she headed straight for her coworker.

***

The Past-2017
Two days later…
The Six Thieves and One Fool

"I'm sick and tired of being sick and tired of being sick and tired, Joe, your parents hate me and no one wants to see a poor little Black woman happy with a well-off white man. I- It's- it's over," the beautiful sista cried, with a passion so heart felt, all who watched became lost in its rapture. The night was pitch black and the only source of light to disturb its purity were the four street lights that they stood beneath.

"Come on, sweetheart, don't do this. Who cares what my mother or father thinks? My heart belongs to you, Betty, and I'll die for you, I swear to God!" Joe declared. He fell to his knees in a prayer's stance and gazed up at the only Black woman who'd ever captured his heart. He studied her.

Her skin tone was the color of light caramel, and her thick, full lips were glossed with a bright- red lipstick. Her thick mane of hair was done up in a beautiful finger waved pattern which was ideal with the fifties' era inspired, spaghetti strapped, sequin mini dress she wore. The glistening beads in the dress were ink black and offset the charcoal-black-and smoke-gray quarter mink fur that graced her bare arms.

The tall buildings in the background were made of a special cardboard, and street lights were another prop we'd used to give the appearance of the play a 'Harlem Nights' feel. We'd rented the building for the night, and thanks to Joey's and my promo skills, we were able to fill nine hundred seats. The atmosphere was festive as I stood behind the scenes, watching my team bring life to the play I'd written.

Tima was the actress I'd hired to play Betty, and Joey was Joe, but the most beautiful aspect of the play was the illusions we'd *implemented. Due to beauty of face paints, soft putty, and faux hair Joey wore to change his appearance, he was able to be an entirely different man.*

"It won't work, Joe, we have no money and you're a member of the Italian Mafia. If they hear that you've run off into the sunset with a colored woman, they'll never stop hunting us, suga," Betty cried, while taking Joe's hand and placing it against her heart. At that moment, I glanced down at my watch. 8:28! I frowned slightly, ole buddy should have already arrived and been escorted through the back to be shown where to drop the ransom. Damn, I know dude ain't gonna leave his baby girls for the reaper? Would he? I thought. But just as doubt was born, what I'd learned of human nature allowed me to abort it. "Two more minutes!" I told myself at the same time Joe scrambled to his feet.

"I don't care, Betty, I love you, baby doll, and for you..." He paused as a thick rope seemingly fell from the heavens, but in actuality, Malcom had dropped it from the rafters up in the ceiling where he was perched. The other end was tied around a full, neon moon we'd hung high in the mock sky. Joe's gaze was intense as he stared into Betty's eyes. "For you I'd go to war with the entire Italian Mafia! I'll defile God and dance with the devil! I'd do it all! What you want, Betty, huh? The moon and the stars?" he asked, before pulling the rope. The false moon drifted down so close that if he wanted to, he could reach out and caress it with his fingertips. "Here," Joe whispered, before placing the rope in Betty's hand. She stared up at him with a hint of confusion intermingled with love in her gaze. He smiled.

"If that's what you want, doll, you can tie the moon to our bed post so it can sleep outside our window for eternity," he declared.

"Awww," a woman in the crowd crooned.

"Beautiful," a masculine voice chimed in. I glanced down at the watch for the sixth time that night. 8:32! And just when my nerves were about to get the best of me, Joey spoke the magic words.

"Is it 'money'? If that's what ails you, sweet cheeks, here..." He waved his hand toward the curtains that separated the front of

the stage from the back. And nothing happened! I frowned, especially when Julio's voice came through the earpiece in my ear. "We're surrounded, Vato, they fuckin called the policia!" he spat. I smirked. I'd expected as much and had a nice surprise for our new guests. A rustling could be heard back stage just before someone came tumbling through the curtains.

"Do you know who I am!" the middle aged Caucasian man shouted, as he was shoved through the curtains, glancing about, with a perplexed expression on his face.

"What-what kind of buffoonery is this! Where are my daughters!" he demanded, with a ferocious glare as he studied Betty and Joe. And then, I watched his studious eyes digest the street light props. Confused, he glanced up at the tall cardboard buildings that were reminiscent of a New York's sky line. Then, the man's vision drifted at the sight of the crowd who were barely noticeable just beyond the dim lights. He could see the first few rows, and at that moment, his mouth fell open in a surprised O at the sight of crowd.

"Is that..." someone from the crowd began, astonished.

"Can't be!" another seconded.

"It's Mayor Michell! Splendid!"

"Bravo! Bravooo!" The crowd erupted with riotous cheers and surprised glee. I studied the man from the side of the stage, and though his eyes briefly trailed my way, I knew he'd only see a white man since my janitor's disguise was perfection.

"Oh my God, what in the name of Christ Jesus is this?" Mayor Mitchell whispered, before spinning toward Betty and Joe. He seemed to strain with the weight of the duffle bag as he glared at them. The shock on Betty's face was priceless, but authentic. She was just as naïve` as the crowd was to the Mayor's part in the play, but the beautiful actress she was, allowed her to cloak her surprise as her beautiful orbs drifted to Joe.

"You want to run away to a faraway place? A beautiful island with a gorgeous château on the edge of the world where the ocean lies only a few feet from our doorstep." He waved toward the man who I, now, recognized as the Mayor of the city. It was a bittersweet

187

moment because though I couldn't figure out how Joey had failed to mention the fact we were taking down the Mayor's daughters, I watched as if on cue, and as if he were truly a member of the cast, Mayor Mitchell dropped the bag of money at my man's feet.

"There's your money, now where the hell are my daughters, daughter, both, oh God!" The man turned to a blubbering fool as tears cascaded down his pale face. An expression of pure surprise fell over Betty's face. She couldn't believe that we'd somehow gotten the mayor to join in on the play, and even more, she couldn't believe he was such a good actor. Neither could the crowd.

"Bravo, beautiful! Beautiful acting," someone shouted to the cheers and agreement of the rest of the audience.

"What the hell is wrong with you people? I want my damn children and I want them now!" Mayor Mitchell declared with a rainstorm falling from his eyelids. Confusion was now very evident in Betty's features; this wasn't a part of the script, but I commended her on her skills. One day lady was gonna take Broadway by storm, but somewhere within the recesses of my mind, I wondered if she would still have the same taste for acting when she realized that the Mayor's tears were as real as the million dollars at her feet. By now, she was a pure actress, no script. She lifted her hands and cupped the sides of Joey's face, gazing so intensely into the gates of his soul, I was sure she could see clear through to his vile thoughts.

"Where'd you get the money, Joe, did you kidnap the Mayor's daughters, suga, is what he saying true?" Her question not only unnerved me, but the look on Joe's face told me he'd been rattled as well. Yet, I commanded my mans for his steel nerves. He smiled sadly and nodded his confirmation at the same time the Mayor's weakened state morphed into madness.

"Enough! I want my damn kids, now!" he raged, before marching straight toward the couple. Betty's look of confusion melted into one of suspicion as she took a step back.

I stood by, waiting for the grand finale. I glanced down at my watch. 8:59.

"Any minute now," I mumbled. And just as the hour and minute changed and nine o'clock appeared, I glanced up.

"They're coming," Julio whispered into the ear piece. I saw the smile that spread across Joey's face as he turned to face off with the Mayor. And just as the man reached out and wrapped his fingers around Joey's neck—

Blam! The doors blew open.

"Freeze! Nobody move!"

"FBI!"

"Everybody down!" A multitude of agents stormed the room with guns drawn.

"Now!" I hissed into the small mic.

"My pleasure!" Malcom's voice responded in my ear. At that moment, the lights went out in the entire building. The crowd exploded in cheers.

"Excellent!" a man shouted from the crowd.

"Marvelous!" someone else shouted, the wonder evident in their voice.

"What the hell?" The Mayor's voice sounded just before I felt a heavy thud land beside me on the side of the stage. I chuckled before snatching the heavy bag up and tossing it in the hidden compartment I'd had installed in the janitor's cart beside me. The lights flashed back on and before I made my exit, I was able to catch the utter shock on Betty's face as her manicured fingers flew to her bright-red parted lips.

"Oh-my-God." The words slipped from her lips in an amazed whisper. The crowd oooo'd and awwwed before a powerful round of applause shook the room. There, standing in the middle of the stage, mouth agape, with a wide-eyed expression on his face, stood the Mayor. He couldn't wrap his mind around how just a moment ago, he'd been on the verge of strangling his daughters' killer, captor to death, and somehow the man had vanished, and in his wake, the only evidence the Mayor held of the man's existence was a lifelike mask and a man's wig. Mayor Mitchell's eyes drifted to the spot he'd dropped the bag of money and fell to his knees when he saw it had vanished as well.

The crowd was beside themselves as people whistled in appreciation, clapped their hands, and gave a standing ovation, yet, *they wouldn't believe the finish. By the time the agents had reached the stage, the Mayor was drowning in a puddle of his own tears. By now, he'd realized that 'he' was the fool in the great play, but though he'd just met one of the six thieves, he still had five more to go.*

"Whyyy! Why did you reveal yourselves? Now I'll never see my daughters again!" His cry was deep ... the things plays were made of. The lead agent rushed over to him as his eyes scrutinized the room.

"Don't worry, Mayor Mitchell, we'll get your children back," he vowed, before speaking into a hidden mic on his FBI vest. "This is, Tyler, block off all exits. I repeat, block off all exits. We're looking for an older white—

"Nooo, dammit!" The Mayor's explosion interrupted him. The agent stared bewilderedly as the elder man slammed the mask and faux hair down against the stage. "It was a ruse, he..." he began, but his words trailed off as Joe stepped from behind the curtain that divided the back of the stage from the front.

"There he-he- it's him! Arrest that man!" the Mayor demanded, and just when the agents moved to do just that—

"Hey, asshole, how do you look like me!" a voice demanded from the front row seats. All eyes shot to the speaker and jaws dropped in a beautiful shock. The speaker was an identical twin to the Joe on the stage, who was also identical to the mask the Mayor had just slammed against the floor. A few agents headed for him.

"Hey stupid, what are we, triplets?" a man from up in the rafters, where Malcom had been perched shouted down. All eyes shot up, and delighted gasps from the crowd told the tale. Another Joe! Identical clothes and all. This played out sporadically until there were five Joes standing in various places around the room, with the last and sixth Joe walking down the center aisle. The agents attempted to go for each replica, but the chase became maddening. Each Joe ran in different directions, save for the one in the center aisle. All eyes drifted to him before impulsively falling to the black duffle bag in his hands. In an instant, many of the agents had drawn

down on the man. Infrared beams and flashlights that were attached to the tops or bottoms of their big guns trained on the sixth Joe.

"Don't move, motherfucker, or I'll blow your brains out your fucking skull," one of the agents spazzed, as he aimed an MP5 machine gun at him. They'd subdued ole Joe in no time, and as soon as they had him on the ground, the lead agent realized something was off. This Joe's clothes were too big, and he hadn't spoken as the others had, and by the time the men realized the sixth Joe's hands were already bound, I was making my way toward my escape, praying the authorities wouldn't think too much of an elderly, white janitor— 'my' disguise!

"Sir, there's something amiss here!" Hawkins, the second agent in charge shouted, before glancing from their captive to the lead agent.

"What you mean, Hawkins, speak!"

"Well," Agent Hawkins began, before pulling the suit coat from around Joe's shoulders. All eyes fell to the knotted rope that bound his wrists together in front. Confused, the lead agent took a step closer as Hawkins pried ole Joe's fingers from around the straps of the bag that we'd demanded him to hold tight to. "I think it's a mask, sir."

"Well, big fucking surprise there, agent! Pull the mask off, for God's sake, Hawkins!" the lead agent demanded, with a frustrating shake of his head. He'd already guessed what they'd find, even before Hawkins snatched the mask off, and the crowd gasped with a generous round of applause.

"Susan!" the mayor cried, as his daughter's blond hair tumbled down. There was a thick piece of duct tape covering her mouth, and her blue eyes seemed haunted as if she'd witnessed firsthand what the seven deadliest sins could do. Someone slowly peeled the tape from over her lips.

"Don't! Don't kill meeeee, Please! I'm not a whore, please, God, don't let them kill me!" she shouted at the top of her lungs. Her eyes were unfocused, stuck in a faraway horror scene. Her poor ole dad rushed over to comfort her, as the head agent made his way over to the duffle bag he'd personally helped fill with a million *dollars of the Mayor's hard earned cash. Kneeling down, he slowly unzipped the bag, and when the contents within were revealed, all the man could do was chuckle in contempt.*

"I don't get it, sir, why would they do 'all this' only to leave behind the money?" Hawkins spoke in disbelief as his vision lifted from the bag of money and studied the lead agent's eyes for answers. But the man merely glanced over at where the Mayor was hugging his daughter as tightly as he could, as if he was afraid she'd disappear again. When his eyes drifted back to Hawkins, he could no longer control it, he burst into laughter as he reached down into the duffle and came out with two fistful of hundred dollar bills.

"Is it the money, sir?" Hawkins was dying to know. The lead man only laughed harder before tossing the bills into the air like he was at a strip club, making it rain harder than heaven could. The bills tumbled and flipped like confetti, and as they rained down, Hawkins plucked a few from the air. The surprised expression on his face was priceless!

"Fucking Barack Obama, ey!" His superior was beside himself with laughter. Hawkins' mouth was fixed into a surprised O-shape as he glanced down at the bag. It had been filled to the brim with freshly printed, U.S. currency—currency that appeared so authentic, that if done correctly, one could actually spend it. Yet, the tale that told the tale of its artificialness was there ... the portion of the bill where the inventor Benjamin Franklin's face usually sat gazing back at its possessor, was replaced by the face of the 44th President, and Barack Obama's face was framed with a big smile.

CHAPTER TWELVE
TNM

Back to the Present- 2020

Two hours later...

♪*Your love is a one and a million / it goes on and on and on / You give me a really good feelin', alllllll dayyy long / Your love...* ♪

Aaliyah's, *One and a Million*, classic played softly as the sweet aroma, of a tender pot roast marinated with chunks of garlic potatoes and diced carrots, wafted throughout the house.

"Turn me inside out, make my heart speed ... need no one else, you're all I need," Oshaya sang along with the iconic songstress. After she'd left the beauty salon, she'd hurried home to prepare a feast for her king. She lifted the top off the crock pot to check her meat. "It can cook a little while longer," she whispered to herself, before replacing the lid. She stepped over to the other dishes she was preparing on the stove. The Cajun seasoned green beans were almost done, and the sea shell macaroni she'd drowned in mozzarella and cheddar with diced jalapeños were complete.

After killing the fire beneath the pot, she headed to the dining room where she'd set the table for two. She smiled at a job well done before her pretty eyes fell to the skimpy, silk, golden robe she had been lounging in. Her nakedness underneath made her feel sexy, as she gently patted the multicolored silk scarf she'd wrapped around her freshly-done hair. The woman's taunt nipples were straining against the fabric of her robe as she sashayed toward the bathroom where she'd prepared a hot bubble bath.

Oshaya shook her head as her mind reflected on the drama of Andrea Styles—*Sissy beat that ass!* she thought with a giggle. Entering the bathroom, a dense fog of steam hovered over the nice sized jacuzzi tub as it whirled with sudsy bubbles. She untied the sash that held the thin material together and watched as it fell open. Her red skin tone was smooth, sensual, and had the hue of cinnamon. Slipping the robe from her shoulders, it fell, pooling at her pretty feet before she cupped her cantaloupe-sized breasts. Glancing down at her chocolate tinged nipples, a chill ran through her, traveling south until settling between her thighs.

Damn, it's been months since he's touched me! Am I losing my touch? He's cheating, but don't 'all' men cheat? Her thoughts were borderline insecure, as her vision fell to her freshly-waxed oasis. At twenty-seven years old, her lower lips were still pretty, juicy, and tight, and as she wondered why Nigil wasn't satisfied with *just* her, the woman made her way over to the mirror. Running a hand across its fogged surface to clear it of the steam, she appreciated her reflection.

She ran her hands down her stomach, hips, and thighs, before turning her back to the glass and staring at her reflection from over her shoulder. Her ass wasn't video-chic fat, but it was naturally juicy. She just couldn't understand *why* her dude didn't yearn to *keep* his dick inside her. With a mischievous smirk, Oshaya begin to make that ass clap.

"Umph! Umph! Umph! Umph!" She grunted with each round of applause. She giggled, and after the moment of innocent fun, lady made her way to the porcelain steps leading up into the fancy bath. She dipped a foot into the almost scalding water to check its temp. "SsSss," she hissed through clenched teeth at its burn. Her eyes did a gentle roll to the back of her head, as the feeling was ecstasy to her. Stepping fully into the water, she paused to allow her body to adapt to the heat, and as soon as it did, she submerged herself within its burning caress. She took a seat on the built-in cushion before resting her head against the inflated headrest. The water rose up to her collar bone, as the music emitting from the surround sound drifted through the open door of the bathroom.

Oshaya hummed along with Aaliyah as her eyes drifted shut. The hot water massaged her flesh as her thoughts carried her away to distant times. To times when she was appreciated and reminded she was attractive. And before she realized it, her hands became Christopher Columbus's explorers of her anatomy's geography.

"Ssss," a beautiful melody escaped from between her full lips. Her soft hands rode the slopes of her succulent titties with an antagonizing slowness. Fingers wet with soapy water, Oshaya traced her areolae before squeezing both her supple nipples between her thumbs and pointer fingers with a hard pressure, creating a painful pleasure. Releasing her jutted flesh, she moaned deeply before squeezing her breasts together.

"I need you, babyyyy," she cried, eyes half-mast. A freak's gaze and bottom lip clenched between her teeth, Oshaya was in her vibe.

♪*I'll give youuuu, everything you want from me / everything you want, everything you need, anything your heart desires / Anythang, 'cause your love is a one and a million*♪

Aaliyah's unique melody added to the sensuous vibe as Oshaya's hand disappeared beneath the surface of the steaming water. Spreading her legs apart, she propped her feet onto the edge of the tub causing her lips to part in ecstasy as one of the jets shot a strong gush of warm water against her femininity. She began to massage the small tongue of her kitten until her pussycat became a lioness with a roar so powerful, its growl surged up and through her. The growl traveled from her South America, danced in her North America, and just before reaching Canada, it escaped from the imprisonment of her clenched teeth in an erotic purr.

"ShiiiiiiitttAh!" Her toes curled as she envisioned her husband giving her essence a sweet punishment. She fantasized of him hitting it from the rearview as she prostrated herself humbly before him as if he were her God almighty. *You want this don't you? You like how I'm giving you this dick, ma, huh? Talk to me!* he growled in a voice that didn't belong to him.

Oshaya frowned in confusion as little beads of sweat appeared on her skin. In *her mind*, she glanced back, glaring at the man who should've been her husband. She attempted to transform the face into Nigil's, but no matter how hard she tried, she just couldn't replace the face that stared back at her. She attempted to, even wanted to stop, but her hands had become violent protesters that rallied for the '*This Nut Matters*' movement (*TNM*). They seemed to scream as her left hand became a claw. Her sharp, pointed nails raked a soft, sensual trail up her stomach, and over the Mount Everest of her slippery left breast, as her right hand became a cyclone against her 'little man in the boat.' Lady's internal waters became the big wave that drowned him. Oshaya gripped, and *squeezed* her left breast, causing her legs to tremble, and her pretty, French-tipped, toes to ball up.

"Yasss! Just. Likeeeee. Thaaaatt," she cried out, in breathless moans, as her hand motion aided the jets in making the water bubble. In *her fantasy*, the man who stood behind her, stroked her hard from behind ... he fucked her in a way that made her wonder if he'd studied her most sensitive spots. Even though she belonged to another man, and even as her mind begged her to stop ... the only thing her body knew was the chant of the rally—*TNM! TNM!* It shouted as her eyes rolled to the back of her head, and as if she'd surrendered to that exact movement, Oshaya whispered rebelliously, "This Nut Matters. . . . Thisssss. . . . Nuttt. . . . Matterrrrrs. . . ."

***

The liveliness of Andrea Styles hair Salon had wound down, but the room was still filled with chatter as the beauticians finished off their last clients. The smell of haircare chemicals and shampoos infused with the telltale smells of burnt hair as women received silk presses and flat irons.

"I'm sayin', Carla, do you spit or swallow?" Juicy asked. The room became as silent as a late night in a suburban neighborhood, and all eyes drifted to Carla in anticipation of her answer. She was cleaning up her work area when both Monay and her client answered for her at the same time.

"Swallow, bihh!" they shouted, before twisting their lips up in that *bitch,- I'm-tryna-tell-you,* kinda way, before giving each other a girlish high five. The nine women shared a giggle. Sissy rolled her eyes in Monay's direction as she curled her client's hair. Though they'd been separated before any real damage could be done, she'd been able to get a few good licks in and busted Monay's bottom lip.

196

I hate hatin' ass women, she thought.

"No comment," Carla declared, before holding up a gloved hand to them.

"Girl, please, ain't nothin' wrong with a little *protein!*" Juicy exclaimed, giggling as she held out a handheld mirror so the lady in her chair could see she'd been beautified.

"Sho' ain't, chile, ain't nothin' like the salty sweet taste of that—

"Uh-un, JuJu, I ain't tryna hear this," Sissy cut him off with *the hand.* All eyes shot to him in wide-eyed stares. JuJu stood a mere five foot four inches. With his milky skin tone and blondish-white dyed hair which he kept done just as the late legend Prince had kept his, he and the singer could've passed for twins.

"Whaaaaaat," he asked, with a look of disbelief on his face.

"I know you bitches not on the brand new, 'cause y'all already know! Me and Romeo does what it does, umph," he declared, with a snake of his long neck.

"You gone head, JuJu, with yo' fast tail. I like those pants, and those boots, girl, you killin 'em," Monay encouraged him. The hot-pink leather pants were a perfect match for the black cowboy boots he had on.

"Girl, thank ya', but you hoes know *exactly* what I'm talkin' about. I know *those* lips done swallowed more cum than a cup at a sperm clinic."

"Boyyy, Boo! Don't do me!"

"Don't be shame, chile … I'm sure all these hussies done tasted that bitter taste. Ouuu, how I use to hate when I told a man not to do it in my mouth, but he *accidentally*—

"Uh-un, JuJu, I'm too through!" Sissy cut him once more, but this time with a giggle.

"Girl, get ouuuuttt! Don't be frontin' like you never had that *accidental it-was- so-good-I-couldn't-control-myself-baby* moment. You *just* told the nikka not to nut in ya' mouth and here he go… *I tried to tell you girl, but you wasn't listenin',"* the woman in Juicy's chair mimicked in a masculine voice.

"Umm, y'all so nasty!" lady in Monay's chair laughed.

Juicy accepted her payment and gave Beunka, the girl whose hair she'd just slayed, a sisterly hug before turning to look at Carla. "Listen, a bitch who's sucking a dick *wanting* to make a man nut in her mouth, sucks that thang better than a timid bitch who's merely sucking his dick because oral is a part of sex. Think about it, C, when you're down there pleasing your man with the *intent* of making him bust in your mouth, you *want* to be nasty!" She held the mirror up to her mouth as if it were a penis and acted as if she were giving sloppy fellatio. The women laughed.

"Umph!" That was Sissy.

"Um-huh, girl, I know Lamar keeps a smile on his face," JuJu added his two cents.

"When you suckin' dick, swallowing is that next level shit," Juicy said, as she laid the mirror down.

"I'm like Mullato, I wanna choke on it till my nose runnin'," Monay cut in, as her and JuJu laughed and high fived.

Carla laughed at the two before adding to the convo. "Bitch, a nikka bust in my mouth, I'm just gonna spit it back on that dick and use my hands to massage it into his skin! Baby will never know the difference, he'll just think I'm being real nasty as I jack him off. A man doesn't have a brain while trapped in the thralls of a good nut, use ya 'hands and a lot of spit, baby, a lot of spit!" Carla was in her act. "I can't stand the taste of semen, so I just spit that shit right back on his dick." She made a face.

"Girl, un-unnn, that just makes *the whole dick* taste salty," Sissy disagreed with a scrunch of her nose.

"Riiiight," JuJu seconded.

"JuJu!" they all shouted at the same time. JuJu was tickled as he styled his clients bangs.

"What- the- fuck- ever! All I'm sayin' is *this* bitch"— he wiggled a playful finger toward Carla— "may as well join the *BSTN* movement 'cause if a nikka busts in ya' mouth, that salty taste is *on ya' tongue*, your taste buds, *not* down your throat. If you can still taste it when it's in ya' stomach, bihhh, *that* man is eating too many veggies and not enough fruit."

"That nigga may be eating *ass* if that's the case!" Juicy giggled.

198

"Uh-un, biiitch, not the groceries," Sissy exclaimed, with a fit of giggles.

"What the hell is *BSTN*?" Carla asked, as her laughter died down. JuJu pointed the rat tail comb he was using.

"Girl, *BSTN*," he reiterated, as if repeating the acronym brought clarity. Everyone in the room frowned and glanced at each other inquisitively. Everyone but Sissy, and Juicy, who'd heard JuJu's phrase before, and as if they were part of a choir, all three of them shouted...

"Bitch, Swallow That Nut!" The room exploded in laughter.

"For real though, Juicy, really?" Carla placed her hands on her shapely hips as she contained her fit of laughter.

"Your man will appreciate it."

"That's why you and Lamar been together so long, even after his ass been locked up for all these years."

"Girl, that man ain't goin' nowhere and neither am I. Jail, home, heaven or hell, we going together, and *no, that's* not why we still together," Juicy corrected. Sissy gave her a curious look.

"Please tell, I can't keep a man even if he locked up. So, what's ya' secret?"

"Maybe if you stop being a hoe you could," Monay mumbled, all eyes shooting to her.

"Don't start, Monay," Carla protested.

"Oh, you ain't had enough?" Sissy sat her curler down on the counter. "My pussy is exclusive. I'm from Tobago where we're taught not to just be a *sample* woman, but *you* need to control that *CSP* you got."

"Here we go with the acronyms, bihh, what's CSP?" Carla was curious. Sissy giggled.

"Carla, now you know this hoe has a Convenience *Store Pussy,* nikkas in and out that mu'fucka like a hood corner store." Laughter exploded in the salon. Except Monay.

Juicy giggled but gave Sissy the eye. Her girlfriend shrugged. "As I was saying, sis, what's your secret?" Sissy reverted. Juicy giggled girlishly. Most of her friends wondered how she could be so beautiful but stay faithful to a man who was locked up. Standing at five six, long, natural curly hair, and a skin tone that was chocolate cinnamon, or depending on her time in the sun, could be as golden as a wheat field in Kansas, Juicy could have her pick of a man. All eyes captured her. Everyone knew she had an old soul and seemed to always have just the right advice. She stuck her tongue out and began to flicker it like a snake before laughing along with her girls. "Naw, for real, as y'all all know, I use to work in TDC as a correctional officer, and girl let me tell ya'!" She fanned herself. "One day that man took me to a closet and did *the wave* in my ocean and—

"Un-unnn, Juicy, I can't deal," Sissy cut her off while laughing.

"Okay, okay, there's no secret to loyalty and commitment. I just *love him,* and when a *real bitch* loves her man, she's gonna be *all in*, no matter the storm, circumstances, or time. It's not that you can't keep a man, sis, it's just that you're trying to keep him with the *wrong* things," Juicy jeweled as she cleaned her station.

"What you mean, Juicy? I cook, clean, and can fuck a man silly, but that doesn't stop him from putting his dick where it don't belong."

"See, *that's* what I'm sayin'! *None* of that shit will *keep* a man. There are *plenty* bitches who will play house with a man. We're taught how to do that with Barbie and Ken dolls! Where you think the game, *playing house*, we used to play with our cousins and friends came from?" Juicy put her hands on her hips as the ladies high fived and giggled.

"You sho' right!" one of the women getting her hair done became verbal.

"There are women who will lick a man's ass, swallow his cum, *and* piss if that's what pleases him. There are also women who will let him stick his thang-thang in her mouth, ass, ear, and between her toes or nostrils if she knew it was his forte, so your pussy will *never* be enough. Your cookie will only make him want more cookie, and after he's stretched out, jumped up and down, allowed his seed to explore it, and done everything a man can do to *your* cookie, he'll become curious about the many other cookies available to him.

Chocolate chip, sugar, macadamia, there are unlimited cookies out here," Juicy proclaimed.

"Umph!" Carla said.

"Dogs!" was JuJu's input. Juicy made her way over to the chairs she had situated in the small waiting area of the salon. Taking a seat, she crossed her left leg over her right knee before returning her attention to Sissy.

"It's you, the woman as a whole that makes a man wanna stay. If you have a street dude, *you know* there's a possibility he'll see a jail cell or two. If he sees or senses you'll become a snake bitch after the Berkin, and other gifts are gone, he's gonna leave you. If you have the nine to five slash business man, and he sees that you're a busybody and not the stay at home bitch he wants, he'll eventually leave. So, it's all about *your* virtue and what you'll conform for."

Have y'all heard about my cousin Pierre?" JuJu cut in. "Excuse me, Juicy."

"Pierre from Third Ward? I thought he was locked up?" Carla asked, as her eyes drifted to Sissy. She knew she and Pierre used to have a thing before he'd gotten sent up the river. She knew they had a big break up about his doggish ways after she'd caught him sticking his private part into other women's private parts one too many times; the type of women whose private parts were more community usage than private.

Sissy's vision trailed to JuJu, but Monay was like Juicy, both had moved to H-Town from Baytown, so though Sissy had told Juicy about her ex, Monay wasn't familiar with dude.

"Who is Pierre?" Monay asked, after catching the looks shared between the homosexual man and Sissy. JuJu smiled.

"Oh, Pierre ? He's just my cousin. He's been locked up ten years, but he comes home tomorrow."

***

2 hours later…

♪ *Wish you would just focus- on meee / can you focus on meee/ baby, can you focus on me . . me . . meee…* ♪

The sweet melody of H.E.R rang out as the music played softly. The lights were dimmed, and the table was set for two. Candles were lit and their flames cast flickering shadows over the four-course meal she'd prepared.

Oshaya glanced down at the attire she'd chosen for the night. She felt sexy. Powerful. The red, see-through teddy was a beautiful display of feminine mischief. As she allowed her small hands to journey erotically down, and over the sheer material that encased the soft mountains God created upon her landscape, her fingers lingered teasingly on her nipples. After seductively massaging the tender flesh, her manicured hands trailed down beyond her stomach which wasn't fat nor flat, and it paused at the tattooed strawberries she had inked just before her pelvic.

The see-through panties connected to the camisole hugged her *personal* garden of Eden so tightly, her lower lips puckered against the material. The small moist spot told a tale all of its own, and the vision of her forbidden fruit was enough temptation to cause Jesus himself to lust for the small piece of fruit that budded at the anterior of the feminine tree of good and evil.

The sound of the door opening caused her eyes to lift and take in the man she loved. Nigil entered their abode looking like a chocolate man delicacy. The suit he wore was a perfect fit, and his West African features could've made him a model on the cover of a GQ magazine. His eyes took in the beautiful woman before him, and the look in his eyes almost froze Oshaya in place, but she was determined to get her marriage back on the right track.

Not today Satan, I rebuke you in the name of Jesus! she thought, as she willed her sexy heels to carry her over to her man with a seductive sashay.

"Heeeeyyy, daddy, welcome home," she purred, once they stood a foot apart. Taking his briefcase from his hand, she tossed it toward the sectional couch before turning to him and undoing the first button on his suit jacket.

"What you doing?" His voice was flat. Oshaya gave an unsure smile.

"Can I not take care of my man? I'm only taking your coat, husband, is that a crime?"

"I got it."

"Why can't *I* do it? Can *I* cater to *my* husband? You are my husband right, husband?"

"I got it," Nigil demanded.

"Your choice," she relented. She crossed her arms over her exposed breasts as she watched him slip his jacket off and extend it to her. Though it was a tight one, she held her smile as she accepted the jacket. "Thanks," she offered, as he made his way to the romantic setting of the table.

Oshaya rolled her eyes at his back before tossing the jacket on the couch. Turning, she found Nigil already seated. In a huff, she made her way to her own side of the table. Chanel N°5 perfume left a delicious trail behind her as she took her seat and crossed her legs. Reaching over and pouring herself a glass of chilled Perrier-Jouët, she took a sip from the flute before fixing her eyes on her handsome husband. He'd loosened his tie and took his phone out of his pocket and began to scroll through it.

"Aren't you gonna eat?" she asked, as she began to bounce her leg.

"Not hungry."

"Fuck you!" She'd had enough.

"That lingerie you're wearing," he said and nodded appreciatively, "it's new, maybe you've been *fucking* some other muther*fucker* in my mutha*fuckin'* house?"

"Fuck you *and* this house."

"Fuck me?" he declared in amusement.

"And this house." Oshaya's leg was now bouncing so hard, her knee damned near knocked against the table. A slow storm built up in her eyes as she glared at the man who was causing her heart not to give a fuck about the things a married woman was supposed to give a fuck about. *I need a drink,* she thought, before reaching for her glass.

Nigil rose from his seat with a contemptuous smirk on his face. The man reached down to the plate and pinched a small piece of roast between his thumb and pointer finger before placing it in his mouth. Oshaya sipped. Nigil chewed. She glared. He smirked. Within the Civil War between husband and wife, there could be no victor. There could never be anything *civilized* about *a war* between two people who held each other's hearts in their hands.

"I ate, see," Nigil mocked her, before opening his mouth wide so she could see he'd swallowed the small piece of meat.

"Fuck- *you*," Oshaya declared as the first trail of salt water leaked from her left eye.

Nigil chuckled as he made his way over to where she sat. He ran the back of his hand down her face, following the path of the liquid pain he'd created.

Oshaya slapped his hand away. "Don't!"

"You know the word *fuck* has two theories on how it derived?" He held up two fingers. "One is that back in the fifteen hundreds, England was detrimentally dying off in population due to sickness and war, so the King issued a decree to *fuck! Fornication under consent of the King!* He wanted people to have babies to revive the population."

"Fuck, *you*," Oshaya spat.

Nigil chuckled before holding up a finger. "You know the word *fuck* is said to have first been used in a poem called *Flem Flys*? You wanna know the other theory, wife. I once read that the word *fuck* gained its sexual connotation because the King of England felt that his title entitled him to *all* things, including another man's wife. So, he decreed, as King, he could *fuck* any woman he chose. Married or not." Nigil's dark eyes explored his wife's anatomy, and the see-through lingerie appeared melted over her flesh. "You fucking another King, *wife*?"

"Fuck-you!" Oshaya gritted, before downing the contents of her glass. Her eyes were leaking faucets that baptized her face, an emotional sacrament which made her wonder if it was *her* definition of love that was crooked, or if love was just meant to have a bitter taste after one had sucked all its sweetness away.

"I won't allow you to turn my heart slimy. I deserve better than this," she hissed.

204

"You *belong* to me, whore, and," Nigil growled and his body language became violent. He took her chin between his thumb and the knuckle of his pointer finger, forcing her to look up at him. "If you need a reminder, I can happily oblige," he gritted through clenched teeth.

" I- hate- you!"

"Clean this shit up." He ignored her proclamation while waving at the spread on the table. He released her before turning and making his way toward their room.

You have to stop this Oshaya, get out before he kills you! Run! Oshaya's thoughts contradicted her actions as she gazed at the candle lit dinner that sat untouched, going cold on the table. The sound of Nigil's phone ringing captured her attention momentarily, and when he answered, she tuned into pieces of the conversation.

"Not tonight. Yes, of course sweety"- His side of the dialogue was enough for her to piece together the other side. Fresh tears blinded her and she hated how weak she was.

"Arrrrghh!" She growled before sweeping her plate, silverware, and the bottle of wine off the table. Food splashed onto the floor as the bottle rolled across the carpet. Oshaya sat there, transfixed as she watched the thick, fermented juice flow out the bottle and soak into the carpet- *Fuck him! Fuck- him! She thought as her tears followed.*

CHAPTER THIRTEEN
CHOPPING GAME

The rec yard on the North Side of the Estelle Unit was packed beyond capacity. A game of five on five was in full swing on the basketball court, and the cling and clatter of the convicts using the universal weight sets intermingled with the numerous conversations being had on the yard. The sun was high and beaming down on that portion of captivity as if God had intentionally situated the fiery ball of gas right there.

"Get that fat bitch up off you, fam! You only got two more to go. Push, nigga," Tay motivated Gambino, as he bench-pressed the two hundred seventy-five pounds they'd put on the bar.

"Ahhhhhhah!" Gambino growled. Chest, arms, and shoulder muscles rippled as he strained to push out the last few reps.

"It ain't shit to a stepper, walk it down, my guy," LeLe, a big speaker on the unit, added his encouragement. The squad was outside. Lil K, Yap, Papa, Lil Woo, Big Vino, Tay's brother Solo, and East Texas TuTu were milling about.

"That's on Woodtown, Oak Cliff, Texas, bro! When I get back to that black top, I'm bossin' up! I'ma write a book 'bout this shit," Lil K declared, before making his way over to the pull-up bar.

"Fuck outta here, bruh, what you gonna call it? *Rec Yard Game?*" Tay joked with a chuckle, as Lil K pulled himself up onto the bar.

"Naw, I'm gonna call it, *From the Rec Yard to the Streets,* bruh. I'ma boss up, fam, I'm tellin' you boys, them niggas out there playin'! I'ma secure that bag, on Blood," he swore between reps.

"Yeah, whateva, nigga. *Everybody* say when they touch they gonna ball and have all the bitches. Dem boys get out and be cappin' with another man's shit!" Tay capped, and the look Lil K gave him would've been threatening if their love for one another wasn't so thick. Lil K jumped down from the pull-up bar.

"Remember you said that. 'Cause you gonna be the first nigga's face I put my nuts in," he declared.

Renta

"Ain't nobody gonna put they nuts in my face. Keep them lil mu'fuckas in yo' Superman Fruit of the Looms!" Tay laughed and that's when Lil K delivered a powerful punch to the man's chest. From there, the exchanging blows could be heard by all in close proximity. They slap boxed until the respect was back in place.

Papa laughed, paying them no mind as he gazed out at the basketball court. A tall dark skinned cat ran down court, and with a mean crossover, sat the man guarding him on his ass, before driving to the basket, leaping high into the air, and getting fancy with a winding dunk.

"Ouuuu!" the crowd roared. Papa's eyes found Lil K in a studious gaze. "Woodtown, Oak Cliff, Texas?"

"Yeah, that's my hood, bruh, wud up!" Lil K was aggressive by nature. Papa chuckled.

"It's overstood that we're gonna rep our lands, but I'm sayin', you boys never think of how calculative them crackas were?" He opened a session the playas knew as *choppin' game.*

"Speak that shit, Big Bro. Jewel us so we can shine bright," Tay chimed in, while taking his position on the bench.

"Think about it, bro … we kill and die for blocks at those project buildings *for a reason* of craziness! We think those reasons are out of love, representation, and loyalty, so we thug for them corners wit' blood in our eyes," Papa talked his talk.

"Shid, them the reasons *I* rep my hood, bruh-bruh. I love my block, SED shit," Solo gave it up.

Papa shook his head sadly as he glanced out at the two hundred plus convicts who were out doing some of everything on the yard.

"I bet every cent I got in my account, all these niggas feel the same, *but* them same niggas we love so hard, we ain't heard from but a few, *if* that! Listen, fam, let me get ya' mental over the fence." Papa pointed to the security fence that separated them from freedom. Sharp razor wire wound over the top and bottom halves ensuring a dangerous climb.

"You boys don't get it? It's all in the name of shit, family, but we done become so lost in the sauce, we overlook the *self* enslavery and instead, poeticize it.

208

Ski Mask Money

Nigga, the projects was actually *a project!* They created low-income housing *projects* because they were beginning to institutionalize our black asses to our own zoo! They knew niggas would run their lazy asses into them and *trap* themselves there!" He shook his head in dismay.

"We happy the apartment is cheap, and they're happy to keep us simple. Fam, somewhere nearby, *in every hood,* you'll find an elementary school and a bunch of stores. The stores were *strategically* placed there so we can recycle our money back to them, and the elementary is there 'cause those teachers need a pretense.

The college is to mock a nigga 'cause they know niggas in the projects not gonna go to no school. Shid, most of us didn't even finish *middle* school, let alone high school. Them crackas built the projects in the hood, far away from their safe and pretty little communities because they didn't want the dirt of their *project* to spill over into their backyards."

"Say, I read 'bout that bizz, bruh, it's called the self-cleaning oven," LeLe interjected. Papa pointed a finger at him with a shake of his head.

"White woman wrote it. She wrote that if they built a place for niggers to live, and built stores around it, and infused it with drugs, we'd spend all our money with them, recirculating it back into their hands. They say the drugs will make us sell to each other; therefore, killing and addicting our own community." Papa chuckled.

"That shit stupid crazy, my dude, I didn't know that," Tay shook his head in shame.

"Family, *that's* why they call their community a *neighborhood* and niggas call our shit *the hood!* Them white folks can break bread, and though they just as trifling as any other race, they trust each other. Bob's wife can go kick it wit' their neighbor Josh without insecurity getting involved.

"Yeah, cuz, white people have no problem fuckin' each other's spouses. They be on some: '*Hey Josh, you wanna fuck my wife?* type shit." Tay got comical, doing a humping motion as if he were sexing an imaginary woman. The bros laughed.

"That too, but us? Them same corners we'll ride, die, and step on somethin' for, we don't trust 'em. So we dropped the neighbor part and just call it our hood. We know our neighbor is just as crooked as we are. Poverty breeds winners and losers, fam, and the losers will do it all to become a winner."

"Say, Gambino," a convict named K-Mo called out, as he walked over and interrupted the game chopping session.

"Sup, LeLe, Papa, Yap, Lil K." He acknowledged the ones he rocked with. The tension instantly shot up, but Gambino knew how ugly shit would get if he didn't intervene.

"Peace, my guy, what's the bidness?" He dapped dude up.

"Say, it's a new cat over here that's raw talent on that mic. Boys sayin' you can't fuck wit' 'em."

"Mane, I ain't 'bout to entertain that lil boy shit. Niggas know I'm—

"I got an ounce of that gas on my guy right here," Tay cut him off.

"Bruh, we ain't from the East Coast wit' all that battle rap shit, we're playas." Gambino wasn't feeling it.

"Naw, y'all just run a few verses. I ain't got no work but I'll put two hundred on dude. He live."

"Suck his dick then, nigga," Tay spat. That gangsta shit instantly bled into K-Mo's gaze. They all knew he'd rep that Hoova Gang with his whole heart.

"Be respectful, lil bruh." LeLe chuckled as he slid from the dip bar. "Let's go check lil daddy out."

***

The Past - 2016

"Que descas hacer en la vida?" La Rosa Peligrosa asked. *Within the last two years, Shay had learned enough Spanish to understand the language, but not enough to speak it fluently. She pondered the question of what she wished to be in life, and as she sat at the vanity mirror La Rosa had gifted her for her eighteenth birthday, she stared at her and La Rosa's reflection as the woman*

she now called mother, brushed her curly hair. The lights were dim in the guest room.

"Free, that's all. Just-Free," Shay whispered.

La Rosa's eyes connected with hers in the reflecting glass. First it was a glare but seeing the truth roaring as loud as an angry lioness in Shay's pupils, the older woman's gaze softened. For a moment, she reflected on the time she was a young, beautiful girl from the slums of La Polvorilla, Mexico. Those were the dark times when her own father had become so enchanted with her beauty, he began to share parts of her body that no father should ever share with their daughter. So, she understood the girls crave for liberty. For the past two years, she'd made a fortune off the girls she'd snatched into her world. And though most had been sold into the hands of filthy rich men from different parts of the cold world, Shay, Alane, and Tresey had been kept. Every six months she held a banquet promoting aid for the poor citizens of the country of Mexico, but the invite-only attendees knew it was merely a front for them to purchase the girl of their desire.

Mexico was a corrupt country ran by the cartels. The corrupt government would turn a blind eye to the darkness they'd created in the country as long as the money continued to grease the right hands, and La Rosa PeligRosa was happy to oblige.

"Everyone has an imprisonment they want freedom from, Shay. Maybe it's a broken marriage that holds a woman captive to the man she can't stop loving, or maybe one is imprisoned to a particular addiction, but it matters not. My point is, all freedoms come with a price, Chiquita."

"What's mine? What price do I have to pay for my freedom?" Shay inquired.

"Tu debes De Usar Tu Hermosura Para Tu Ventaje." La Rosa told her she had to use her beauty to her advantage.

Shay dropped her head in shame. For the past few years, she'd been forced into a life that turned a girl into a woman too quickly, and she'd been fucking older men since she'd been stolen from home. Though they'd praised her on how beautiful she was, all she knew was sex. No feelings. No sense of attractiveness. Only

211

defilement. The action of fucking without the feeling of being appreciated. La Rosa stepped around her and placed a finger beneath her chin, causing her to look up into a pair of eyes that were as cold as the polar caps.

"Do you know why I've kept you? Tresey and Alane?"

"No," Shay whispered.

"When a girl becomes a woman, that woman can recognize tings in a girl, that girl won't understand until she's a woman. You two friends are fighters, and one day they be very beautiful women, but they will never be who you are, Chiquita. You are a girl with thoughts." La Rosa PeligRosa paused to rest the brush on the counter. Pointing at her head, the woman turned and made for the door, but paused in the threshold, again, tapping her finger against her head. "A thinking woman is more powerful than ten giant men, but an ignorant woman only sees the power of the ten giant men rather than seeing how she can use those men's power to place her in a powerful position." La Rosa paused to smooth non-existent wrinkles from her beautiful, heaven-white cocktail dress that molested her every curve. "Te Digo La Verdad, Tu Talvez No Podras Irte Viva." Her words were low, but clear. Shay nodded slightly as the words translated in her mind. "I tell you the truth, you may not make it away alive."

"So, why not just let me go?"

"Eres Bonita, Pero El Dinero Que` Recibo De Tu Panocha Es mas Bonito." La Rosa Peligrosa told her that she was pretty, but the money she made from her pussy was prettier.

Shay's eyes misted, she hated her. She despised the woman who coined herself, the 'Deadly Rose'. She hated God for the hand she'd been dealt. She just hated period. La Rosa's departure left a lingering fragrance of Jimmy Choo Illicit perfume dancing on the air.

Shay took the brush into her nimble fingers, and staring in the mirror, she began to brush her long hair. Soft tears dripped from her eyelids as she stared at her reflection, and as if an evil spirit had suddenly overtaken her, she hurled the brush at the image staring back at her. The glass spider webbed, causing her reflection to split into multi-dimensions. Transfixed on the mirrored image, it converted to multiple reflections of herself, trapped within one big reflection. And as she took deep breaths to calm herself, the image reminded her of her heart. Shattered. In a million pieces.

***

The Present- 2020

A convict by the name of OF One Eighty used two spoons he'd stolen from the prison's kitchen to create a live beat, and humming, he began to beat box along with the rhythm of the spoons. The rec yard was alive with different activities, but in that corner, about thirty convicts had gathered around to vibe to the rap session.

"Yeah, Klutch A million, nigga," dude vibed, while getting lost in the beat.

Gambino's eyes studied the slim, dark skinned brotha as he rocked and nodded his head to the beat. Playas recognize playas, so the two men smirked at each other as they faced off, ready to show their skills over the jail-house beat.

"Klutch!" Playboy repeated, before getting animated with his hand gestures as he spit his verse:

"My mama was target practice for twenty-five years, so I was born a marked man/ The black sheep, *Dark Skin*, move smoother than a shark's fin/ With that metal, make a car bend, or cut Goliath down to a short man/ Real life no fable. . . I'm live like exposed wires, we been stealin' cable/ Kuz mama wasn't able, I sold crack but granny stole it, dawg, my house wasn't stable/ I'm from Dead End, the Dead Land/ where a dead man ain't sayin' shit/ can't thug on my corner if you ain't sprayin' clips/ West Coast customs we ain't sprayin' whips/ walk niggas down and get personal, *like, what you sayin' pimp / Broad Day /* Got 45 the hard way / It's ending with a car chase, and whackin' my codefendants woulda been the smart way/ But listenin' to what my heart say/ Got me lost in a dark cave / I enjoyed the game until I realized prison was the arcade!"

The crowd was hype, loving dude's vibration, but when Gambino stepped forward, it was as if someone had lit a fuse.

"Crash that boy, G, breathe on that beat, Bro Bro," Tay encouraged, as Gambino eyed Klutch. Both men bobbed their heads to the beat.

"You niggas listen up." Gambino was in his act. The crowd was lit, and the correctional officers who patrolled the yard stood by, watching the activity as if it were a live concert. C.O Givens and another officer nodded their heads to the beat but kept their distances from the crowd.

"Go, Gambino, you better do yo 'thang!"

"Heyyy!" Two homosexual men, Peaches and Cookie, rooted.

"Shut y'all punk ass up!" Lil K spat with a glare. The two he/shes rolled their eyes like females, but it was Peaches who gave him the hand with a dramatic roll of his neck.

"Boy Boo!" he sassed. C.O Givens laughed, she was too tickled at the murderous glare Lil K gave the two other men. Peaches and Cookie had both permed their hair with a mixture of lie soap, magic shave, and hair grease the inmates dubbed *slick fifty*. The two men's pants were so tight, it was a wonder they still had circulation in their legs. However, they knew Lil K was a savage, so when his glare didn't waver, and he took a step toward them ...

"Come on girl, our presence ain't wanted at they little concert." Peaches rolled his eyes once more before dragging Cookie away. Givens' giggles caused Lil K's gaze to capture her, but Gambino's verse allowed him another focus.

"Got an addiction for chasin' blue cheese, I'm on my Steve Urkel/ ya' bro a rat like Master Splinter, you related to the Ninja Turtles/ we no fuckey wit' rodents, he say he hard to kill like he Arnold Schwarzenegger the terminator/ My shootas on speed dial, will mask up and exterminate cha/ Meech was only tryin' to feed his team and Trump didn't wanna pardon him/ crackas justify the choke hold, look how they did Eric Garner/ I can only imagine how his family felt gettin' that call from the coroner/ got our grass filled wit' too many snakes like we fired all the gardeners/ crackas stormed the capital, waved rebel flags, nobody stopped 'em/ If they were black the police would've smiled before they slaughtered 'em/ Illuminati, Illuminati they'll give a nigga life for being robbers/

Ski Mask Money

Donald Trump won't get found guilty, he connected to Russian mobsters/ And playin' like you a big chief / will have niggas runnin' up in yo' tepee/ Mad Max wit' that machete, scalp a nigga like a Cherokee/ Lil Wayne got my dudes in skinny jeans, but I thug wit' Future, I'm the future in designer/ Christian Louis Vuitton's with gold spikes, kick you in the ass and leave you with a reminder...

***

The past- 2016
Mexico City – 9:45 PM

In the country of Mexico, the ghettos are far different from the hoods of the United States. In most of the country's rural areas, the economy is poor, and the sewage infrastructure is weak, adding to the foul stench of dog, chicken, and goat shit.

A lot of times, the dirt roads that run through these poverty stricken cities are tainted and moist with piss and shit, due to the lack of proper plumbing, but the same can't be said about the nation's capital.

Mexico City is a beautiful city and a lair for dangerous and powerful men of the country's elite residents. Loma's de Chapultepec is an influential neighborhood comprised of Mexico City's politicians, Narcos, and retired men in the know. Just Northwest of downtown, this wealthy section of the city was a world of its own. And on this night, the moon was full and glaring down upon mansions like the home of La Rosa Peligrosa.

The night was festive, and La Rosa was the perfect hostess to the many men who were mostly important and high ranking Narcos. Rosa Tapia was beautiful. Her long, black hair hung down passed her shoulders and framed her native Mexican face. Though many admired the way her perky breasts sat up behind the silk material of her Atelier Versace cocktail dress, no one dared verbalize their lustful desires. The million dollar home was made of many parts, but there in the makeshift ballroom, tables were set out to give each man a sense of space.

"Good Evening, Deadly Rose, you're beautiful, as always." A masculine voice stopped her in her tracks. La Rosa's eyes took him in, and though she despised Diego del Rio, she smiled, nonetheless. He wore the typical Narco's attire. His long, oily black hair was tied back into a ponytail and topped with a seven hundred dollar cowboy hat. And the black, pearl-snap button-up shirt he'd worn was tucked into the waist of a tight pair of Wranglers. La Rosa's eyes fell to the rattlesnake skinned cowboy boots on his feet before lifting back up to meet his appraising gaze.

"And you, Diego Del Rio, are not too hard on the eyes yourself," she spoke to the Zetas' general in Spanish. For some reason, a snakish feeling danced over her body as they gave each other false smiles. She didn't trust him. He lusted for her, always had. Furthermore, she knew he wasn't supposed to be in her home that night. He knew she knew as well. There were rules in the Cartel, and she knew Diego del Rio's presence meant something wrong. Something evil.

"A lot of people talk," he said, without losing his smile.

"Of?"

"Don't like a woman in the ranks of the family."

"I've proven how much gender matters, have I not?" The threat was blatant. Diego del Rio chuckled as La Rosa smiled.

"Enjoy your night, Señor del Rio. I'm sure we'll be seeing a lot more of each other before the night ends, si?"

"Si, señorita La Rosa Peligrosa, si," Diego del Rio confirmed as Rosa excused herself. With a forced smile, she greeted the other guests.

On top of her own girls, she'd brought in some of Mexico City's most beautiful working girls. Pretty prostitutes. The drinks were plentiful, and everyone seemed to be enjoying themselves, but La Rosa Peligrosa could feel the gazes of the hunters ...the secret eyes of the people who watched her every move. As she made her way through the crowd, the live band she'd brought in for the occasion began to sing about her life. She listened to the corridos.

"Shes a deadly rose from the beginning of our beginning/ of the deadly kind. A poisonous flower from Matamoros."

They sang as the unique sounds of their instruments filled the room. The table she headed for was occupied by a lone man who held up his glass of whatever his pleasure was for the night. She nodded in acknowledgement of the toast, and as a slim waiter passed with a tray of drinks, she stopped him and took two shot glasses of tequila before taking a seat at the table. She crossed her legs in a feminine gesture before tossing the first shot down her throat.

"Evening, Señorita La Rosa," the gentlemen across from her greeted. What made him unique was he was the only African American present that night. Draped in an expensive, double breasted Celine suit that complimented the thousand dollar John Lobb Williams double monk shoes, the man was as GQ as a man on the cover of an Esquire magazine.

"Evening, Señor," she responded, before a Mexican call girl sashayed over and handed her a thick portfolio. La Rosa Peligrosa waved the girl away with a flick of her fingers before sliding the leather bound book to the dark skinned American.

"In a hurry? Does my company bore you?" he asked, before accepting it.

"There's a demon in the air. Tonight is the night of the dead."

"Huh?" Her words confused him and the expression on the man's face was a testament.

"There's been some sort of shift in power, I sense it. Santa Muerta watches over me and I can feel death on the air." She spoke cryptically as her eyes studied the room. Every man in the room was either a powerful drug lord, a heartless murderer, or a lot of both. She watched as they paired off with the beautiful ladies and began to dance to their homeland music, and though the mood was festive, La Rosa couldn't shake the feeling she'd invited the devil into her home.

"There's nothing that can touch you. You're the dangerous rose and your connections are too political." The man attempted to rationalize as he opened the portfolio to the first page. It was filled with pictures and every piece of info she had on each of her girls. There was a picture of each girl in a beautiful evening gown, and

beside it were two other photos—both nude—one of the front view and the other of the back. The ages ranged from anywhere between thirteen to thirty years old. All races. All for sale. Each woman, a sex slave.

"Si, señor, but here in Mexico, our government is corrupt, our country is ran by the Cartels, Los Narcos. El Chapo Guzman was only a layer of the monster my beautiful country breeds." La Rosa's words were low as her eyes drifted to him. The man's vision was studious as he appraised the pictures. All the women were beautiful. "You see anything you like, Señor, time is of the essence." La Rosa's patience was short. The American man's gaze lifted to her, but before he could respond, his eyes shifted, just as most of every other man's eyes in the room did. Curious, La Rosa would follow their gazes until she found poetry in motion.

Shay made her way down the spiraling, floating steps that descended down through the middle of the room. The velvet mini dress she wore was strapless, and her thick, red boned legs and thighs, and shapely hips set fire to every man's imagination. Her long hair flowed down her back in a cascade of wavy ripples, and her face was flawless—no makeup needed.

"I want her." His words were low, but sure.

"Not for sale."

"Fifty thousand."

"Not. For. Sale."

"Hundred grand." The man was persistent and La Rosa's eyes left Shay to capture the American. She studied him as her mind came to a wicked conclusion. Her vision drifted to the table in which Diego de Rio sat in the company of a beautiful, blue-eyed blonde. As if his eyes hadn't left her during the time passed since they'd spoken, their gazes connected. Diego smiled connivingly before he lifted his shot glass in a toast. And though it hadn't been verbalized, La Rosa Peligrosa believed she knew exactly the cause for the unofficial celebration. She lifted her second shot glass and both she and her enemy downed their drinks.

"Mother," Shay acknowledged, after making it to their table. Her eyes trailed to the handsome man across the table from the

woman who had turned her life upside down. Their eyes bore into one another's, both wondering.

"Tu Han Comprado Por Un Hombre Generoso Que` Esta` Enamorado De Tu Hermosura." La Rosa's words cracked through their chemistry.

Shay's eyes grew wide in shock and the American man's face revealed his ignorance of the Spanish language. La Rosa rose to her feet as the words translated in Shay's mental... 'you've been bought by a generous man who is in love with your beauty'. Shay's eyes ping ponged from La Rosa to the American man and back to the woman who had held her captive for the past two years.

"No! You promised to free me, not sale me. I won't go!" she screamed, drawing unwanted attention as she spun on her heels and ran out of the room.

"That didn't turn out so well," the man mumbled, before downing his drink.

"Have the money wired to my account. I must go now," La Rosa spoke before turning to leave.

"Why such a rush?" The American was curious.

"This matter no concerns you, but I suggest you be very careful. Leave this place quickly. Do you have a gun?"

"Why?" He wanted to know. La Rosa thought on it for only a moment.

"There are very dangerous men here tonight who want me dead before sunrise, and they will slaughter everything breathing. There's no such thing as innocence in my world, only death," she warned before making a hasty exit.

***

The present- 2020

They'd spit verse for verse and Gambino was raw talent. Klutch was hands down the rawist between the two. His "Liquid Gold," and " Been a While" tracks was what murdered the competition so Tay grudgingly had to fork over that bread. It was all fun amongst real dudes, and behind that wall, men won and lost on the daily.

"Let's go, gentlemen, recs over! Recs over," one of the officers shouted repeatedly.

"Aiiight, Gambino."

"Fuck wit' me Tay!"

"LeLe, I'm gone swing through and pick that up, big bro!" If you can imagine two hundred people attempting to show love, flex for the female officers, and make plans *all at the same time*, you can get an idea of how the ending of a recreational period in prison is.

For two hours, those men had sold drugs, done drugs, plotted on how to get the contraband in, some worked out, and some had even gotten their ass beat. It was the prison way. Gambino and his dudes were saying their farewells when he excused himself. He made his way through the throng of convicts, dapping some and ignoring many, until he'd made it over to where CO Givens stood, passing the inmates their IDs She glanced at him curiously before smiling.

"Didn't know you could rap. Maybe that should've been your thing instead of a life of crime."

"We all have hindsight, but it's foresight that saves a mu'fucka from the crack in the street. I'm sayin' though, you never got back at me." He got straight to the business. The shocked expression on Givens' face got a chuckle out of him and Givens' eyes took him in before returning to the IDs. "Did you at least read it?" Gambino was referring to the kite she'd taken from him when he was in lockup.

"Yeah."

"And?"

"And? I mean, what you want me to say? This is my job and you're a- a—

"Prisoner? Convict?" The tone of his voice as he completed her sentence caused her to glance at him once more.

"You big mad or lil mad?" She smiled before laying ten IDs out on the rec table so the convicts could retrieve their own.

"So, since these chains holdin' me—"

Ski Mask Money

"That's not what *I* said. *You* made yourself a prisoner in my conversation. *I* was trying to say that you're a *stranger!*"
"Oh . ." He felt like, *lame-lame, be quiet.*
"Yeaaah, ohhh." She giggled.
"My fault, but I'm sayin', what's *wrong* with rockin' with a stranger?" He was curious, but the look Givens gave him was one of those *nigga, are-you-crazy* expressions.
"My mama taught me not to talk to strangers, let alone attempt to establish a relationship with one. That is *a case*, you know." She bobbed her head with her words in a feminine way that turned Gambino on, but he concealed it with a chuckle.
"In all due and respect, yo' mama is either a liar, or she never grew up from the bullshit lesson that was only meant for children."
"What!" she snapped, on the verge of serving him proper. Gambino held up his hands in a calming gesture.
"Naw, see, the thing with people is that we react wrong because we hear words, but emotions blind us to *the purpose behind them.* All I'm sayin' is, if you lived your life not talking to strangers, you wouldn't know *nobody.* Before a family member can be truly family, they start in the stranger category, right?"
" I guess, but—"
"No buts, ma, before you call someone a friend, they're strangers. You gotta give a mu'fucka a chance to get familiar in order to move 'em out the stranger zone. When you was a *little girl* you wasn't 'pose to talk to strangers because as a little girl you were naïve and you could've fallen into the hands of a dangerous man."
"Boy, whatever! I'm a *grown ass woman* and can *still* fall into the hands of a dangerous man." Givens gave him the eye before looking him up and down with a sexy smirk.
"Or, you can fall into *the heart* of a *perfect stranger.*" He smiled.
"A perfect stranger, huh?" She giggled before laying the rest of the IDs out faceup. Convicts retrieved their IDs before making their exit. Gambino found his, and to her surprise, he extended it to her. A moment of deja` vu washed over her as she gave him a suspicious

221

look, and though he smiled, Gambino's eyes were trained on the approaching groups of convicts.

"Take it," he suggested, without looking at her. She did, and as soon as she had it in her hand, she felt the folded up piece of paper he'd hidden beneath it. Inconspicuous as ever, CO Givens cuffed the kite before tossing the ID back into the pile. She glanced around to ensure no one had witnessed the exchange.

"I have to go."

"Look, this place is a cemetery, ma. *This* ain't living. A concrete casket." He waved his hand around the gym area. CO Givens reached beneath the table were the guards kept their things and retrieved her see-through purse.

"What do you want *me* to do, Ridge? *I* didn't put you here." She addressed him by his government. "You want me to break you out?" She laughed but realizing he didn't see the humor, she composed herself." That was a joke, you know, ha-ha?" She rolled her eyes before slinging the purse over her shoulder.

"You might can't take me physically, but spiritually and mentally you can." He pointed at his head.

"I don't get it."

"Think about me. I just wanna be wherever you are, mama. Even if I gotta live inside your mind. If you go to church, I wanna sit on the pew wit' you. You go to the gym, I wanna be on your mental, the motivation that makes you work harder to keep that ass right and ya' thighs tight. You go to the moon? Shiid, I ain't tryin' to go waaayy up there, but just tell me the time, and at that same time, I'll stare out the window of my cell and search for a shooting star wit' you. The mind, ma, that's where I stop being a stranger at."

"Givens, you okay?" one of her coworkers asked, as he made his way over to where they stood.

"Uhh-yeah, we—"

"Like I was sayin', Ms. Givens, you ain't always gotta be a bitch! I know I'm an inmate, but I'm still human." Gambino shocked her.

"You watch your fucking mouth when you're talking to her, offender!" CO Smith was a redneck, police, son-of-a-bitch who hated inmates, and when he took a step toward Gambino...

"Sup, bleed, you good?" Tay asked, as he and the gang made it to the table for their IDs. Gambino saw the look of uncertainty on CO Smith's face and the fear in CO Givens' eyes. He chuckled before finding his ID and nodding his confirmation. Papa strolled over and put an arm around Gambino's neck before leading him toward the door.

"Always be sharp, lil bruh, appreciate even the smallest of victories," he whispered knowingly.

***

The Past - 2016

"Holy Death, protect me from the hands of my enemies," La Rosa whispered, as she made her way into the part of her house she'd had converted into a small chapel. Glancing behind her to make sure she hadn't been followed, she slipped into the massive room. The lights were off, but as she kept it, there were ten black candles lit at the altar, casting dancing shadows across the walls.

La Rosa Peligrosa paused midway and glanced up at the huge shrine of Santa Muerte, The Goddess of Death that Narcos prayed to. Where most churches would have a cross depicting the crucifixion of Christ, or even a weeping statue of The Virgin Mary, the black monument of the Holy Death stood proud. The statue resembled the reaper, but with a beautiful face that was half woman and half skeletal. As La Rosa Peligrosa took slow steps toward the only God she believed in, the shadows around her seemed to come alive.

"For I've lived a dark life, but I've always paid my respects to you, in blood." Her voice was a whisper as she glanced down at the sacraments she'd dedicated to her God. As if an unforeseeable force had beckoned her, when La Rosa's eyes lifted, they shifted to the seven rows of church benches she'd had installed, more for show than sitting.

223

At the front of the chapel, though the rest of the body was obscured by the mahogany lacquered bench, a pair of freshly shaved legs jutted out into center aisle. Yet. even without seeing the girl's pretty face, her long lush raven-black hair, or even without the girl's favorite perfume lingering in the air, La Rosa Peligrosa would still recognize the six-inch violet crocodile-skinned heels she'd gotten Alane for her birthday.

La Rosa's knees almost buckled, but in her lifestyle, fear wasn't an option. A thick trail of dark blood slowly leaked away from the dead girl's form, and though tears bled into her glare, La Rosa Peligrosa lifted and focused her vision on the dark shrine. The candles melted slow and flames flickered as if a soft breath of wind had blown through the room. Black wax dripped down the black candles as she made her way to the edge of the shrine where they were situated in an outward arch.

"My enemies are here for blood, Muerte, my blood. I don't fear death for I am your servant," she whispered, head bowed, and eyes drifting closed as she fell to her knees in prostration. As she prayed, she sensed the reaper's presence the moment he entered the room. Still, she prayed to her deity. Behind her, she could hear a tumbling sound as if her killer had rolled something toward her. And though she heard the squishing, wet sound as the object tumbled, still, La Rosa Peligrosa prayed. "If I shall die, reveal my murderer so my soul may haunt him ... so I can repay him in blood in the afterlife. Holy Death..." She tensed as the rolling object bumped and came to a rest against her leg, without pausing in prayer, La Rosa smiled wickedly.

A lesser woman would've run for her life, but not the cartel princess. Not the dangerous Rose from the slums of La Polvorilla Mexico. Not the woman who had murdered her husband at their breakfast table and made her bones in the city of Matamoros, Mexico. Not the woman who knew in her lifestyle, men were expected to die like warriors and woman were just as fierce. She didn't run because La Rosa Peligrosa, name meaning 'The Dangerous Rose', knew that not only would running shame her

Ski Mask Money

entire family, but running would be useless. The Gulf Cartel could find her anywhere!

*****

Shay had slipped off her heels and held them in her hands as she ran. She'd exited the house. She'd ran and ran until she reached the guesthouse that was about sixty feet behind the main house. And just as she'd made it to the front door, she tripped and fell, scraping her knees in the fall. Her dress was ruined but she didn't care. Her knees bled. She didn't care. She buried her face in her hands and cried right there on the welcome-home mat at the door of a house that could never be her home. Moments passed before the door cracked open and a dim light spilt out.

"Señorita Bonita, Shay, what's wrong?" a man-child spoke in broken English. Hector Berrera was La Rosa's nephew whom she loved more than life.

After her sister had died from cancer, La Rosa took the woman's only son in and raised him as her own. She'd kept him away from the worst parts of "the life," and had even paid for him to be home schooled by a very expensive teacher she had flown in from the U.S. Hector was set and though he was being groomed to take over her business, La Rosa Peligrosa had made him vow on his mother's grave that he'd remain chaste until he was twenty years of age—until she'd been able to teach him all that she could about a woman and the power their lower lips had over men.

"Prometeme que te vas ah esperar atener sexo, Mijo. La panocha ser mala, tienes que aprender antes." She'd told him to promise her that he'll wait for sex. She told him pussy could be evil, he must learn first. She told him she's telling him the truth. So he'd vowed to wait until he was twenty calendars old before partaking of the pleasure of a woman's treasure. And though he had turned the big eighteen at twelve o'clock that night, just two years away from being the man of his word, Jesus Christ was the only man to ever have remained chaste under the fire of temptation. Hector was no Jesus, fuck forty days and forty nights. The devil had barely tempted

225

him for forty "seconds" and his nature betrayed him. Shay had always been his weakness, and over time, he'd convinced himself that he was in love with her.

"Are you okay, Señorita?" he questioned, as his gaze lifted to study the night. The main house was aglow with the light from numerous octane fueled lamps, but everything outside of that space was bathed in pure darkness.

Shay willed herself to get it together before her head lifted, and she ran her hands down her face to wipe away the wetness. She studied him, not truly understanding "why" she'd gone there. Though they were the same age, her experiences gave her a gorge wide length of maturity over him, and though he was being sculpted for the life, there were powerful things about a woman he would never understand.

Some men had a gift in pussyology, but most became so smitten with pussy, they missed the entire ology part. Hector was one of "those" men. Shay sniveled as he helped her to her feet, still confused.

"You're bleeding." He spoke the obvious as both their eyes fell to her right knee.

She waved him off. "It's nothing."

"Why are you crying? Is someone after you?" His tone was protective. Shay's vision took him in. Curious. A black woman ... in Mexico. He lusted. She smiled as her mind gave in to resolution. She'd been sold to a stranger. She'd been fucking grown men since she was a young girl. Shit was crazy. Without verbal, she gently pushed him back into the house, before crossing the point of no return, and kicking the door closed behind her. Little did she know, she had an unwanted audience who watched through binoculars. About a hundred armed men watched while surrounding the mansion from every angle.

The lead man smirked before lifting a handheld radio to his lips. "We take them in ten minutes."

"Copy," came the response.

CHAPTER FOURTEEN
Beauty and The Beast

The Present- December 23rd

The cell block was lit that Wednesday. Two days before Christmas and two days before Pierre was to discharge his sentence. The men on cell block G1 were turned up. LeLe and Papa had provided the Ganja to be smoked and in their own section of the dayroom, a group of Eses who repped the Tango Blast Gang had a trash bag filled with that jailhouse hooch. Almost every man in the dayroom was lifted off of some kind of drug or alcohol. And though that type of shit, combined with too many rival races was known to be destructive, it was still a vibe.

"I'm tellin' you young niggas," a convict known as V-Dub shouted over the noise, before pausing to take a gulp from his cup. "Y'all betta enjoy dem young gals while you got 'em, 'cause they won't be around too long! Especially if you got more than a lil skid bid. I had an ole gal that promised to never leave, and the dirty hoe even claimed to love the shit stains in my dirty draws." He talked his jailhouse blues before pausing once more to hit the hooch in his cup. "Then, a year into my bid, the funky bitch left me high and dry! She took the money, sold the house, and gave my dog away. I loved that dog, funky, bitch!" he declared, as Gambino and the gang laughed. Gambino "G'd" for V-Dub. He knew the old timer had been locked up since 1990 for a string of murders around Dallas, Fort Worth, and in thirty years, wasn't no telling how much a man could lose.

"She say she loved ya' draws, huh?" J-Bo, Gambino's neighbor was beside himself with laughter.

"Youngin', don't act like you ain't ever had no doodoo streaks." V-Dub pointed his finger at him.

"Naw, I'm sayin' though, Dub, I don't believe *all* women like yours was. I think it depends on the *type* of bitch you got that determines what you can expect from her. You can't just say *every* woman will leave their dude down bad. Some bitches were built to last, and others weren't *taught* real loyalty," Tay interjected.

"Young nigga, I done lived fifty-six calendars, I been your age, you just gotta live to see mine. I'm tellin' ya', some women wear cotton panties and some wear dem-dem, Jennifer Secrets panties, the real sexy kind. But no matter the size, the fashion of heels, or level of intelligence, in the end, all dem gals are the same."

"Hell are Jennifer Secrets?" Gambino was curious.

"Mannn, quit jivin' me, y'all know dem real sexy panties the ladies wear these days." V-Dub was as intoxicated as a downtown drunk. Papa, LeLe, Tay, and Gambino glanced at each other confusedly, but Pierre burst into laughter.

"Bruh-bruh, the nigga talmbout *Victoria* Secrets!" he exclaimed between fits of laughter. The others exploded like timed bombs when it dawned on them that the old head was too gone off that penitentiary brew. V-Dub didn't get the joke and gave the men a wide-eyed look of confusion.

"Who? Ohhh, the bitch name is Victoria! Yeah, that's right, Victoria. The bitch that make the secret panties that don't keep no secrets! Bitch got crotchless panties, backless panties, G-Strings, titties-out corsets and thangs, and got the nerve to call that shit *secret*! More like Jennifer *no secrets*!" He chuckled before downing the rest of his cup.

"Victoria," Tay corrected.

"Yeah, whatever the bitches name is!" V-Dub sputtered before stumbling off toward the Mexican's at the back table.

"Say, Pelon, I got a chili with beans for another one of them bottles, that's some liquid fire!" he declared. Gambino laughed as he shook his head, amused. They all knew V-Dub was a stone cold killer and a very vital voice to the Mandingo Warrior faction, a prison based family comprised of killers. Very seldom, a man with anything less than a life sentence could join, and that was rare.

"Aw shit, I see that boy's words done struck a cord wit' our boy. Look at 'im. V-Dub got this cat stressin' 'bout baby." LeLe chuckled with the words as all eyes drifted to Tay. He shrugged.

"Bruh, you and Drea straight. You know lady down by law when it comes to you. Fuck you always *dry* stressin', bro?" Gambino chastised, before lighting the tip of a stick he'd just rolled.

"Brooooo, I ain't heard from baby in a whole week, that ain't like my bitch, dawg, and all y'all know it." Tay shook his head in disappointment. Gambino hit the stick a few times before passing it to him.

"Damn, a week?" His words were muffled due to attempting to hold the weed smoke down in his lungs. "You right, that ain't like sis. See, *that's* why I don't trust females. Their emotions too fucked up and ain't no tellin' when they'll twist the blade in a nigga chest." LeLe chuckled at Gambino's admission before giving his.

"Lil bruh, if she gone leave or stay, *you* can't influence that decision. All you can do is be a real nigga and take it how it comes," he added.

"Fuck a bitch," Gambino declared, exhaling the smoke with a few coughs, "she'll be down as long as you can pipe that pussy and blow a bag, but soon as you outta bounds, lady do magic and disappear on a nigga."

Papa shook his head in amazement. He and LeLe were the elder of the four. Both men had been gone over two decades *and* both men kept their hands in something that could lead them to the money.

"Why you say that, G?"

"Bruh, 'cause it's a buck! Think 'bout it, Papa ... When we were free, females broke their necks just to slide, but as soon as shit got ugly, where they at?" Gambino asked, before lifting his hands as if to say *explain that shit!*

"Naw, lil bro, see ... that's where you got the game fucked up. I happen to know some very solid women, bruh. What about you, Le?" LeLe nodded his confirmation.

"Tay?" Papa had a point to prove.

"Mane, I know a few, but—"

"Naw, ain't no *buts*, I don't wanna hear your *insecurities*. See, when we in them streets, we thuggin'. We not spendin' our time gettin' to know them girls. Gambino, them girls didn't truly *know* us! They only knew who the streets knew... *The type of nigga* we gave to the street. The..." His words trailed off as he waved the stick away Tay was attempting to pass him. Weed wasn't his hype. "All those girls knew was the designer clothes, the foreign cars, the bread, and the rest of the *bullshit* we can't take with us when that fat bitch starts singin'. Niggas come to the pen talmbout folks forgot 'em, but what's real is we never really *knew* them folks morale just like they didn't know ours."

LeLe dapped him up, feeling the gospel being spoken to the small church of real niggas.

"How many people knew your government names, bro? Not ya' street shit, but the shit ya' mama and ya' loved ones call you?"

Tay and Gambino glanced at each other before bursting into laughter.

"See what I'm talmbout?" Papa chuckled. "Most of them folks didn't even know our real names, but we expect them to sit down and write a letter! What they gonna put on the envelope? Tay from Denton? Oak Cliff? Fuck outta here! If one of those women was to write *right now*, you wouldn't even know who they was unless they *described* they self. Guess why?" The men snickered at the truth.

"Shid, 'cause a nigga never even knew most of them girls *real* name either," LeLe chimed in. "All we ever knew was females nicknames, MoMo, NeNe, Tika, and shit like that. Bitch real name be Monique, but she calls herself Nikki! Bitch, how you get Nikki out of Monique?" He burst out laughing and the action was contagious. The bros had found a piece of sunshine within that dark place.

"Brooooo, why them girl's mama's be giving them all those hard to pronounce names?" Tay added to the vibe. "Bitch name be so complicated *she* can't even pronounce it! Woman's name be A'Ziamondia, you be like, say, what's ya' name, lady, and she like, uh-uh, just call me Zia," he mimicked in a girlish voice with a feminine wave of his hand. "Bro, how a bitch name have syllables, verbs, and a noun! Shit crazy!"

***

CO Givens tucked her feet beneath her when she took her seat on the couch. Her husband had to work late, and she had the house to herself. So, in nothing but tee shirt and panties, she unfolded the kite Gambino had given her. Smiling as her eyes swept over his words, and though it seemed so juvenile to be reading a note, she liked the feeling of it. As if she could hear his voice whispering in her ear, the man's words took form.

Egypt,

On my Pop Smoke vibe, what you know 'bout love shit. I'm man enough to admit that I'm in search! Not just "any" kind of love. I know that love is a tailored emotion expressed and given in personalized doses. She or he may love in their own version of the notion and label it unconditional, but 'I' don't want that kind of love. A pretense love. All love has a condition. If love can decrease, increase, or transform into something else, it means that 'something' changed it! Rather for the good or bad, some sort of condition can transform or deform the unconditional. And though you may be wondering 'why' I'm speaking on love, it's simply because your vibe has me in love with 'the idea' of what 'your' love will be like. FRFR! Let me ask you something. If I was given five minutes in a locked room with you, what you think I'd want to do? NNNNTT! Wrong answer, mama. You assume I'd be spending that five minutes attempting to explore that pussy, but even though some of my wildest fantasies are of fucking you into submission, I'd rather hold your mind for ransom and demand your time and attention for the payment. I'd hold tight to your every thought and convince you that this was never about a hostage situation, but more of me wanting you to see that Mr. Wrong can sometimes be Mr. Right. Vibe wit' me real quick though. Can you do that? Hey . . . you . . . yes . . . you, the pretty mu'fucka reading this. You remember the story of the beauty and the beast? I'm sure you do. But allow me to give you the street nigga's version. See, just like every other female, the beauty was warned about being fast. She was warned about the beast— a vicious, good for nothin' type that was busted and couldn't be trusted. Yet, one faithful day as the beauty sashayed down the block, even while all the hustlas were shootin' their shot, lady paid 'em no mind ... didn't look ... didn't smile .. and surely didn't stop. It was only one nigga on her mind, and that moment was the right time for her to see what all the hype was 'bout! It had to be something about him that people feared, but maybe it wasn't 'him,' maybe it was merely their misconceptions. So, the beauty traveled through the gutta where the wolves howled, and life as she knew it ended. She was scared as a mu'fucka, but with determination in her pursuit, those corners she kept bending until she finally arrived. At the den of the beast, the man that was feared by the streets, and even had her mama telling her to never meet. At that moment, mama's opinion became meaningless, the naysayers became being-less, and curiosity may have killed the cat, but for a woman, it may lead her to discover the type of shit she can hold onto for a lifetime. So, she rolled the dice with curiosity, and as soon as she entered that house, she found the meaning of what most people fear. She encountered a talking clock, which was really a metaphor that means time speaks to us even though it waits for no man, woman, or child. Then beauty met a talking candlestick, which was the metaphor meaning that no matter how dark a moment may be, there's light, 'you' just have to find what 'your' light is. Even though the beauty didn't understand these things at the time, the one thing she did understand was their warning of the beast! Yet, just as she decided to heed the warning, just as it always does, at the wrong time, time ran out on her. And, there came the beast! Fucked up attitude, gold teeth, a monster! He roared and revealed to her exactly what the streets had turned him into, and at first? The beauty was terrified! Yet, just like any other woman that finds it in their hearts to give a man from the slums, a street nigga, The Mr. Wrong, a chance, the beauty had to first set to the side, 'everything' she thought she knew of his kind, and allow the beast to show her 'how' to rock with him. Only then was she able to humble him. Only then was she able to show that beast who he was in spite of the armor he wore for the streets. And guess what, love? There was only 'one' thing that allowed her to say, "fuck all she'd heard!" 'One' thing that allowed her to see beyond all the attitude, tattoos, gold teeth, and dark eyes. Can you guess what that one thing was? Fuck it, I'll tell you! It was 'understanding'. The beauty understood that just 'cause a man had been outcasted by society, didn't mean he was undeserving! People do crazy things in order to protect what makes them weak! Understanding allowed the Beauty to not only kiss the beast, but also, to fall in love with him. Why? It's 'cause just as she'd thought, as soon as she gave him a chance to be more than a beast, when she kissed him beyond what she saw, the Beast turned into a handsome Prince.

Kiss me, Mama, there's a boss that resides beyond my gangsterisms. I've just hidden myself behind so much armor, I can't find my way out. Trapped in beast mode! Take a chance with a beast?

-Mr. Wanna be yours, The Beast-

Givens' eyes watered. "Damn," the word slipped from her lips.

***

The Past- 2016

"You are my protector, Santa Muerta, I offer my soul to you," La Rosa Peligrosa whispered, as her eyes slowly opened. The flames of each candle swayed sideways as if a dark spirit had blown a kiss with a gentle exhale of wind. La Rosa's eyes lifted to the huge statue of her Goddess, and it was then that Santa Muerta` spoke to her. Upon the wall, just behind the shrine, a shadow 'slithered across in the slippery motion of a snake. A sign of betrayal! A lone tear dripped from her left eye even while she smirked evilly. "De la Serpiente." The name parted her lips like a vile taste. Treason! she thought.

"Yes, my dear, La Rosa Peligrosa, it is me," her general whispered. "Forgive my 'gift' to our Goddess, but de girl was just too feisty." He chuckled, and that's when La Rosa's vision fell to the moist thing that had bumped against her leg. A head!

233

Alane Ortiz's severed head rested bloody beside her. The girl's eyes were wide in shock, seeming to study her. La Rosa had seen and done much worse, but La Serpiente's treason was the testament that in Mexico, just as it were in every other country, gang, or faction, 'everybody' wanted to be the boss. Even if it meant whacking the very same mu'fucka who trusted them and gave them a seat at the table.

"You betrayed me," La Rosa Peligrosa whispered.

"I am the serpent, the snake, Peligrosa."

"They will kill you after they kill me. The Sinaloa is loyal to no one."

"No, not the Sinaloa. I've made a blood pact with the Jua`rez."

"Our enemy," she hissed, before spitting on the floor.

"They're giving me part of the Jua`rez valley, but you must die first."

"The Jua`rez and the Zetas are allies, but—

"They all have a common goal, La Rosa, they—

"Want to see me dead!" La Rosa Peligrosa cut him off. Her eyes fell to the gleaming blade of the knife she used to make blood sacrifices to her Goddess. It lay just beyond the nearest candle, and she was sure her training in combat would come in handy if she could get it.

"May I finish my talk with our Goddess before I face my killer? Will you grant me that, La Serpiente?"

"Si, La Rosa, Si," De la Serpiente whispered with a nod. He watched her bow her head so low, it touched the cold stone of the floor. He never noticed her inching hand as he bowed his own head out of respect. The man crossed his chest like a Catholic before bringing his knuckle to his lips and kissing it.

He watched, with a slight frown, as La Rosa Peligrosa climbed to her feet before reaching down and twisting her nimble fingers within the bloody tresses of Alane's severed head. She stood with her back to him. Beneath the soft, flickering light of the candles' flames, the scene was demonic. The man known as the Serpent stared in fascination, his vision briefly falling to the decapitated head. Strung up by its long hair with streaks of blood dripping down its pretty face, Alane stared at him with her mouth ajar, in the exact scream of horror she'd cried out when he'd sliced through her tender neck.

"La Familia, De la Serpiente, theres no more honor, no loyalty." La Rosa's words were low and sad.

"No, Ya No lo hay." His response was 'No, not anymore'.

"I was good to you, no?"

"Jesus was good to the Jews and they repaid him with a day of crucifixion." His response was treacherous, and that's when the devil smiled. La Rosa Peligrosa became a blur of speed when she spun on her heels.

"Judaaaasss!" she growled, before hurling the decapitated head at him. And though the move surprised him, De la Serpiente's trigger finger was steady when he squeezed over and over and over.

Boom! Boom! Boom! Boom! Boom!

The Glock .27 exploded, yet as bullets flew, the scene slowed within the man's eyes. It was as if he could see each slug as they exited the barrel. And as the head flew toward him, mouth ajar in that silent scream, one of the fiery balls of led entered her open lips before bursting through the back of the skull. Coated with blood, it pierced La Rosa Peligrosa's chest. The impact knocked her back, and just as the remaining balls of led lifted her off her feet, De la Serpiente noticed the flashing gleam riding the air with deadly precision. The bloody head struck him in the chest, and though he spun in an attempt at dodging the assault, the sharp blade buried itself in his shoulder.

"Fuuuucck!" he growled, as La Rosa's body crashed into the statue of her Goddess before crashing to the floor, atop of the black candles.

For a moment, all was peaceful. Eight of the candles lay melted and smashed beneath La Rosa's body, but the two candles that were still upright, burned a slow burn. De la Serpiente glanced at his shoulder where the short blade had embedded itself. A trickle of blood leaked slowly as he reached up and took hold of the knife's handle. His eyes lifted to the toppled statue of the Goddess he praised as he yanked the blade out with a brutal force. "Arrrruuh!"

he growled, as it pulled free, followed by a squirt of blood. His eyes trailed to where La Rosa Peligrosa had fallen, and his mouth fell open in shock.

Where the woman had just lay was a thick puddle of blood. Yet, La Rosa's body was gone, and in her place lie a single black rose. De la Serpiente took a step back, cautiously. His eyes shot to the shrine where prayers were sent up to the Holy death and that's where he noticed the trail of blood leading toward the back of the chapel where he knew there was an exit door. He took a step in the direction his prey 'had to be' crawling, but paused.

Something was wrong. De la Serpiente began to see spots and his throat had suddenly become dry. Pistol clutched in his left hand, the man's eyes became suspicious. His legs became shaky and unsteady as he stumbled over to the ruined shrine. His eyes grew wide when he noticed the silver bowl with a blackish paste in it. He knew. De la Serpiente knew La Rosa liked to experiment with poisons, a mixture of the Bella Donna herb infused with a trickle of potassium Cyanide which was said to kill in less than sixty seconds. At that moment, he smiled.

"Puta!" He cursed La Rosa Peligrosa. The gun fell from his hand as his esophagus contracted. Both hands went to his throat as he fought for air, and at that moment, the doors to the chapel blew open, and twenty men stormed the room with their guns drawn.

***

The moon was bright outside the window as they stood naked, staring at each other. It was Hector's first time having a naked woman in his room. It was Shay's uncountable time being naked in a man's room. He was unsure. She was aware. He was in love. She didn't know what love was. She took his hands and placed them on her breast.

"Touch me." she whispered.

"You're beautiful, Señorita, I—

"Shiiish." She shushed him before gripping the back of his head and pulling his face to hers. Her tongue slipped inside his mouth,

and though he'd experienced juvenile foreplay with other girls his age, Shay's tongue dance was a different kind of eroticism.

His mini me was on salute, pre-cum leaked from its tip as Shay's hand slipped passed his stomach and pelvic, reaching his South pole. She gripped it so tightly he flinched.

Breaking the kiss, she led him to his bed before lying on her back, legs spread to reveal her slightly fuzzy peach. Hector stared in amazement as she began to molest her breasts before her hands traveled south. Shay's red skin seemed to glow in the darkness of the room as her fingers began to create a song against her clit that pulled a sensuous melody from between her lips.

"Ouuuuu," she moaned. Head thrust back, legs in a v-shape, she played with her pussy as Hector watched with his mouth ajar as her legs began to shake. "Uhhhhhhh- uh huh! Uh huh! Uh huh!" She cried as she polished her pearl with an erotic massage. Dipping two fingers inside her island of paradise, she began to explore the places within herself that only she knew would burst her dam. Her juices wet her fingers as she played.

"Ohhhhh!" She quickened her pace. "Yesssss!" Ecstasy arrived. "Oh...my...G-Go," she moaned as her stomach quivered, "God!" Explosion! A short squirt exploded from within her. "Myyyy!" Another quick squirt escaped her essence. Hector's knees became weak.

***

"Policia! Policia!"

"D.E.A, D.E.A.!"

Get the fuck down!" Numerous Law enforcement rushed into the chapel. With flashlights on top of their weapons, they were able to see, but confusion quickly stole their element of surprise. All they found was one headless girl and one dead man.

"Fuck!" the head agent spat. "Johnson, take care of this." He nodded toward the dead. The man beside him nodded before turning to study his partner.

"What will you do?"

"I'm going to find the Dangerous flower."

***

Their bodies were covered in sweat as Hector collapsed beside her, spent from his first nut. Shay smiled, glad she'd pleased herself before the deed.

"I'm leaving," she proclaimed, after propping herself up on an elbow, gazing down at him. Hector lay on his back, eyes closed until her sudden revelation. His eyes shot open.

"Leaving? Why? No need to fear my aunt, she will be angry, bu—

"I'm running away, your aunt sold me tonight."

"Sold you? I no understand." He glanced up at her, confused. Shay smiled down at him. Under the glow of the moon, Hector looked so innocent.

" I-I- I love you, Señorita Shay. I have for very long time."

Shay's smile slipped away as she gave him a penetrating look. Without a word, she climbed on top of him; pussy on top of dick. Human nature. She began to rock gently, his muscle becoming powerful beneath her.

"Don't love me, Hector, please don't."

"Why?"

"I don't believe in it."

"Why?"

"I'm a whore."

"You're beautifu..."

"I don't know how to love or what being made love to feels like."

"Señorita," Hector moaned, as his nature became buried within her after she'd risen and impaled herself.

"All I know how to do is fuck, Hector, that's all."

"Señorita."

"Fuck, Hector!"

"Sen-or-ita!"

"This is- all- I- know, how to fuck!" She cried as she began to ride that bull as if she were contending at a national rodeo. Then...

Blam! The sound of the front door crashing in caused her to roll off of him in fear. Shay hurried out the bed thinking they'd been caught doing the nasty. Just as she was going for her clothes, the door to the room caved in.

"Down! Down! Policia! Policia!" someone demanded.

***

The Present – 2020

"AHHHH!" Patrese fought for her right to breath after exploding upright in the bed. Her petite body was saturated in sweat and her eyes were wild and unfocused.

Just a dream, get a grip, Patrese," she told herself, as her heartbeat slowed, and she shook the ruminants of the dream. The bedside clock read *9:03 A.M.* and the sun was already high in the sky.

"Damn," she mumbled. Ever since things had turned sour, her life seemed to be as Twisted as Keith Sweat's song, but Patrese was solider. She was resilient. She'd fought her way out of the funk, and though she still loved her, her and Tabitha was no longer friends. As she sat there, wondering the why's, her phone chirped, alerting her to her Facebook notifications. She retrieved the phone and touched her finger to the popped-up notification. The screen melted into the madness of social media and sucked her right on into it:

Last post- A week ago-
Friends and Stalkers, I have a few questions for the ladies:

1. *Why do we as women, disrespect ourselves for the sake of momentary gratification?*

Drea Ridge with friends: Girl, we don't know how to appreciate ourselves! The thing is, most of us believe appreciating ourselves involves dick, doing the most for a no good ass man that measures our worth with a Birkin or jewelry.

Beunka T: Shit we can get on our own! SMH! Oh, and Girl, I stopped the clubbing and partying long ago! When a woman obtains responsibilities, it's time out for the extras!

2.   *If you had a homeboy/*
friend and you saw his girl out being disrespectful, I mean, outright
hoish, do you tell him or wait and let someone else?"

Drea Ridge with Friends: Mind your business, telling him will
only make you look messy. Especially if he truly loves the girl, you'll
look like the bad guy.

Tay Lamar: Expose that hoe, mane, treachery has no room
amongst real ppl. If you don't tell the homie, he can't be your friend
nor homeboy. Real is real in every season, mama, and if ole buddy's
gal is a snake, fuck bruh's feelins, Keep it a buck with him.

Drea Ridge with Friends: SMH! STHU Lamar!
Tay Lamar: 100
Oshaya: I agree with Drea
Tay Lamar: I bet you do! : /
Drea Ridge with Friends: SMH! Get ya' life, Husband!
Tay Lamar: #NoFakeshit2021 #streetniggaslivesmattertoo
Beunka T: KMSL

An incoming call shrunk her screen and though she'd been
dodging *everyone's* calls, she needed to talk to her sister.
"Hey, girly," she answered.
"Patrese Marie Vaentine, where the hell you been! You got time
to be active on Facebook, but no time to answer your phone?"
Oshaya spat in relief. "You've had me worried sick!"
"I Know, I know, sis, it's just, I've been going through soooooo
much, Oshaya. I just needed some me time, but now I'm feeling like
this apartment is closing in on me! I just- just need to get away!"
She moaned exasperatedly before falling backwards onto the bed.
She curled up into a ball as her vision became blurry from the tears.
"It's still bothering you, huh?" Oshaya's question only made
the tears fall.
"I've been having nightmares, Oshaya."

"You know what, pack a bag, you're coming to stay a few nights with me. Nigil's never home anyway, it'll be just like old times."

"I've been having nightmares, Oshaya."

"We can glut on ice cream and binge watch Raising Kanan and—

"*Shay!*" The calling of the name Oshaya hadn't used, heard, nor cared to remember was reciprocated by a thick silence. Patrese could hear her friend's soft breathing, but the only thing to reveal how much of the woman's attention she now had was the one word that she murmured.

"*Tresey?*"

"I've been having nightmares."

"Of?"

"Our past, when we were young girls." Patrese exhaled a long breath.

"Of?"

"Once upon a time in Mexico."

To Be Continued ...
Ski Mask Money 2
Coming Soon

Lock Down Publications and Ca$h Presents assisted publishing packages.

BASIC PACKAGE $499
Editing
Cover Design
Formatting

UPGRADED PACKAGE $800
Typing
Editing
Cover Design
Formatting

ADVANCE PACKAGE $1,200
Typing
Editing
Cover Design
Formatting
Copyright registration
Proofreading
Upload book to Amazon

LDP SUPREME PACKAGE $1,500
Typing
Editing
Cover Design
Formatting
Copyright registration
Proofreading
Set up Amazon account
Upload book to Amazon
Advertise on LDP Amazon and Facebook page

***Other services available upon request. Additional charges may apply

Lock Down Publications
P.O. Box 944
Stockbridge, GA 30281-9998
Phone # 470 303-9761

Submission Guideline

Submit the first three chapters of your completed manuscript to ldpsubmissions@gmail.com, subject line: Your book's title. The manuscript must be in a .doc file and sent as an attachment. Document should be in Times New Roman, double spaced and in size 12 font. Also, provide your synopsis and full contact information. If sending multiple submissions, they must each be in a separate email.

Have a story but no way to send it electronically? You can still submit to LDP/Ca$h Presents. Send in the first three chapters, written or typed, of your completed manuscript to:

LDP: Submissions Dept
Po Box 944
Stockbridge, Ga 30281

DO NOT send original manuscript. Must be a duplicate.

Provide your synopsis and a cover letter containing your full contact information.

Thanks for considering LDP and Ca$h Presents.

<u>NEW RELEASES</u>

GRIMEY WAYS 2 by RAY VINCI
AN UNFORESEEN LOVE 3 by MEESHA
BORN IN THE GRAVE by SELF MADE TAY
MOAN IN MY MOUTH by XTASY
SKI MASK MONEY by RENTA

Ski Mask Money

BAE BELONGS TO ME III

TIL DEATH II

By **Aryanna**

KING OF THE TRAP III

By **T.J. Edwards**

GORILLAZ IN THE BAY V

3X KRAZY III

STRAIGHT BEAST MODE III

De'Kari

KINGPIN KILLAZ IV

STREET KINGS III

PAID IN BLOOD III

CARTEL KILLAZ IV

DOPE GODS III

Hood Rich

SINS OF A HUSTLA II

ASAD

RICH $AVAGE II

By Martell Troublesome Bolden

YAYO V

Bred In The Game 2

S. Allen

CREAM III

THE STREETS WILL TALK II

By Yolanda Moore

SON OF A DOPE FIEND III

HEAVEN GOT A GHETTO II

SKI MASK MONEY II

By Renta

LOYALTY AIN'T PROMISED III

By Keith Williams

I'M NOTHING WITHOUT HIS LOVE II

SINS OF A THUG II

TO THE THUG I LOVED BEFORE II

IN A HUSTLER I TRUST II

By Monet Dragun

QUIET MONEY IV

EXTENDED CLIP III

THUG LIFE IV

By **Trai'Quan**

THE STREETS MADE ME IV

By **Larry D. Wright**

IF YOU CROSS ME ONCE II

ANGEL IV

By **Anthony Fields**

THE STREETS WILL NEVER CLOSE IV

By K'ajji

HARD AND RUTHLESS III

Ski Mask Money

KILLA KOUNTY III

By Khufu

MONEY GAME III

By Smoove Dolla

JACK BOYS VS DOPE BOYS II

A GANGSTA'S QUR'AN V

COKE GIRLZ II

COKE BOYS II

By Romell Tukes

MURDA WAS THE CASE II

Elijah R. Freeman

THE STREETS NEVER LET GO II

By Robert Baptiste

AN UNFORESEEN LOVE IV

By **Meesha**

KING OF THE TRENCHES III
by **GHOST & TRANAY ADAMS**

MONEY MAFIA II

By **Jibril Williams**

QUEEN OF THE ZOO III

By **Black Migo**

VICIOUS LOYALTY III

By Kingpen

A GANGSTA'S PAIN III

Renta

By J-Blunt

CONFESSIONS OF A JACKBOY III

By Nicholas Lock

GRIMEY WAYS III

By Ray Vinci

KING KILLA II

By Vincent "Vitto" Holloway

BETRAYAL OF A THUG II

By Fre$h

THE MURDER QUEENS II

By Michael Gallon

THE BIRTH OF A GANGSTER III

By Delmont Player

TREAL LOVE II

By Le'Monica Jackson

FOR THE LOVE OF BLOOD II

By Jamel Mitchell

RAN OFF ON DA PLUG II

By Paper Boi Rari

HOOD CONSIGLIERE II

By Keese

PRETTY GIRLS DO NASTY THINGS II

By Nicole Goosby

PROTÉGÉ OF A LEGEND II

Ski Mask Money

By Corey Robinson
IT'S JUST ME AND YOU II
By Ah'Million
BORN IN THE GRAVE II
By Self Made Tay

Available Now

RESTRAINING ORDER **I & II**
By **CA$H & Coffee**
LOVE KNOWS NO BOUNDARIES **I II & III**
By **Coffee**
RAISED AS A GOON I, II, III & IV
BRED BY THE SLUMS I, II, III
BLAST FOR ME I & II
ROTTEN TO THE CORE I II III
A BRONX TALE I, II, III
DUFFLE BAG CARTEL I II III IV V VI
HEARTLESS GOON I II III IV V
A SAVAGE DOPEBOY I II
DRUG LORDS I II III

CUTTHROAT MAFIA I II

KING OF THE TRENCHES

By **Ghost**

LAY IT DOWN **I & II**

LAST OF A DYING BREED I II

BLOOD STAINS OF A SHOTTA I & II III

By **Jamaica**

LOYAL TO THE GAME I II III

LIFE OF SIN I, II III

By **TJ & Jelissa**

BLOODY COMMAS I & II

SKI MASK CARTEL I II & III

KING OF NEW YORK I II,III IV V

RISE TO POWER I II III

COKE KINGS I II III IV V

BORN HEARTLESS I II III IV

KING OF THE TRAP I II

By **T.J. Edwards**

IF LOVING HIM IS WRONG…I & II

LOVE ME EVEN WHEN IT HURTS I II III

By **Jelissa**

WHEN THE STREETS CLAP BACK I & II III

THE HEART OF A SAVAGE I II III IV

MONEY MAFIA

Ski Mask Money

LOYAL TO THE SOIL I II III
By **Jibril Williams**
A DISTINGUISHED THUG STOLE MY HEART I II & III
LOVE SHOULDN'T HURT I II III IV
RENEGADE BOYS I II III IV
PAID IN KARMA I II III
SAVAGE STORMS I II III
AN UNFORESEEN LOVE I II III
By **Meesha**
A GANGSTER'S CODE I &, II III
A GANGSTER'S SYN I II III
THE SAVAGE LIFE I II III
CHAINED TO THE STREETS I II III
BLOOD ON THE MONEY I II III
A GANGSTA'S PAIN I II
By J-Blunt
PUSH IT TO THE LIMIT
By **Bre' Hayes**
BLOOD OF A BOSS **I, II, III, IV, V**
SHADOWS OF THE GAME
TRAP BASTARD
By **Askari**
THE STREETS BLEED MURDER **I, II & III**
THE HEART OF A GANGSTA I II& III

253

Renta

By **Jerry Jackson**
CUM FOR ME I II III IV V VI VII VIII
An **LDP Erotica Collaboration**
BRIDE OF A HUSTLA **I II & II**
THE FETTI GIRLS **I, II& III**
CORRUPTED BY A GANGSTA I, II III, IV
BLINDED BY HIS LOVE
THE PRICE YOU PAY FOR LOVE I, II ,III
DOPE GIRL MAGIC I II III
By **Destiny Skai**
WHEN A GOOD GIRL GOES BAD
By **Adrienne**
THE COST OF LOYALTY I II III
By Kweli
A GANGSTER'S REVENGE **I II III & IV**
THE BOSS MAN'S DAUGHTERS I II III IV V
A SAVAGE LOVE **I & II**
BAE BELONGS TO ME I II
A HUSTLER'S DECEIT I, II, III
WHAT BAD BITCHES DO I, II, III
SOUL OF A MONSTER I II III
KILL ZONE
A DOPE BOY'S QUEEN I II III
TIL DEATH

Ski Mask Money

By **Aryanna**
A KINGPIN'S AMBITON
A KINGPIN'S AMBITION **II**
I MURDER FOR THE DOUGH
By **Ambitious**
TRUE SAVAGE I II III IV V VI VII
DOPE BOY MAGIC I, II, III
MIDNIGHT CARTEL I II III
CITY OF KINGZ I II
NIGHTMARE ON SILENT AVE
THE PLUG OF LIL MEXICO II
CLASSIC CITY
By **Chris Green**
A DOPEBOY'S PRAYER
By **Eddie "Wolf" Lee**
THE KING CARTEL **I, II & III**
By **Frank Gresham**
THESE NIGGAS AIN'T LOYAL **I, II & III**
By **Nikki Tee**
GANGSTA SHYT **I II &III**
By **CATO**
THE ULTIMATE BETRAYAL
By **Phoenix**
BOSS'N UP **I , II & III**

Renta

By **Royal Nicole**

I LOVE YOU TO DEATH

By **Destiny J**

I RIDE FOR MY HITTA

I STILL RIDE FOR MY HITTA

By **Misty Holt**

LOVE & CHASIN' PAPER

By **Qay Crockett**

TO DIE IN VAIN

SINS OF A HUSTLA

By **ASAD**

BROOKLYN HUSTLAZ

By **Boogsy Morina**

BROOKLYN ON LOCK I & II

By **Sonovia**

GANGSTA CITY

By **Teddy Duke**

A DRUG KING AND HIS DIAMOND I & II III

A DOPEMAN'S RICHES

HER MAN, MINE'S TOO I, II

CASH MONEY HO'S

THE WIFEY I USED TO BE I II

PRETTY GIRLS DO NASTY THINGS

By Nicole Goosby

Ski Mask Money

TRAPHOUSE KING **I II & III**

KINGPIN KILLAZ I II III

STREET KINGS I II

PAID IN BLOOD **I II**

CARTEL KILLAZ I II III

DOPE GODS I II

By **Hood Rich**

LIPSTICK KILLAH **I, II, III**

CRIME OF PASSION I II & III

FRIEND OR FOE I II III

By **Mimi**

STEADY MOBBN' **I, II, III**

THE STREETS STAINED MY SOUL I II III

By **Marcellus Allen**

WHO SHOT YA **I, II, III**

SON OF A DOPE FIEND I II

HEAVEN GOT A GHETTO

SKI MASK MONEY

Renta

GORILLAZ IN THE BAY **I II III IV**

TEARS OF A GANGSTA I II

3X KRAZY I II

STRAIGHT BEAST MODE I II

DE'KARI

257

TRIGGADALE I II III

MURDAROBER WAS THE CASE

Elijah R. Freeman

GOD BLESS THE TRAPPERS I, II, III

THESE SCANDALOUS STREETS I, II, III

FEAR MY GANGSTA I, II, III IV, V

THESE STREETS DON'T LOVE NOBODY I, II

BURY ME A G I, II, III, IV, V

A GANGSTA'S EMPIRE I, II, III, IV

THE DOPEMAN'S BODYGAURD I II

THE REALEST KILLAZ I II III

THE LAST OF THE OGS I II III

Tranay Adams

THE STREETS ARE CALLING

Duquie Wilson

MARRIED TO A BOSS I II III

By Destiny Skai & Chris Green

KINGZ OF THE GAME I II III IV V VI

Playa Ray

SLAUGHTER GANG I II III

RUTHLESS HEART I II III

By Willie Slaughter

FUK SHYT

By Blakk Diamond

Ski Mask Money

DON'T F#CK WITH MY HEART I II
By Linnea
ADDICTED TO THE DRAMA I II III
IN THE ARM OF HIS BOSS II
By Jamila
YAYO I II III IV
A SHOOTER'S AMBITION I II
BRED IN THE GAME
By S. Allen
TRAP GOD I II III
RICH $AVAGE
MONEY IN THE GRAVE I II III
By Martell Troublesome Bolden
FOREVER GANGSTA
GLOCKS ON SATIN SHEETS I II
By Adrian Dulan
TOE TAGZ I II III IV
LEVELS TO THIS SHYT I II
IT'S JUST ME AND YOU
By Ah'Million
KINGPIN DREAMS I II III
RAN OFF ON DA PLUG
By Paper Boi Rari
CONFESSIONS OF A GANGSTA I II III IV

CONFESSIONS OF A JACKBOY I II
By Nicholas Lock
I'M NOTHING WITHOUT HIS LOVE
SINS OF A THUG
TO THE THUG I LOVED BEFORE
A GANGSTA SAVED XMAS
IN A HUSTLER I TRUST
By Monet Dragun
CAUGHT UP IN THE LIFE I II III
THE STREETS NEVER LET GO
By Robert Baptiste
NEW TO THE GAME I II III
MONEY, MURDER & MEMORIES I II III
By **Malik D. Rice**
LIFE OF A SAVAGE I II III
A GANGSTA'S QUR'AN I II III IV
MURDA SEASON I II III
GANGLAND CARTEL I II III
CHI'RAQ GANGSTAS I II III
KILLERS ON ELM STREET I II III
JACK BOYZ N DA BRONX I II III
A DOPEBOY'S DREAM I II III
JACK BOYS VS DOPE BOYS
COKE GIRLZ

Ski Mask Money

COKE BOYS
By Romell Tukes
LOYALTY AIN'T PROMISED I II
By Keith Williams
QUIET MONEY I II III
THUG LIFE I II III
EXTENDED CLIP I II
By **Trai'Quan**
THE STREETS MADE ME I II III
By **Larry D. Wright**
THE ULTIMATE SACRIFICE I, II, III, IV, V, VI
KHADIFI
IF YOU CROSS ME ONCE
ANGEL I II III
IN THE BLINK OF AN EYE
By **Anthony Fields**
THE LIFE OF A HOOD STAR
By Ca$h & Rashia Wilson
THE STREETS WILL NEVER CLOSE I II III
By K'ajji
CREAM I II
THE STREETS WILL TALK
By Yolanda Moore
NIGHTMARES OF A HUSTLA I II III

Renta

By King Dream

CONCRETE KILLA I II III

VICIOUS LOYALTY I II

By Kingpen

HARD AND RUTHLESS I II

MOB TOWN 251

THE BILLIONAIRE BENTLEYS I II III

By Von Diesel

GHOST MOB

Stilloan Robinson

MOB TIES I II III IV V VI

By SayNoMore

BODYMORE MURDERLAND I II III

THE BIRTH OF A GANGSTER I II

By Delmont Player

FOR THE LOVE OF A BOSS

By C. D. Blue

MOBBED UP I II III IV

THE BRICK MAN I II III IV

THE COCAINE PRINCESS I II III IV V

By King Rio

KILLA KOUNTY I II III

By Khufu

MONEY GAME I II

Ski Mask Money

By Smoove Dolla
A GANGSTA'S KARMA I II
By FLAME
KING OF THE TRENCHES I II
by **GHOST & TRANAY ADAMS**
QUEEN OF THE ZOO I II
By **Black Migo**
GRIMEY WAYS I II
By Ray Vinci
XMAS WITH AN ATL SHOOTER
By Ca$h & Destiny Skai
KING KILLA
By Vincent "Vitto" Holloway
BETRAYAL OF A THUG
By Fre$h
THE MURDER QUEENS
By Michael Gallon
TREAL LOVE
By Le'Monica Jackson
FOR THE LOVE OF BLOOD
By Jamel Mitchell
HOOD CONSIGLIERE
By Keese
PROTÉGÉ OF A LEGEND

Renta

By Corey Robinson
BORN IN THE GRAVE
By Self Made Tay
MOAN IN MY MOUTH
By XTASY

BOOKS BY LDP'S CEO, CA$H

TRUST IN NO MAN

TRUST IN NO MAN 2

TRUST IN NO MAN 3

BONDED BY BLOOD

SHORTY GOT A THUG

THUGS CRY

THUGS CRY 2

THUGS CRY 3

TRUST NO BITCH

TRUST NO BITCH 2

TRUST NO BITCH 3

TIL MY CASKET DROPS

RESTRAINING ORDER

RESTRAINING ORDER 2

IN LOVE WITH A CONVICT

LIFE OF A HOOD STAR

XMAS WITH AN ATL SHOOTER

Renta

www.ingramcontent.com/pod-product-compliance
Lightning Source LLC
Chambersburg PA
CBHW071234260626
47161CB00003BA/940